ReVeNGe CaKe

SKYLER MASON

Cover Design by Cover Couture **www.bookcovercouture.com**
Editing: Rachel Daven Skinner at Romance Refined

Visit the author at **www.skylermason.com**

To Nicole, for all those Closure Cakes we shared

CHAPTER 1

Present Day

Leilani

"I'm just going to get straight to the point. I can't do this anymore."

There it is.

He finally said the words I've been dreading.

I inhale a shaky breath, desperate to calm my racing heart, but it's futile. I'm too far gone already. My pulse pounds like a canon in my ears, while a feverish cold sweat sends trickles of moisture down my chest. That familiar sick feeling twists at the pit of my stomach, just before it grows—spreading like wildfire—thrashing through my limbs until I can't keep them still.

I wish I could burst out of my skin to escape just the feeling alone. At my worst, I have actually clawed myself with the jagged edges of my chewed fingernails, or at least I gathered as much hours later when I saw the welted lines stretching from my collarbone to the edge of my bra. But even if I could break free, the fear is so all-consuming I almost believe it would follow me anywhere, even into death.

"You're shaking," Logan says, and it sounds like a simple observation. Long gone is the concern he once felt for my suffering. He resents me for it now.

"Yeah, I'm having a fucking panic attack." I try to keep my voice light, but it only sounds brittle, like a tightly wound guitar string.

"It's not going to make me feel sorry for you. I hope you realize that." His words are matter-of-fact, free of the vicious anger from last night, but still they kill me. He's never looked at me like this before, his face a rigid mask, his posture so languid he almost looks like he's melting into the couch. Even at our worst, when I wanted to die of shame over the frantic behavior I couldn't control, at the very least I had his pity.

And I'd take even that over this cool detachment.

He lowers his eyes to my chest. "And that shirt has no effect on me either. I don't know if you thought it would bring back memories or if you're just being passive aggressive, but I really couldn't give two shits."

I glance down at iron-on letters across my chest—*My Boyfriend is a Feminist*—already starting to peel and curl at the edges from too many washes. If I could feel anything other than panic, it might make me sad to look at it. The boy who made this shirt adored me. I miss him. I miss his kind, self-deprecating warmth. Where did he go? I don't even recognize this hateful person next to me.

"Passive aggressive," I say, though he wasn't asking for a response.

His smile doesn't reach his eyes. "Good to know."

"Just finish saying whatever it is you have to say." I can't bear the anguish of drawing this out. I knew it was over the moment he stormed out of my house last night. Even through my drugged haze, I could feel his hatred.

And the betrayal I overheard when he pocket-dialed me shortly after only confirmed it.

I'm about to mention the phone call, but when I lift my eyes to meet his, I'm seized with an overwhelming ache in my chest. This may be the last time I'll ever see his face in person, and I miss it already. Thirteen months together has made it almost as familiar as my own. I love the way he looks, and not just because he's beautiful. He has a kind face, with heavy-lidded eyes that make him look perpetually sleepy, and full, pouting lips that tilt up at the corners, suggesting a smile that isn't there. And when he does smile, it's so sincere, so full of goodwill—one eye crinkling more than the other, a lone dimple popping out. Even in his rage, he doesn't look mean. Not really. I wish I could reach out and touch his cheek.

"Alright," he says as he stands up from the couch and turns to face me, his six-foot-three form blocking the sunlight from the living room window. "I think we can both agree that after last night, things cannot continue this way any longer."

"I agree," I say.

He puts his hands on his hips as he stares down at me. I clench my hold around my upper arms, as if to shield myself from his judging gaze.

"I'm glad we're on the same page. Seems like the first time

we have been in *months*." He spits out that last word.

Months of my constant panic attacks, he means. Months of taking too much Ativan. Months of ignoring my responsibilities and retreating even further into my own head. Months of looking like a bedraggled, sunken-eyed waif. Months of embarrassing him in front of our friends.

"I think I need to give you some time to figure things out."

I blink once. "What do you mean?"

"I mean you have to get your shit together if we're going to stay together, and I know that sounds harsh, but after last night I don't have a lot of sympathy for you."

I can only stare back at him with my lips parted. I didn't expect that. I was certain this was the end. I shift my gaze to my lap, considering his words. Maybe he does feel a small measure of guilt, and it's preventing him from showing me the full force of his rage. Maybe he feels obligated to give me another chance.

The hope that springs in my chest gives me pause. Have I really become this pathetic? I never would have accepted this even three months ago. I don't want to be chosen out of guilt. I want him to want me with the passionate intensity of those first few months, when he was so desperate for my love he refused to let me push him away.

Besides, if he's still hanging on to me after the misery of the last few months, he's just repeating his old mistakes.

This is exactly what he did with Brittani.

Because this is what Logan does. He plows through relationships like he'll get a reward for sheer volume. He repeats the same mistakes over and over again in a never-ending pattern of fevered infatuation that steadily dims with growing intimacy before exploding spectacularly into total disillusionment. He's on an eternal quest for love, as his twin sister Lauren aptly pointed out.

And I'm done with him. Done with it all.

I lift my gaze from my lap, about to tell him what I know about last night, but just as I open my mouth, my tongue freezes. I can't do it. I'm gripped with the same reservations that kept me from confronting him last night.

I can't do it like this.

I can't do it while I sit here with my shoulders hunched and my arms hugging my body, my hair in a messy knot on my head, and my eyes probably red and veiny from lost sleep. I look exactly like the mess I've become.

I just can't do it.

So instead I probe him. "What exactly do you mean by giving me time to get my shit together?"

"I mean I'm going to give you one month to work on yourself. And you'd better look into a twelve-step program or something. Like, you need to seriously figure your shit out."

A heat of rage surges at his continued contempt, but I can't show it. Not if I'm going to wait a month to confront him. Instead, I smile sweetly, blinking up at him slowly. "Of course I do," I say in a breathy voice.

My sarcasm incenses him. He grits his teeth before saying, "I have every right to be pissed off. You were a fucking shitshow. The very least you can do is acknowledge it."

I lower my gaze to my lap. Those were the exact words he used last night, but at least then I had the aftereffects of my boozy, Ativan haze to dull the stinging pain in my chest.

"And all the stuff you said…" He breaks off. For the first time I hear an emotion other than anger in his voice. "I don't

9

think I'll ever forget it."

Even in my indignation over the injustice of it all, guilt grips me. I don't know why I said those awful things—those mean, nasty, hurtful things—that weren't even true. I must have lost my head in my drugged rage. He's right that I'm a shitshow.

"So I'm going to give you a month to figure your shit out, and then we can reassess. We'll meet up exactly a month from today, which will give us three weeks before graduation to figure everything out." He settles hard eyes on me. "I sure as fuck am not moving to another city with you if you're still doing all this shit a month from now."

"Fair enough," I say lightly, and I'm surprised that it didn't take effort.

It occurs to me that I no longer feel the physical toll of trying to keep it together—the rigidity in my poster, the tightness in my throat. Sometime after he told me he's giving me time, my body relaxed, my breathing steadied. The dreaded panic retreated when I realized I might be able to exit this relationship with a shred of dignity.

Maybe even more than a shred! Maybe I can make him regret what he did. The realization makes my body feel lighter, but I can't indulge it just yet. This will be no easy feat.

It will take careful planning.

"Can you give me more than two-word answers, please?"

I'm startled by the question, but I try to sounds calm when I ask, "What else is there to say?"

When I stand up from the couch, Logan's expression shifts. "Are you leaving?" he asks, an unfamiliar shrillness in his voice.

"Of course." Two words. Intentionally this time.

I walk to the door, but hesitate when a thought occurs to me.

I school my face into an expression of innocence before turning around and facing him. "Are we allowed to be with other people during our time apart?"

He stares at me blankly for almost a full five seconds before my meaning seems to dawn on him. "What the fuck kind of question is that? Are you just trying to piss me off?"

I fight the smile rising to my lips, trying my best to appear cool and aloof. "No, I'm really not. A month is a long time for me to go without sex, and I obviously won't be having it with you."

His lips part. "Are you fucking serious right now?"

"I am." Two words.

He walks slowly toward me, his expression growing harder with each step. "It's a strange thing for you to say when it's been about a month now since we've had sex." A humorless smile rises to his lips. "Are you sure your Ativan won't be enough to get you by?"

The question makes my teeth clench, but unfortunately he's right. I try to remain expressionless as I ask, "Is that a yes or no?"

The smile vanishes. "Of course we're not allowed to have sex with anyone else. What the fuck is wrong with you?"

I stare steadily back at him, fighting the urge to sneer. "Fine. I suppose I can handle celibacy for a month." I move toward the door, but hesitate once more. I turn to him. "Oh, one more thing." I grip the bottom of my T-shirt and pull it up over my head. With a flick of the wrist, I toss it into the air. Logan's green eyes dart to the red fabric as it drifts to the floor in front of his feet. He stares at it for a moment before lifting his head and meeting my eyes.

"I won't be needing that," I say.

His eyes dart to my chest then back to my face. "Lani, what the fuck?" he shouts. "Are you really going to walk out of here in your bra?"

I glance down at the lacy fabric cupping my small boobs. I smile innocently as I look back up at him. "It's more of a bralette." I shrug before turning toward the door.

After setting my hand on the knob, I hesitate at the sound of his voice. "Oh my god," he mumbles. "You are seriously unhinged right now."

The contemptuous statement propels me out the door.

Blinding sunshine that makes me sneeze. Lines in the sidewalk passing under my feet. The rustling of leaves from the ocean wind. An effusive conversation between a group of college students on the other side of the street. "I literally died of alcohol poisoning," a boy says. Incorrect use of "literally."

If I take inventory of my surroundings, hopefully I'll be too distracted to cry before I make it to my car.

"Lani!" Logan's distant shout tells me he didn't follow me.

He didn't even step outside his front door.

I take a slow, steady breath, realizing for the first time that I'm not going to cry. Something inside me shifted today. Of my range of emotions over the past few months—fear, humiliation, despair—the only one markedly absent was anger. And it feels great as it pulses through my body like the buzz from a strong cup of coffee. I'll be just fine without you, Logan Henderson.

And thanks for giving me a month to prove it to you.

CHAPTER 2

Past—The Meet-Cute

Logan

"No need to thank me now," Armaan says, his head turned from my view as he parallel parks on the neighborhood street, "but I'm about to introduce you to two potential rebound lays. Both of Brenna's roommates are hot. Just wait till you meet Mia." He shuts his eyes as he shakes his head. "Smokeshow. It's a shame I met Brenna first."

I sigh heavily, exhausted at the prospect. I know he's just trying to cheer me up by bringing me here tonight, but I wish I'd stayed at home. My breakup is still too fresh for me to start pursuing another girl, even only as a "rebound lay."

"I just hope you told them that I'm not up for anything serious."

Armaan snorts as he twists the key and turns off the ignition.

"Sure you aren't."

"I'm serious. I'm done with relationships for the rest of college."

"Right."

I fight the urge to groan. "No, I really mean it."

"I know you do. That's why it's funny." With that he exits the car.

I can't blame him for not believing me. I've had probably ten relationships just since he and I met in the Anacapa dorms three years ago, and I've had at least forty since seventh grade.

I'm well known among all of our friends as The Relationship Sociopath—a title earned mostly from a few impulsive words said to a girl I met during a spring break trip to Cabo (and who among us hasn't told someone they love them when they were drunk, only to take it back the next day?)—but it's not really true. I'm not in relationships all the time because I treat women like conquests, but because I don't see the need to hold back when I meet a beautiful girl I love to be around, and there are smart, interesting, beautiful girls everywhere, especially in a college town like Santa Barbara.

I feel like my friends should be explaining why they *aren't* in relationships all the time.

But my disastrous breakup with Brittani was a wakeup call. I shouldn't need to justify being in healthy relationships all the time, but toxic relationships are exhausting, and I need time to recover.

"What are we even doing tonight?" I ask after catching up to him on the sidewalk. I put both hands in my pockets to fight the cold. It's an unseasonably chilly day for late March in Santa Barbara.

He stops in front of the baby-blue Victorian house with the white shutters and wraparound deck. "Just hanging out. Mia stalked you on Instagram and thinks you're pretty."

I nod. Nothing new there.

"But she was even more excited to meet you when I told them what a wreck you've been since Brittani keyed your car…"

He trails off when I throw my head back and groan. "Was that necessary? Couldn't you have just said we broke up and left it at that?"

He shakes his head. "I think the pity angle works really well here because it deflects from the real issue, which is that you're super needy and incapable of being single."

I smile. "Thanks for having my back."

"No problem."

We resume our walk up the warped wooden stairs to the front porch. When we reach the front door, Armaan turns to me. "Oh, I almost forgot to tell you the best part," he says in a lowered voice. "The girls made you a cake."

I frown. "Why would they make me a cake?"

"It's this tradition between Brenna and her best friend Leilani—one of the roommates you'll meet tonight. After every breakup, they bake a cake together and call it 'Closure Cake.' They put the person's name on top in frosting letters and thank it for all the good times. And then they eat it and supposedly feel at peace about the breakup and as one with the universe…" He breaks into a smile when he sees the look on my face.

"You're fucking with me, right?"

"I'm one hundred percent serious. Dude!" he whisper-shouts and then grins. "Leilani is out of her fucking mind. Like, I think she might secretly be a serial killer. She's definitely crazier than

Brittani. You'll be in love with her by the end of the night. Mark my words."

I only get the chance to roll my eyes, saved from the necessity of defending myself when the door opens and Brenna sings out, "The boys are here!"

As we walk into the front room, I see two girls sitting on a couch, each with a glass of wine in hand. My eyes don't linger long enough to catch any details, but I have an overall sense of pretty. I shoot Armaan a look acknowledging that he delivered, and he answers me with a stoic nod.

Brenna introduces me to both of them. Armaan was correct about Mia. She *is* a smokeshow with her long, wavy blonde hair, but my eyes linger on Leilani, the one he said was secretly a serial killer. My brow furrows. This can't be her. Even unsmiling, she looks like an angel with those giant brown eyes, full cheeks, and heart-shaped lips.

I don't have time to contemplate that further when Mia approaches me. She asks if she can get me anything to drink, and if I need something a little stronger than usual because of my rough breakup. I glare at Armaan for telling the girls everything, but he only smirks back at me.

"We're here to take care of you," Mia says with a smile.

"That's sweet, but I don't really need it. My breakup was a long time coming."

Mia winces as she says in a lowered voice, "I heard she vandalized your car."

This time I shoot Armaan a much more menacing glare, and he cackles.

"'Vandalized' is kind of a strong word," I say. "She keyed it."

"And poured jungle juice through the crack in your window,"

Armaan says.

"Yes." I sigh. "And that."

When a smirk forms on Armaan's lips, I just know he's about to be an asshole. I brace myself for whatever he's about to say. "Tell the girls *what* she keyed into your car, Logan."

My eyelids flutter, but I don't respond.

"Come on." He pats me hard on the back. "This is a safe space. We're all here for you."

"Armaan, seriously, fuck off."

He only grins.

When I glance around the room, I see riveted eyes staring back at me. Of course they're intrigued with an introduction like that. Oh well. There's nothing to do about it now. "She keyed 'fuckboy' into my hood."

Armaan is the only one who laughs—his signature cackle—because the girls are too polite to show amusement, though I notice a collective pursing of lips, likely to fight smiles. I can't blame them. If I hadn't been so distraught over the sharp deterioration of my relationship, I might have laughed too. My poor little white Prius looked so pathetic with those slanting letters across the hood. And having to drive it through my small home town of Coronado to get the paint fixed was the icing on the cake. I think at least five people I grew up with saw me before I made it to the body shop. I knew even in the moment that I would laugh about it someday.

Plus, it's not like it's true, so why should I be troubled by it? I'm not a fuckboy. I'm the opposite of a fuckboy. I'm a relationship-boy.

"Why did she call you a fuckboy?" one of the girls asks, as if she read my mind.

My eyes dart around the room to find the angel face Leilani. Heat shoots into my groin at the sight of her direct, unblinking stare. She looks like she's trying to hypnotize me. "I have a lot of friends who are girls," I say. "Brittani was always really jealous, but it got really bad toward the end there. I think she knew I had checked out already, so she freaked out."

"Armaan said Brittani was a little…" Mia trails off.

"Crazy," Armaan fills in.

At this, Brenna places her hands on her hips and looks up at Armaan with a scowl. "Armaan Singh, this is a house of women. If you ever call a woman crazy again, you'll be shown to the door. I'm not kidding. We don't make exceptions for boyfriends. Don't do it again."

"Yes, ma'am," he says, reaching out his hand and patting her head. Tiny little Brenna barely reaches Armaan's pecks.

"I don't really like saying she was crazy either," I say to Brenna, "because she had some legit mental health shit going on, but let's just say that she kind of…spiraled. Like, the person she was when we first started dating is not the person she became at the end there. It was kind of alarming."

"She's not crazy," a husky voice says. "You're just weak."

Momentarily stunned, my lips part. When I glance around the room to find the speaker, I'm arrested again by the angel face. God, she's beautiful, and in such a soft, sweet way. A sharp contrast to the voice that just insulted me, but there's no doubting that challenging stare. That single brow lifting as if to say, "You heard me right."

"Lani!" Mia shouts before turning to me. "She's very blunt. She doesn't realize that it comes across as rude sometimes."

Finally starting to recover, my lips lift into a faint smile.

"What makes you say that?" I ask the angel face. Mia called her "Lani." I like it. It's short, sweet, and to the point. Just like her.

Still unsmiling, Lani shrugs. "Armaan told us the whole story. He said you've been technically broken up for a month, but you've still been going to her house at night to comfort her. Who does that?" She grimaces. "What kind of person are you?"

When abrupt silence fills the room after her question, I realize I'm not the only one shocked. I'm so caught by it, I can't even be mad at Armaan for apparently telling these girls every humiliating detail of my breakup with Brittani. Heat creeps into my cheeks, but my smile stays in place. I'm embarrassed, yes, but I can't help feeling a little thrilled at her assessing, skeptical gaze. I love the way she looks at me, like I'm the most interesting person in the room.

"I don't know…" Her hard eye contact makes it difficult for me to find the right words. "I guess I was just worried about her. She wasn't doing well after we broke up and I kind of felt responsible for it. I've always been a sucker for crying, and she was leaving me these voicemails where she was literally sobbing, begging me to come over. Jesus…" I shake my head at the memory. "It was fucking terrible. I felt like she needed me."

Lani isn't moved. If anything, she looks even more disgusted. "You understand that the breakupper isn't supposed to comfort the breakuppee, right? Brittani knows this too. I don't think she really needed you. She was trying to punish you."

A faint smile rises to my lips as I squint at her skeptically. "You know this from the stuff you heard secondhand from Armaan?"

"Yes," she answers instantly.

My smile widens at her confidence, though I have to

contradict her. "Brittani's not a very manipulative person. Or, at least, she's not very good at manipulating. She kind of wears her heart on her sleeve, you know? Almost to a fault. Like, when I go over there, she wants me to hold her on her bed while she cries. That's all we do. She cries and I hold her. Don't you think that's kind of embarrassing?"

"For you or for her?"

My mouth drops open for the second time in as many minutes. Did she really just insult me again? Holy shit, this girl has balls. I stare at her dumbly for several seconds, vaguely registering that Armaan is chuckling quietly.

"I think it's more embarrassing for you," Lani says, as if she didn't already make that clear. "Brittani is making you her bitch. You humiliated her and now she's punishing you for it. Punishing you turns her on. I get it." She smiles for the first time, a slight lift of her heart-shaped lips that draws my eyes to her mouth. "Her methods aren't my style, but I would punish you too."

In a rush, heat fills my belly, clenching my stomach muscles so tight I have to fight the urge to hunch. Is she really implying what I think she's implying? My eyes dart to Armaan, if only to make sure I heard her correctly, and his eyes are as wide as mine must be.

"Lani," Mia says, her tone pleading. "This conversation is getting weird. I think you're making Logan uncomfortable."

It's true, but God Almighty not in the way Mia thinks. My face feels as hot as a furnace, my pants growing tighter by the second. If there wasn't a group of people around us I would be tempted to ask Lani to take me into her bedroom and punish me now.

Lani looks hesitant for the first time, as if she only recognized her audacity after Mia pointed it out to her. As if she thought nothing before about picking apart the intimate details of the life of a complete stranger and handing him his balls on a platter.

God, she's amazing. "Why do you think I humiliated her?" I ask, desperate to keep her talking.

The hesitation vanishes from her face. She lifts a brow. "Armaan told us about the best friend."

"He sure did," Brenna says, lowering her chin.

I don't know why I have to fight the urge to flinch. I have nothing to feel guilty about. Nothing even happened with Brittani's best friend Olivia. Can I help it if I liked talking to her, and that she happened to be around? Can I help it if I didn't like talking to Brittani after she lost her fucking mind and started demanding that I account for my every movement? After she started tracking my location on her phone and asking me about every place I went. My whereabouts were the only god damn thing she ever wanted to talk about, and I never even gave her a reason to mistrust me. Jesus Christ, our relationship was a nightmare.

Recovering myself, I say, "Nothing happened with the friend. That was all in Brittani's head."

Lani narrows her eyes. "Things are rarely *all* in a person's head. I'm sure you gave her some reason to be jealous."

I sigh heavily. "There was one night after we came home from a party and Brittani passed out early. Her friend and I weren't tired, so we stayed up watching *The Office* together. We were laughing. Brittani woke up and heard us. That was it. That's the extent of my 'cheating' with best friend Olivia."

Lani nods slowly, but she still seems a little skeptical.

She looks like she's about to respond when, to my immense aggravation, Mia interrupts again. "Okay, why don't we change the subject, Lani? This is really awkward making Logan talk about all of this personal stuff in front of us."

"I'm fine," I say, but Mia isn't swayed.

"No," she says knowingly, as if certain I was only being polite. "Lani will interrogate you for hours if you let her. She loves this kind of stuff."

Please interrogate me, I want to say. *Take me to your bedroom and interrogate me.* But I can see from Lani's body language that she's done too. She seems to have withdrawn into herself. Irrationally, I hate Mia for it.

Lani starts talking to one of her roommates. Since I'm out of earshot, I can't jump in to keep my conversation with her going. I glance back at Mia to see eager blue eyes fixed on my face. I should be relieved that I still seem to hold her interest after the less-than-flattering information I just shared, and yet I can't help but be annoyed. If Mia stakes her claim on me, will that drive Lani away? Armaan wouldn't hesitate to steal a girl I liked first, but girls tend to be more sensitive about this kind of thing.

As we make polite conversation—discussing the typical stuff like our majors and where we grew up—I make a conscious effort not to seem too enthusiastic, inwardly vowing to make my interest in Leilani apparent before the night is up.

Our conversation is interrupted when Brenna calls me into the kitchen to look at the cake. I had forgotten about it, and that it was she and Lani who made it for me. My stomach flips at the thought. It makes me wonder if Leilani, like Mia, was interested in me before we even met tonight.

When I walk into the kitchen, everyone else follows. Brenna

gestures to the cake on the wooden table. It's a fancy cake, like something you'd see in a bakery—tall with white frosting and curling calligraphy letters at the top. I'm warmed by the image of Lani making this just for me.

"Armaan told us we spelled 'Brittani' wrong," Brenna says.

I nod. "She spells it with an 'i' instead of a 'y.' I don't care, but Brittani would definitely make you fix it if she were here." I can't fight the cynical smile rising to my lips.

"Would she really?" She turns around and frowns at the cake. "What a cunt," she mumbles.

Lani rushes over to the cake. My eyes are drawn to her brown legs, surprisingly long for her petite stature. They look soft too. I can already imagine what they'd feel like wrapped around my waist…

"No, she's not." Lani's voice drives my eyes to her face. Good timing too. I don't want to get too carried away when the night has barely started. "If it's something she would care about, we need to fix it." After lifting a serving knife from the table, Lani scrapes off the frosting "y." She walks over to the fridge and pulls out a plastic bag with a metal cap. I watch her long fingers as she writes a frosting "i" with a deft twist of her wrists. When she's done she turns to me, and I'm overcome again by the intensity of her unblinking stare. "This is not an exercise of spite," she says. "Closure Cake is a celebration of your relationship. We need to be respectful to Brittani. Logan." My dick twitches at my name on her lips. "Brenna and I are trusting you by including you in our ritual. No more shit-talking Brittani."

My lips quirk. "Got it."

She raises a brow. "Good. Now, before I cut the cake, I want you to shut your eyes and think about your happiest memory with Brittani."

Collective giggles erupt around the room. Lani's face is still serious, but maybe she's just not a giggler. Or a smiler. I glance at Brenna for guidance, who has a repressed smile on her lips. I look back at Lani. "Um…" I squint at her. "Are you fucking with me?"

"No," she says. "And I won't cut the cake until you do it. It's part of the ritual." She gestures with the cake knife in her hand as if to say, "Go on." And just like that, my dick stirs again. It takes so little with this girl. All she has to do is look at me with those intense eyes and order me around with the stern primness of an elementary school teacher.

"Okay," I say. I shut my eyes tight, torn between embarrassment for doing this in front of so many eyes—Armaan's especially—and the strong desire to please Lani. I take a slow, steady breath, trying to ignore the whispered chuckle I know belongs to Armaan.

I'm not thinking about my ex-girlfriend. Brittani Vaughn feels like ancient history already. Instead, my head is full of stern eyes and prim, heart-shaped lips. Memories of that high, husky voice floating in and out. *I would punish you too.* When heat shoots into my groin, I figure I've been closing my eyes long enough. I don't want anyone around me to guess my thoughts.

The first thing I see when I open my eyes is Lani's concentrated stare looking back at me. Warm pleasure spreads through me. She looks like she's fascinated. Like I'm as interesting to her as she is to me.

"What did you think about?" Brenna asks.

I smile faintly. "Something personal."

"That means blowjob," Armaan says. "Although, he's already

told me that Brittani was pretty stingy with oral. One of her many wonderful qualities."

"I never said that!" I exclaim, hating him for the millionth time tonight for his god damn mouth.

He smirks. "You did, though."

I'm saved from arguing when Lani intervenes. "Armaan! None of that. I told you this is a ritual of respect."

"Seriously, no more!" Brenna shouts. "I'll banish you from this kitchen. You won't get any cake!"

Armaan shrugs before taking a sip of his Stone IPA. "I'd rather just have beer anyway—no offense, Lani."

"More for us," Lani says, stepping closer to the cake. She takes the serving knife and cuts into the white frosting, bending slightly at her hips. My eyes run up and down her body. She's thin and muscular, but not without curves. Her hips flair gently and her legs are shapely. She moves gracefully, like a dancer, even while doing something as unathletic as slicing a cake.

She turns around with a slice of cake and a fork on a small plate in her hand. She approaches me slowly with that unblinking gaze, and I wish I could ask her to feed me. "Don't take a bite yet," she says as she hands me the plate. "I want to watch you eat it."

Giggles erupt around the room, and I fight the urge to drop my jaw. *I want to watch you.* Her words make me hot everywhere. Nothing about her serious tone would suggest that she was trying to arouse or fluster me, but she could not have been more successful had she knelt in front of me and unzipped my pants. I can't help but wonder what else she might want to watch me do.

After handing out slices of cake to everyone else in the room,

Lani walks back over to me. "Okay," she says. "You can eat. And you don't need to tell me if you like it or not, because I'll see it in your eyes."

I smile. "Is that why you want to watch me?"

"Yes." Her eyes roam my face. Heat fills my belly as her eyes fix on mine. I take a forkful of the cake and slowly lift it to my mouth, enjoying her gaze now on my lips. After I finish chewing and swallowing, she smiles. "You like it."

"It's delicious," I say, though I'm not really sure. I barely paid attention to the cake. All I can think about is her. It makes me impatient. "Let's hang out tomorrow. Let's go see *Deadpool 2*." When she continues to stare at me blankly, I add, "With Armaan and Brenna." A double date. She can't be opposed to that.

Her body language shifts. She seems more remote and aloof than she has all night. A slight notch forms between her brows. She looks away from me, seeming lost in thought. "I've never seen the first *Deadpool*," she says quietly.

"Well, we need to correct that because it's amazing. I've actually heard *Deadpool 2* isn't that great, but I'm a Marvel completist, so I have to see it. We should watch the first one together before going to the theater."

I realize my mistake when she lifts her eyes and I see the surprise behind them. I'm too forward for her comfort. For all her candor, she's reserved. Slow to warm up.

"I don't like Marvel movies."

Changing tactics, I wince. "That hurts. Did I really need that after everything? After you told me I'm weak and an embarrassment to myself?"

Though she tries to smile, she looks unsure of herself for the first time. "I'm sorry I said all of that. Mia was right. I say rude things without thinking sometimes."

"Oh, I wasn't asking for an apology. I was actually thinking about asking you to marry me."

I feel like howling in victory when she gives me a small smile, lifting her hand to tuck a strand of dark hair behind her ear. The nervous gesture makes her seem human for the first time. Shy and wanting my approval. Suddenly less intimidating. "I mean I know it's kind of sudden since I just got out of a toxic relationship, and I literally just met you an hour ago, but I don't know… It seems right. What do you say?"

Abruptly her smile fades, her large brown eyes narrowing. "If I say 'no,' will you need me to come over tonight and hold you in bed while you cry?"

My lips part into an open-mouth smile. "I think rude is an understatement. You're vicious!"

* * *

"I'm going to need your help with Leilani," I tell Armaan on our drive home later that night. "I scared her off tonight."

"Finally!" he shouts, lifting one hand from the steering wheel. "Every girl you meet should be scared of you."

"Probably," I say. "But this is much more intense than usual, and I got way ahead of myself. I asked her to hang out tomorrow, and it freaked her out."

"So she shot you down. Good for her."

"I know. She's incredible. The way she talks… The way she commands your attention… She's like, 'I've got shit to say, and you're going to listen! Sit your ass down while I tell you what a worthless piece of shit you are.'" I shake my head, in a daze.

"She's amazing."

"You have serious problems."

His gaze on the road, he can't see when I roll my eyes. He'll never admit it but he likes the same thing. We're both just a couple of chill guys who enjoy it when a woman bosses us around. I just happen to be more open about it. I don't see anything wrong with it.

When we get to a stop sign, he turns to me. "You could have had Mia!"

"No way. She's every bit as boring as she is hot. She's your type. You should go after her."

He shakes his head dejectedly. "I already ruined my chances."

"Speaking of the ruiner-of-your-chances," I say, annoyed that he continues to downplay his infatuation with Brenna, "do you think Brenna likes me enough to help me out with Leilani?"

"I don't know, and I really don't want to ask. Do you think you could just chill out for once and let things happen naturally?"

"No, I really can't. I think I might be in love with her already."

"Oh my god! You told me just three hours ago that you weren't going to be in another relationship for the rest of college."

"Yep, and I meant it, but that was before I met Leilani."

And I feel like my entire life could be divided into Before Leilani and After Leilani, like pursuing her might be the most important thing I ever do. I knew it in my gut the moment I looked into those severe brown eyes as they saw right through me.

CHAPTER 3

Present Day

Leilani

"I want to make him regret it," I tell my psychologist.

Dr. Scott's eyes widen minutely. He uncrosses his legs, then crosses them again. The moment therapy started, I launched into a calm, almost robotic recitation of the events of the last thirty-six hours, and Dr. Scott just finished complementing me for respecting Logan's boundaries. Instead of rolling my eyes—as I was sorely tempted—I got straight to the point.

When he doesn't comment, I continue. "Which means I need to get healthy. He's not going to regret losing this shell of a person I've become, so I need to fix things. And since I only have thirty days, I need you to tell me what to do without any placating bullshit—no offense. I'm not that fragile anymore. Just tell me what I need to do to become the woman I was four months ago."

He doesn't flinch at my rudeness. I've always appreciated that about him. He has the perfect demeanor for a psychologist— pleasant and unflappable.

If only he also had helpful things to say.

"That's not really a question I can answer. If you want to 'get healthy'"—he makes air quotes—"we can talk about strategies, but I can't guarantee you'll become who you once were. I'm an existentialist." He smiles. "I believe we are who we are right now. It's impossible to become the Leilani of four months ago."

I fight the urge to scowl at him. Isn't there some psychology rule where you don't allow your personal beliefs to guide therapy?

"Well, I'm the one seeking therapy right now, and I'm a nihilist. So nothing matters, and nothing you tell me will have lasting consequences in a world that may not actually exist. So just tell me what to do to make my soon-to-be ex-boyfriend suffer."

He smiles faintly, because he thinks I'm being facetious. It's annoying how he always assumes the best of me, that all the snark I throw his way is just playfulness. Even three solid months of weekly therapy hasn't taught him my vindictive streak.

"Up until today," he says softly, "you weren't open to weaning your Ativan use. Is that still the case?"

Startled by the question, my eyes dart to his face. There's a wealth of understanding behind the dark eyes staring back at me. My throat freezes when I realize he knew. He knew all along. Apparently, he's not as dense as I've always thought he was. He knew I was taking too much. Was it that obvious, even to someone I see for fifty minutes once a week at ten in the morning on a Monday?

"No," I answer, my voice strained. "I'm willing to cut back. Even cut it out entirely if necessary."

"In that case," he says, and suddenly his voice sounds very loud, like he's shouting at me. "I recommend cutting out daily use, at the very least. That medication was never meant to be taken every day, as I'm sure your doctor has already explained."

My doctor prescribed it at your recommendation, I want to say. "Yes," I say instead.

"If you feel a panic attack coming, use the other strategies we've practiced instead. Try to cut your use to every other day at first." In a lowered voice, he adds, "even if it means allowing yourself to have a panic attack."

I want to shut my eyes in despair, but instead I nod faintly.

"And if you find you can't do that, Leilani, and you may find that it's very difficult, then we should talk about other options."

"Like a Narcotics Anonymous program?" I ask, my voice just above a whisper.

"Yes."

* * *

My heart pounds as I leave the counseling office, but even fear can't curb my anger. On the contrary, I'm energized with rage. My body feels so light, I could almost skip to where I parked my car this morning in Lot 22.

When I step into my bedroom, I glance at the clock on my desk. 12:06. Over twenty-four hours since my conversation with Logan, and yet my exhilaration hasn't waned. How can brain chemistry change so drastically from one moment to the next? I remember sitting there in silent panic, waiting for him to

31

deliver the final blow, and then storming out of his apartment in righteous fury not ten minutes later.

How is this happening? Losing Logan was my greatest fear!

If only I had known that losing him would actually become the solution, at least temporarily, to all of my problems. Instead of panic thrumming through my limbs, I feel simmering anger. Instead of fear of abandonment, I feel the rage of injustice. I once was a dying woman, but now I'm a soldier marching into battle.

Granted, I know this feeling won't last. Euphoria is as short-lived as the blissful feeling of peace from my Ativan.

And speaking of Ativan, I took two before bed last night. Oh, I had a list of rationalizations that all seemed completely legit before I washed those pills down my throat.

1) It had only been twelve hours since my conversation with Logan, and who was I to say this euphoric feeling wouldn't disappear into the night, that I wouldn't jolt awake in a gasping fit at the weight of my loss? 2) One Ativan wouldn't be enough, not if I wanted a dead, dreamless sleep, and 3) Don't I deserve that? My sweet, beautiful, perfect boyfriend just broke my heart, for fuck's sake. And, finally, 4) I have a prescription, yo! Would my doctor have given it to me if I didn't need it?

What a bullshitter I've become. And is there anything more pathetic than bullshitting yourself?

Also, I'm pretty sure I took three Ativan last night.

Brutal self-reflection would have decimated me twenty-four hours ago, and yet now I embrace it with such force I can hardly believe what I'm about to do. Without giving myself a chance to second guess, I rush to my dresser and yank open the top drawer. I frantically rummage through a pile of underwear until I feel the plastic tube beneath my fingers. After gripping it tightly, I jog to the bathroom.

As I stand over the toilet, I rattle the bottle, cringing slightly at the sound.

There are so many in there.

I'm frozen in hesitation, feeling like I might stand here forever staring hypnotically into the toilet water. How can I open the lid and dump out my sole source of relief and contentment?

When I took my first Ativan three months ago, I felt those magical rom-com sparks—*Now I know why nothing ever felt right before. It was you I waited for.* It made me the person I always wanted to be—my body relaxed, my mind sharpened. The anxious thoughts were the same but without the catastrophic effects. What once was fragile like glass became as indifferent as water.

It's always been you. Only you.

Even then, I wasn't an idiot. I knew it was a dangerous love. I was cautious. I only took it when I sensed a panic attack coming, which was exactly what my doctor instructed me to do. Could I help it if I had multiple panic attacks a day? And I only combined it with alcohol out of necessity. I'm a college student. It would seem peculiar if I didn't drink at a party.

Or so I told myself.

And I almost forgot about that nearly full bottle of Xanax I swiped from my parent's medicine cabinet on my last visit home, the one I told myself over and over again in an almost hypnotic daze that I needed more than they did. "Acute panic disorder is much more urgent than the fleeting anxiety of an infrequent flier. They probably won't even notice it's gone for another year."

Oh. And I guess I also forgot about the fifteen Valium I was able to score from my family's idiot primary care doctor in Palo Alto, when I told him I needed something to get me through mid-terms. He even gave me the strong stuff, probably the exact same prescription he's been handing out since the mid-70s.

Those pills were heaven.

God, I'm a mess.

Suddenly, a memory is summoned. The memory of hunching over this very toilet while Logan said all of those ugly words. "You're a fucking mess, do you know that? You seriously should win some kind of sloppy drunk girl championship ring for your performance tonight."

A fresh wave of rage propels me into action. After twisting off the cap, I watch the pills fall in a clamoring stream into the toilet water, while only a distant part of me clenches at the sight.

I toss the empty bottle into the trash before turning slowly to the sink to stare at my reflection.

I don't look like a femme fatale yet. I'm too wan and thin and my shoulders still hunch, but I'll bring that golden hue back to my skin. I'll bring back that dancer posture, those full cheeks, and barely B cup size. I'll bring it all back by will alone.

I'll get revenge on Logan Henderson if it's the last thing I do. The next time we meet, he'll see a different girl than the one who begged him not to leave her on that wretched night. The quirky, brainy, classy as fuck Leilani of the past will be back, even if I have to use black magic to resurrect her.

Only she'll no longer be his for the taking, and if there's one thing Logan can't stand, it's being told he can't have something.

CHAPTER 4

Past—The First Non-Date

Logan

Armaan's phone buzzes. He picks it up, swipes it, and furrows his brow while his eyes scan the screen. I clench my teeth in anticipation of what he's about to tell me, my eyes straining to read his pensive facial expression. "She agreed to come out with us tonight," he finally says. "But she doesn't want you to think it's a date."

I exhale slowly and feel a mixture of relief and disappointment at this new development. I ought to achieve sainthood for my restraint in my pursuit of Leilani Girard since I met her three days ago, and I'd be lying to myself if I didn't admit I expected a greater reward than this for my efforts. Aside from asking Armaan to get her to hang out with us, I pretty much left the ball in her court.

I've literally never done that before.

Armaan looks at me pityingly. "She's understandably…" he tilts his head to the side as if searching for a word, "*nervous* to agree to go on a date with someone who likes to go to his ex-girlfriend's house and hold her in bed while she cries."

I glare at him. "Yeah, thanks a lot for telling them all of my relationship problems before they even met me. Great strategy on your part. Now Leilani thinks I'm a fucking lunatic."

"You were the one who told her about the crying in bed thing, not me." He shakes his head. "You did it all yourself, bro."

"None of it would have even come up if you hadn't told them everything first. Now I have to undo all the damage you've done."

"It probably won't even matter. You always find these gorgeous girls who somehow don't realize something is wrong with you when you tell them you're in love with them after three days. It's so annoying."

"One girl!" I shout, my hand gesturing a "one." "I told *one* girl I loved her after three days because I was out of my mind drunk. Thanks to you and Miller and your fucking tequila beer pong! I'm so fucking sick of hearing that story told over and over again." When a thought occurs to me, I shoot him a menacing glare. "You will *never* tell Leilani the Cabo story. Are we clear about that?"

He rolls his eyes. "I don't need to tell her. She probably knows just by looking at you. And what do you mean it only happened one time? You're in love with *her* already."

He's right, but it's different. I can't seem to convince anyone that falling in love with Leilani at first sight has more to do with her exceptionality than the fact I'm a relationship sociopath.

"That's different," I say.

"Sure it is."

* * *

Leilani

Brenna shoots me a sympathetic look from across the table. Great. That means my nervousness is painfully obvious.

I can't believe I agreed to come tonight. The situation is exactly what I expected. Armaan, Brenna, Kyle, and Mia all huddle together at the other side of our long bar table, leaving me to fend for myself with The Relationship Sociopath.

Sensing his gaze, I dare a glance across the table. My sixth sense was correct. He's staring with *that* look, those pouting lips curling at the edges, those heavy lids nearly shutting, like he's in love with me already.

I fight the urge to glare at him. Why won't he just leave me alone?

It would be so much easier to resist him if he wasn't so beautiful with his thick dark hair, tan skin, and angular jaw. If only I could fuck him just once…

But that's a terrible idea. Then he'd never leave me alone.

He's far more tempting than I expected from everything Armaan told us, like that wretched Cabo story. It's easy to see why he's had so many girlfriends. Logan has that annoying ability to talk to anyone he meets with the same steady friendliness and ease. His pale green eyes are expressive and sincere, alighting his face with warmth. He even seems trustworthy. Then again, there's a reason they call him a relationship sociopath. Women trusted Ted Bundy too.

"You're nervous," that drawling voice says, pulling me out of my head. I clench my teeth as I lift my eyes to meet his. His smile has changed. His eyes are gentler, as if he's trying to put me at ease. And how like someone without social anxiety to use a line like that to put me at ease. *You're nervous.* Oh thanks. I feel much less nervous now that you pointed it out to me. Why don't you draw attention to the rings of armpit sweat on my dress while you're at it?

"Yes," I answer, unsmiling.

"Why?" It might be my imagination, but I catch a hint of triumph in the question, as if he thinks making me nervous is a good sign. A sign that he's important to me.

It's time to dispel that assumption.

I stare at him in a moment of indecision, wondering if I should just go for it and bare all to him. What do I have to lose? It's not like I have to be around him in the future, and this might send him for the hills sooner, sparing me the effort of avoiding him. "This situation is my nightmare."

"Your nightmare?" I'm delighted by the apprehension in his voice. "What do you mean?"

I glance around the table before meeting his eyes again. "It's a set up. I'm only here because you harassed Armaan into making me come, and everyone else is ignoring us so that we can get to know each other. For a person with social anxiety, this is a nightmare. I'm under everyone's scrutiny, and they all expect something of me that I won't be able to perform. I can't just get to know you like a normal person would. I'm not capable of it even if I wanted to. I have no social skills. I don't know how to laugh if you tell a dumb joke, and judging by that ever-present smirk of yours, you'll probably tell a lot of them. I can't smile and say 'oh, she's a doll' when you show me pictures of your niece, because I have even less interest in small children than I do in you. If I'm being forced to talk to you, I'd much rather have a conversation about the Coen brothers or super volcanoes, though I doubt you'd have anything to say on either subject that would interest me, and feigning interest is yet another of my social weaknesses. I'd rather you just go away. Go pester someone else." I turn my head and glance pointedly at Mia.

Logan's already wide eyes became saucers at that last statement.

"Although…" I start, feeling a twinge of guilt for my harshness. "Maybe you would have something interesting to say about the Coen brothers. Maybe I'm stereotyping you because you have a dumb face. And a dumb voice. And you like superhero movies."

He chokes out a laugh. "Dude! You're savage! Apparently, I'm not just weak. I'm also dumb, unfunny, and you have zero interest in me." He lifts his hand and ticks each item on his fingers, a wide grin on his face. "Is there anything else?"

My lips lift at the corners of their own volition. It's hard to dislike him when he accepts my rudeness with such grace. It makes me realize that I've been using my gaucheness as an excuse to be deliberately mean. I'm compelled to offer some form of an apology. "I didn't say you were dumb, only that you have a dumb face and a dumb voice, which is completely different."

"What exactly do you mean by that?"

My eyes roam his pretty face with those bedroom eyes and half-smile. "You just look like the stereotype of a handsome, dumb guy, but it has nothing to do with your actual intelligence. Your voice sounds dumb, but it has nothing to do with the content of what you say. You speak slowly, kind of out of the side of your mouth. It's the most Southern California accent I've ever heard. I'm from the Bay Area, and I didn't even realize our accents differed that much until I heard you speak."

He narrows his eyes, as if considering my words, and I can't help but notice that he only looks dumber.

"It's not an insult," I say. "People are drawn to dumb people, often to their detriment. It's why Trump was elected, against all odds."

He ticks his fourth finger. "And I'm like Trump."

I roll my eyes. "I didn't say that."

He grins. "Leilani's a super pretty name. I read online it's Hawaiian."

"It is."

He stares at me with his brows raised, as if expecting me to elaborate.

"Are you Hawaiian?"

I sigh. "Yes. My mom grew up in Maui. My grandparents still live there."

He grins. "I fucking love Maui, dude! Have you visited there a lot?"

"Yes," I answer, averting my eyes from his.

I can't have this. Now that he's broken the ice, he wants to get to know me. He'll want me to tell him about the summers I spent on my grandparents' avocado farm in Hana and why I chose my major and what sports I played in high school. "This conversation is boring."

His eyes widen a little. "Okay," he says, but he sounds like he's holding back laughter.

"This is what I meant earlier. I don't want to talk to you about things like that. If I had any interest in dating you, I might make the sacrifice of stating autobiographical facts one by one. Since I'm not, I'll only talk about things I find interesting, or nothing at all."

"Okay," he says, and this time I hear laughter in his voice.

It's amazing how undaunted he is. No one in my life has ever reacted to my candor this way. He almost seems like he likes it.

"Look," he says, leaning his broad shoulders into the table. "We can talk about anything you want. I'm just happy to be hanging out with you. I like you a lot, but I don't want you to feel like I'm pestering you. If you want me to go away, I will."

My eyes fixed on the table, I purse my lips, deciding whether or not to believe him. It could be a trick. He could be using humility to make me lower my guard. The problem is that I don't want him to go away. I wish I wasn't so drawn to him against my better judgment.

"I don't just love superhero movies, by the way. I fucking love *No Country for Old Men*."

I blink once, momentarily forgetting my earlier reference to the Coen brothers.

"I think it's a masterpiece," he continues. "And you were right—I'm probably not smart enough to say much about the Coen brothers, except that I fucking love movies about assassins, and Anton Chigurh might be my favorite of all time."

I smile wide, impressed that he actually knows the name of Anton Chigurh. "*No Country* is definitely their masterpiece."

He nods. "They make the best weed movies. I have probably five of their movies on my list."

I frown. "Your list of…weed movies?"

"Yeah, it's pretty straightforward. Just a list of the best movies to watch when you're high. Or…I guess the concept is straightforward, but Armaan and I have gotten into some heated arguments about what goes on the list. He would say that *No Country* shouldn't be on it because it's hard to follow when you're really high, but that doesn't make sense because *2001*— the Stanley Kubrick movie—is the holy grail of weed movies, and I'm not a hundred percent sure I even know what it's about when I'm sober, and I've seen it like a hundred times."

"You've seen *2001: A Space Odyssey* a hundred times?" When he nods, I ask, "Do you like any other Stanley Kubrick movies?"

"Oh, hell yeah!" He frowns, as if offended by the question. "I fucking love Stanley Kubrick. *The Shining* is the greatest horror movie of all time, and the second-greatest weed movie."

I stare at him, arrested. I realize I must be insulting him by my shock, but I never expected to be so thoroughly entertained. Or to share his taste in movies.

He smiles. "I feel like you just put me through some hipster test and I passed."

I don't even bother correcting his assumption. "You passed. You should know ahead of time that I judge people for not sharing my taste in art. It's irrational, but I have no desire to change."

He shrugs. "All hipsters do that, but I've never met anyone as honest about it as you. It's actually very un-hipster to admit it like that. And I'm relieved you want to talk about the Coen brothers. Armaan told me you're deep into your sociology major. I was worried you'd want to talk about Noam Chomsky or something and I'd have to work really hard to sound smart.

Apparently, it would have been extra hard for me too, with my dumb face and dumb voice. I'd already have a handicap going in."

A smile tugs at my lips. "Why would I want to talk about Noam Chomsky?"

"I don't know. I just thought maybe you'd want to talk about sociology shit."

"He's a linguist. Do you know anything about sociology?"

"Not really, no."

I smile as I roll my eyes. "Don't worry, I won't be talking about sociology tonight. I'm not *that* socially inept. You won't have to try to sound smart."

"That's a legitimately huge relief." He follows that with a smile that makes my insides turn to mush. I can't stop my lips from lifting into a wide, girlish grin. His self-deprecation is utterly disarming. I can't imagine being so comfortable in my own skin.

An idea occurs to me. I glance around the table to assess the situation, to see if people in our group are keeping an eye on us. As I suspected, Armaan is looking in our direction, a slight smile on his face, likely at the progress Logan has made with me. The sight of it propels me to make my next move. I turn to Logan. "I hate this bar. Let's go somewhere else. Just the two of us."

His eyes widen in surprise, but he quickly schools it away. Clearly trying to look casual, he nods once. "Sure. Let's go."

* * *

Logan

"Why do you always have to be in a relationship?" Lani asks with that unblinking stare that hypnotized me on the night we met. "What's wrong with you?"

I shut my eyes as I chuckle. This is probably the tenth time she's insulted me in the last hour alone, and yet I don't remember having so much fun talking to anyone in my life. "You're a delight, Leilani."

She frowns as she crosses her arms. She leans back into the iron bar stool as if to give herself the space to examine me. "Don't be evasive. I'm genuinely curious."

Heat creeps up my neck as I try to fight the smile tugging at my lips. I don't think I've ever met anyone who seems to find me this interesting, and certainly never anyone like her—someone I'd lie to impress if I had to. I've been smiling so much this past hour, my face almost hurts.

"I know you well enough by now to know that you wouldn't have asked me if you weren't. Um…" I purse my lips to the side, trying to think of an answer that would satisfy her. "I don't think I *have to* be in a relationship, I just tend to be in them, but I'm fine being single too. I don't know… I think I'm more decisive than most people. When I meet someone and it feels right, I'm confident in my gut instinct, and I just go for it."

"Why? If you've been the one to break up with all of your girlfriends—and usually after a very brief amount of time, according to Armaan—then your gut instinct has always been wrong. You're an incredibly poor judge of what's right for you."

God, she's amazing. I smile slowly, hoping that my feelings

for her aren't all over my face. "I don't think I was necessarily wrong about them just because I wanted to break up with them later. I think the night we met gave you a bad impression of my past. None of my other relationships ended as disastrously as my relationship with Brittani. I've had a lot of good times. And I broke up with them because I'm just as confident in my gut instinct when it tells me things are wrong."

She rolls her eyes. "Your gut instinct ought to be telling you that things are wrong between us."

I exhale as quietly as I can, trying not to show her how much her continued resistance irritates me. Leaning into the table, I lower my voice when I say, "I don't know how you could say that. I've never had this much fun talking to anyone in my life. Is it just me? Are you bored right now?"

When the question came out, it was rhetorical. I know she's having fun. She's barely taken her eyes off of me since we ditched the others an hour ago. I've made her smile and even laugh, which is no easy feat. But when she doesn't answer right away, I start to feel nervous. I run my eyes over her face, trying to read her thoughts.

Abruptly, she meets my eyes. "No, I'm not bored," she says, her tone almost resentful.

Relief washes through me, another smile spreading across my face. I'll take it. I'll take her resisted attraction over her indifference any day.

"I like that you let me say exactly what's on my mind," she says. "I like that you let me ask rude questions."

My smile grows lazy. "You can ask me rude questions anytime you want." I reach my hand across the table and grab hers. She looks startled, but she doesn't withdraw. My stomach jolts in victory. Her hand is soft, but I try not to think about her skin just yet. With my other hand, I grab my beer and take a sip, feigning nonchalance.

"Do you want to have sex?"

I choke on the beer I just swallowed. My chest heaves in a violent coughing fit, my throat on fire. Leilani reaches out her hand and pats me on the back several times in a row, but it's futile. By the time my coughing dies down, my throat is itchy and my vision a watery blur.

Through my foggy vision, I see a wide, pretty smile. "You look like you're crying."

My throat is raspy when I speak. "If you said that just to make me choke on my beer, I might actually start crying."

She laughs, a husky sound that sends shivers down my spine. "I've never seen that happen in real life! I thought it only happened in movies."

"Speaking of movies... No. Not speaking of movies. Speaking of the only thing I can think about right now, can you repeat your question? Maybe with more detail this time."

She smiles at my lack of finesse. "I asked if you wanted to have sex. What other details do you need?"

"When and where would be helpful."

"Now," she answers right away. "Or as soon as possible. At your place."

I shut my eyes for a moment, unable to believe my good fortune. I thought I had an uphill battle in winning her over. I had already resigned myself to not even kissing her for a few weeks at least, which is an eternity compared to my usual timeline. Never in my wildest dreams did I anticipate this. "Oh my god," I mumble before opening my eyes and meeting hers squarely. "You're my favorite person in the world, Leilani."

* * *

We don't even make it to my apartment.

Halfway up the stairwell, she pins me to the wall. The breath I'd been holding escapes me in a whoosh. She lifts her hand to my nape and curls her fingers into my hair. My eyes pop open when she yanks back suddenly and presses soft kisses over my neck. "Holy shit," I mumble, my voice strained.

"Am I hurting you?" she asks.

"God, no."

She presses her other hand against my waist, slipping it under my jeans and into my boxers. I hiss as her cold hand wraps around my dick. She releases her grip on my hair to look me in the eyes. "You're hard already," she says, smiling.

"Yeah." I release something between a gasp and a laugh. "I'm not even sure what's happening right now, but I don't want it to stop."

She looks over her shoulder and glances around the stairwell, the dim light casting shadows over the soft contours of her face. As she turns back to me, she strokes my dick up and down. The tickling pleasure that radiates into my belly is so overpowering I nearly whimper.

Shit. I need to get this under control. She already thinks I fall instantly in love. I don't want her to think I instantly come too.

"Have you ever had sex in a stairwell?" she asks, and the question alone sends another shooting pleasure into my groin. "Uh…" I begin, my brain barely functioning. "No." It sounds like a question.

She nods once before releasing her grip around my dick. I groan at the loss of contact. Her eyes fixed on my hips, she unbuttons and unzips my jeans. With a swift yank, she pulls my pants and boxers down, exposing my dick and ass to the damp air. My lips part. Is this really happening?

"We should probably be quick." Her tone is all business.

I release a whispered laugh. "That won't be a problem. For me, I mean."

Turning away from me, she lifts her purse from the concrete floor. After unzipping it, she pulls out a small square package.

"You keep condoms in your purse?" I ask.

"Yes." It's all she has to say about it.

Her eyes on my exposed dick, she approaches me slowly and drops to her knees. Her face is inches from my dick as she tears apart the condom wrapper with her teeth. I look away, unable to stand it. "I seriously might last thirty seconds," I find myself admitting. "Sorry in advance."

Even the slight pressure of her hand as she slips the condom over my dick sends a wave of heat into my belly.

"I don't mind," she says. "You like novelty just as much as I do. I've never had sex in a stairwell either." My eyes fix on her hips as she stands up and slips her hands under her sundress, removing tiny black underwear. To my surprise, she unzips her purse and slips them inside. She's not even trying to be sexy. She's swift and methodical, which only pushes me closer to the edge.

I lean back into the wall, shutting my eyes tight. "It's not the stairwell…"

Tossing her purse aside, she places her hands on my

shoulders. "Brace yourself. I may be short, but I'm not light."
With that she leaps onto me, gripping my shoulders and
wrapping her legs around my waist. My knees nearly buckle, but
not from her weight. In an effort to gain some self-control, I
turn around and press her against the wall, burying my head in
the crook of her neck. The slight brush of my dick against her
inner thigh calls to my senses, but I try to push it away.

"Logan…" Lani says, likely confused as to why I'm just
standing here holding her thighs and not moving.

"I need like…a solid minute before we start. Is that okay?"

"Sure." Her voice is gentle.

"Like, I literally need to count down from sixty seconds."

"Okay." She sounds like she's restraining laughter. I would
probably laugh too if I wasn't so fucking turned on. Jesus Christ,
will it always be like this with her?

After counting down and trying to think of unsexy things
like what I plan to eat tomorrow, I feel a little more in control.
I take a deep breath and release it slowly as I pull away and
look down at her face. "Okay. I think, at the very least, I've
successfully avoided embarrassment."

She smiles up at me, her full cheeks dimpling. "I wouldn't
mind if you lasted thirty seconds."

"Oh, I'm still going to last thirty seconds. I was worried
about jizzing all over you before we even started."

She laughs loudly, filling me with a different kind of pleasure.
This is the first time I've heard her laugh this hard, and the sound
of it flows through my body like a drug. This is how I want her.
As much as her cold severity turns me on, I want much more
from her, and I want it greedily. I want her to reserve this side of
herself only for me—a version of Leilani who actually seems like

the twenty-one-year-old girl that she is, with that unfeminine laugh and open-mouth grin.

"I'm ready now," I say.

She smiles coyly as she slips her hand between us. I brace myself for her touch, but I can't help groaning as she wraps her hand around my dick and guides it forward. She's wet, but I can't think about it or I'll tip over the edge.

I press forward and enter her. She's tight and slippery and the feeling makes my teeth clench.

Don't think about her pussy. Think about a grocery list or an email or that paper you have to write for Cultural Anthropology.

Distraction doesn't work. Her little gasp as I press all the way in is heavenly torture that sends a surge of heat that builds like a wave and…

Oh shit. No. Not now. Please not now.

Pressing her closer to the wall, I force my body to go very, very still. I shut my eyes and clench my teeth, begging my dick to let the wave recede.

"Why did you stop?" It sounds like a scold.

Even in my agony, a smile forms on my lips. "I can't be the shortest fuck of your life. It's just unacceptable."

"And I told you I don't care." Her voice is hard. "Do you think I asked for sex in the stairwell because I wanted a slow, leisurely fuck? I don't care if you last ten seconds. We have all night. Right now I want you to pound into me, slam me into the wall—"

"Jesus Christ! Stop talking!"

She narrows her eyes, a smile tugging at her lips. "I want your giant cock to plunge into my tight, wet pussy—"

"You're the fucking worst!" I shout as I pound into her. She makes a sound that starts as a laugh but drifts into something more like a whimper and suddenly I forget my embarrassment and become lost in the haze. I manage three hard thrusts before exploding with the most overwhelming pleasure of my life.

I take minutes to recover, and I'm still a panting, sweaty mess by the time I slip out of her and set her down.

It's not until we make our lazy tread into my apartment that I realize I haven't even kissed her yet.

* * *

Leilani

"When I was a little kid," he says, stroking my collarbone with the tips of his fingers. "I thought that basements didn't exist. Like, I thought they were just a movie thing. You know, like me choking on my beer earlier. It wasn't until I spent the summer with my great grandma in Missouri when I realized, holy shit, these things are real."

I smile, loving the hushed sound of his voice, and the way he keeps that same tone no matter what he shares. It's a tone of openness, steady and even because he has nothing to hide. I love that about him, and I feel like I could lay like this, with my head on his shoulder and his fingers running lightly over my skin, and listen to him talk forever.

I lift my head to smile at him. "Was your mind blown?"

He smiles ruefully. "It legitimately was. When I saw her basement for the first time, it was like the ending of *Fight Club*. Or Bruce Willis finding out that he's dead at the end of *The Sixth*

Sense—"

"Brad Pitt saying 'What's in the box?' at the end of *Seven*."

He grins, squeezing my thigh with his other hand. "Yes! I fucking love that movie." He leans forward and gives me a peck on the nose. "Anyway, my Grandma Louise was legitimately the best grandmother who ever lived. She was the kind of grandma who let you do everything your parents never let you do just because she was like, 'I'm older 'n hell and y'all can go fuck yourselves.'"

"That's a good southern accent."

"Thanks, but apparently it's inaccurate. My mom says Lauren and I remember her accent being way thicker than it actually was."

"Memory's funny that way." I lift my hand to stroke his hair, surprised at my own gesture of intimacy. I'm rarely this touchy with anyone, but then again, he's touchy with me. Most guys find me too cold to dare stroke and pet me like a lapdog. "Tell me about her basement."

His pale green eyes alight with warmth. "It was my little kid fantasy come to life. It was this giant room, and it was all cold and dark, and had this pullout bed and old school Nintendo. My cousins and Lauren and I could play video games all night long and be as loud as we wanted and no one could hear us. When I buy a house someday, it's going to have a basement."

My smile spreads across my face. I wonder if that basement is actually bigger and colder and darker in his memory than in real life, just like his grandma's embellished southern accent. Joy tends to do that to our memories. It makes me wonder if I'll remember Logan being even sweeter than he is right now, years from now, long after he's forgotten me. "Do you think you'll stay in California after college?"

"I don't know. Engineering jobs are everywhere, and sometimes I think of looking for one far away just to try something new, but then I'm not sure if I could live without Mexican food."

"I've thought the same thing!" I whisper-shout, not wanting to wake Armaan and Brenna in the next room over. "And I'll probably have to move to the Midwest for graduate school. I don't know how I'll survive."

This gets his attention. He lifts his head as if to get a better view of my face. "So graduate school is a set thing for you?"

"Oh, yeah. I knew it from the beginning when I chose sociology. But I don't mind. I love school. I'm a nerd."

He nods thoughtfully, and I wonder what he's thinking, why my after-college plans seem important to him. It couldn't be that he's thinking of our future already…

But then again, I almost forgot he's The Relationship Sociopath.

Well, whatever. Even if he's thinking about a relationship, he'll be long gone by the time I leave for graduate school.

The melancholy that overcomes me at that thought gives me pause. What's wrong with me? I just met this guy three days ago. It's unacceptable to be feeling this much already. I need to get a hold over myself.

I twist away from him, reaching for my phone on his nightstand. "It's after five," I say after tapping the screen. "I should probably head out." I hop off the bed and start searching for my dress, the cold air making my bare nipples hard.

"What?" He sounds shocked.

"I think we're long past actually sleeping—"

"Hell no, we're not! We're going to sleep in until noon and then I'm going to make you waffles."

I smile at his vehemence. "I'm not a good sleeper, and I don't like cuddling."

He scoots to the edge of his bed, gesturing to the wide-open spot next to him. "Then we won't cuddle, but you're not leaving. Come on. You know that's bullshit."

I stare at him steadily. "Logan, I won't be your next crazy ex-girlfriend."

He holds my gaze for a moment before snorting out a laugh. "I don't remember asking you to be my next crazy ex-girlfriend."

I lift a brow. "You know what I mean."

"No, I don't."

"You're thinking about our future already."

"I was actually just thinking about waffles." When I continue to stare at him skeptically, he shrugs one shoulder. "I don't know what to tell you, Lani. I'm a simple guy. I have a dumb face and a dumb voice and I like waffles. I want to make you some in the morning, which means you'll need to come back to bed. So, get over here." He pats the mattress. "And I've been having to stare at you naked for the last minute"—he gestures over my body—"so I can't promise you'll get to sleep right away. And I'm not really sorry about it either."

A small smile tugs at my lips as I make my slow walk back to the bed. He makes me feel light and easy, I realize, and that's why I like him so much already. I'm not a light and easy person. I'm dark and twisty most of the time, and being with Logan Henderson is a welcome reprieve.

But when he shifts his body over mine and plants a hard kiss on my lips, I realize his trick. Those friendly eyes don't fool me as they stare back at me with hard, possessive triumph.

He does want me to be his next crazy ex-girlfriend. And he wouldn't have so many crazy ex-girlfriends behind him if he wasn't good at luring us in, and lowering our guards. He knows exactly what to say to make our icy hearts melt.

I refuse to fall for it

CHAPTER 5

Present Day

Leilani

Rage gets a bad rap. Not only does it feel so much better than fear, it's also far more motivating. I've known all along how to aid my recovery in the long-term, but I had no desire to do it. Eating well, exercising, and daily meditation take effort, and I was perfectly content to wallow in a hazy Ativan fog of self-pity. I sought only immediate solutions to fear and loneliness, like junk food, mindless TV, or pathetic texts to Logan.

When my worst fear was finally realized and the anger settled in, the brain fog cleared. I now see a straight path to getting better, and all I have to do is move my feet one at a time. Who knew that revenge could do such wonders for mental health?

It's been three days since the dreaded conversation with Logan, and my ire hasn't cooled in the slightest. On the contrary, it's nearly consumed me.

I'm reminded of those blissful weeks after we met, and how I thought about him constantly when he wasn't around. I thought about running my fingers through his soft, wavy hair, caressing the smooth skin on his face, and kissing those full pink lips. I imagined his smile more than anything, and every single time I did, heat pooled in my belly.

Now, the thought of crushing that smile turns me on almost as much.

Granted, it hasn't been a picnic. I've had a near constant headache since I flushed my pills down the toilet two days ago. I haven't stopped sweating, my hands twitch, and even as I sit here my pulse races like I just got back from a run. The symptoms are almost identical to panic. And yet somehow, against all odds, I haven't had a single attack.

Revenge has been my savior.

Revenge has given me distraction, purpose, and even joy.

I smile wickedly as I stare at my completed list.

It's perfect. Worth the thirty minutes I spent on Pinterest learning how to make these calligraphy letters. I even wrote it on pink stationary to embrace femininity. This list, after all, is about the empowerment of women.

It's about reclaiming my dignity.

I relish completing each item. Nothing, not even sex in a stairwell, could give me more pleasure.

And it's not as if I wrote a *Kill Bill* Death List. None of the items on my list will cause a fuckboy like Logan Henderson any long-term damage. I have no reason to feel guilty, especially after everything he's done to me.

I don't ask for much.

It's hardly a surprise that I want to look hot again when I've been dressing like a slob for the last three months (Item 1—Makeover). And wouldn't it be nice for Logan to see this hot, self-possessed woman and wonder how his next crazy ex-girlfriend could ever live up? If I want that to happen I'll have to find a way to see him before the break is over (Item 2—Lure him back), because thirty days is an eternity in fuckboy time. I could be fully replaced if I wait the full month. Obviously, I'll need to seduce him (Item 3), which isn't too out of line because he's still technically my boyfriend. Finally, I want to be the one to deliver the breakup speech, preferably while he's still inside me (Item 4).

Oh. And I want to make him cry (Item 5).

Notably, the meanest part of the list.

But, really, is that too big of an ask? Is it sadistic to want a small sign of regret after he abandoned me in my darkest hour?

CHAPTER 6

Past—The T-shirt

Logan

"Oh, Logan." Armaan cringes. "This should be the funniest moment of my life, but it's just too sad."

"Mhmm," I answer absently, lifting another letter patch from the pile. I squint as I try to peel off the thin plastic backing with my thumb, nearly breaking my nail before eventually getting a hold of it. "Fucking Michaels makes cheap shit," I mumble as I place the "T" on the red fabric. I groan after placing the iron down, realizing I didn't properly align the "T" with the "S" to its left.

"You do realize that this is some really pathetic shit, right?" Armaan asks.

"Yes."

Today is the Santa Barbara Women's March, and Armaan

and I were invited to come along with a large group of Lani and Brenna's girlfriends. Lani told me to make a sign, "Either something feminist or anti-Trump," she said. "Just make it clear that you're a feminist." And I decided to go out on a limb by making this T-shirt.

The last two months with her have been heavenly—near perfect, with one glaring exception. She still refuses to label our relationship. It's a bizarrely stubborn move on her part considering she's given in on everything else.

We have a whole routine now. I make her breakfast in the morning before she leaves for class, and she comes back in the evening to sit on my bed with her laptop and do homework. We even go to Farmer's Market on Tuesday nights to get produce and her favorite oatmeal pancake mix, like we're a fucking married couple. And when we wake up in the middle of the night with our limbs entangled, she doesn't pull away, even though she still claims she doesn't like cuddling.

She's warmed up to me. In all ways but one, but god damn it I'm a greedy bastard, and I can't stand it. If she's going to basically be my girlfriend, she should *be my god damn girlfriend*.

After ironing the last letter, I lift up the shirt to show Armaan the final product. "My Boyfriend Is a Feminist" in bold letters. "What do you think? Should I start my own Etsy business?"

Armaan groans. "I changed my mind. I don't think you're a relationship sociopath. I think you might just be a regular sociopath."

"You said that Lani might be a serial killer, so I guess that makes us perfect for each other. Trust me, this will make her laugh. That was the whole point in making it." When the words ring hollow to my own ears, I wonder if I'm trying to convince myself more than Armaan.

He lifts a brow. "I think the point is that all of their friends will be at the March and you want a sign across her tits announcing that you're her boyfriend."

It's not a leap for him to come up with that, given that I've been whining about my predicament whenever I get the chance. I'm envious of his relationship with Brenna. He hasn't known her much longer than I've known Leilani, but she's given him none of the same stubbornness, and he doesn't even appreciate it.

"You should have made her some yoga pants. Then you could have ironed 'Logan was here' on her ass."

I roll my eyes, wishing that my possessiveness wasn't so glaringly obvious. I wish I had control over this frustrating itch to stake my claim on her. It's a really bad look, especially since we're going to a fucking Women's March today.

With that thought, I fix Armaan with a glare. "Don't say any of that sexist shit in front of the girls. Not even as a joke."

"I won't need to. She'll know as soon as she sees that stupid T-shirt."

* * *

We arrive at the Blue House an hour early to pick the girls up for the March. Armaan knocks the ornate wooden door once before walking in, and I envy the sign of intimacy. For as much time as I've spent with Lani these last few months, I still wouldn't have the balls to enter her house without being let in first, like a fucking vampire, but Armaan doesn't have to worry about seeming presumptuous to their roommates because he has the "boyfriend" label.

Armaan immediately walks toward Brenna's room, but I wait in the living room, wanting Lani to come to me. I walk over to the coffee table and pick up a book, pretending to skim through it as she calls my name from the hallway. When I look up to see her standing in the entryway, I melt at her delighted smile. A voice at the back of my mind asks why she won't just admit what's all over her face.

"Do you want to borrow that?" she asks, referring to the book in my hand. "You'd love it."

"I've already read it actually. And I've read like three nonfiction books in my life that weren't for school, so I'm kind of impressed with myself."

"You always do that."

"What?"

A faint smile twinges her lips. "You downplay your intelligence. At every opportunity."

I shrug, smiling. "I'm not that smart, Lani. And it's okay. I'm totally fine with it."

"You're very smart," she says firmly, though still with that ghost of a smile. "You just have a dumb face."

I smile warmly at the memory of our first non-date. "And a dumb voice." I narrow my eyes at her. "It almost sounds like you're trying to talk yourself into my intelligence. I wonder if you have something against dumb people. Maybe you're embarrassed that you have a dumb boyfriend."

She lifts a brow. "But I don't have a dumb boyfriend, because I don't have a boyfriend."

I force my smile to stay in place, fighting the urge to clench my teeth. This playful argument is still fun to her, and I can't show her how annoyed I am after a month of it. I'm about to respond when I hear Armaan interject from the hallway. "Uh oh," he sings out. "Sounds like someone doesn't like the shirt you made her."

"What shirt?" Lani asks, as Armaan and Brenna walk into the living room.

"Oh, yeah." I chuckle, trying to make the shirt sound like an afterthought, like it hasn't been foremost on my mind since I made it this morning. "Instead of making a sign for the March, I made you a T-shirt."

I lift up the folded red material from the coffee table and let it fall open, clenching my teeth as I wait for her reaction. "I was hoping you weren't set on wearing what you already have on."

"My boyfriend is a feminist…" She says it under her breath. For a moment, she only shakes her head slowly, but luckily I'm not left hanging for too long when she snorts out a laugh. She covers her mouth as giggles burst out.

Thank god. I exhale the breath I didn't realize I was holding.

"I see you took my instructions literally," she says. "I'm confused, though…"

I narrow my eyes in playful exasperation, trying not to show how actually annoyed I am at what *I know* she's about to say.

"Because I just told you I don't have a boyfriend, so how could I have a boyfriend who's a feminist?"

I frown, tilting my head to the side in mock confusion. "But you do have a boyfriend. His name is Logan Henderson."

"Oh, I know him. He's cute, but he's not my boyfriend."

"I think he is actually. He just made you oatmeal pancakes this morning, and I don't think he makes oatmeal pancakes for people who aren't his girlfriend."

"Logan," Armaan says. "This is really uncomfortable for Brenna and me."

"Too bad," I say, my eyes still fixed on Lani in our stand-off.

"We're both over here crossing our fingers you'll show a little respect for yourself, and you keep letting us down."

"Armaan, shut your mouth," Brenna says. "Stop speaking for me like you're my patriarch. We're tearing that shit down today."

"You can't seriously expect me to wear this," Lani says, her eyes roaming over the rubber letters. "I would never wear a T-shirt like this even if I had a boyfriend. My friends will think I've lost my god damn mind."

I shrug one shoulder, smiling with effort. "That's the part I'm most looking forward to. When my hands started getting tired from ironing on those letters, I thought of how embarrassed you'd be trying to explain this shirt to your feminist friends who don't know me, and it kept me going. I knew it would all be worth it in the end."

She shuts her eyes, smiling as she shakes her head. "You're the fucking worst."

"I know," I say gravely, setting my hand on her shoulder to give it a squeeze. "You should also know in advance that I'm going to make you feel really guilty if you don't wear it. I spent like an hour making it—"

"He literally did!" Armaan interrupts. "I had to set up the iron for him because he had never used one before. Then he ironed the letters one by one, making sure that each one lined up with the other. It took him *over* an hour, and that's not including all the time he spent at Michaels. And it still looks like a five-year-old made it."

Leilani's coy smile widens into an affectionate, almost

piteous grin. "That's so cute. Alright fine, you sneaky bastard. I'll wear your stupid T-shirt."

I'm almost lightheaded with relief, but I try not to show it. Instead, I shrug one shoulder. "You can just tell everyone your feminist boyfriend lives in Canada."

Lani smiles reluctantly, taking the shirt from my hand before walking to her room. When she walks back into the living room with "My Boyfriend" plastered across her small, perfect tits, I am flooded with a triumphant thrill of possessiveness so powerful I have to look away from her, terrified that she might see it on my face.

* * *

It's evening by the time we make it to the beach. Our group dawdled during the March, and we're some of the last to arrive. Mia suggests we all go out to eat, but I persuade Lani to stay at the beach. It's a beautiful day and, now that the crowd of the March has died down, it's unusually vacant for a Saturday.

We walk over to a swing set near the wharf. "Did you have fun?" she asks, plopping down on the black rubber swing next to mine.

"I did. It was awesome. I can't believe there were so many people."

My eyes drift to the writing on her chest. My gaze catching her attention, she glances down at her tits. She frowns as she lifts her head to look at me. "Logan, this T-shirt was a bullshit move."

My stomach plummets, and yet I knew this conversation was coming. Her original amusement died almost as soon as we left the Blue House. She's been reticent all day when people have asked her about the T-shirt.

"It was a joke," I say tonelessly.

She whips her swing around to face me. "No it wasn't! You want everything you want in the moment you want it and you expect everyone else to bend to your will."

Anger rises at her accusation, but I try to maintain an almost bored tone. "Nope. I want you. That's a lot different than everything."

She turns away, shaking her head. "You want more than I'm ready to give you, and instead of respecting my wishes, you tried to bulldoze me. And you did it in front of Armaan so I couldn't say no. It was devious."

I glare at her. "When have you ever let the opinion of other people stop you from busting my balls? The night we met you told me I was weak. It was the first thing you ever said to me, in front of like seven people! I couldn't bulldoze you even if I wanted to, and I do respect your wishes, but I can't help it if I want things to be different. And I'm not going to keep my mouth shut about it. Lani…" I pause to take a deep breath, bracing myself for her reaction to what I'm about to tell her. "I've never had feelings this strong before for anyone. I think you're the most remarkable person I've ever met in my life."

My lips part when she snorts loudly. Even given her resistance, that wasn't the reaction I was expecting.

"I've known people like you before," she says. "You fall hard and fast with no perspective. You think every new love is special and you can't remember anything that came before it. Every new girl is the one you feel strongest about. Every new girl is the most remarkable person you've ever met in your life."

"That's absolutely not true."

"How would you know? You can't remember. You have relationship amnesia."

"I don't even know what that means."

"It means you can't remember your past relationships. You may remember the facts, but not the feelings."

"That isn't true—"

"It is! You think you remember, but you can't remember all the things you can't remember."

I grunt. "That's such a bullshit thing to say. How can I defend myself if you say I can't remember?"

"You can't. Relationship amnesia is your blessing and your curse. Every new relationship is magic, but then you never learn from your mistakes."

I turn away from her, shaking my head. "Doesn't sound like a blessing. Sounds like I got the shitty amnesia. I'd rather be able to kill someone with a pen."

When she makes a gulping sound, I realize she's probably choking back laughter. I didn't even really mean it as a joke, and only in retrospect do I recognize what a ridiculous thing it was to say. A sheepish smile tugs at my lips.

"*The Bourne Identity* is a great movie," she says in a patronizing tone, though I hear a smile in her voice.

I whip around to face her, my own smile spreading into a grin. "It's the greatest! In my top five, easily. I fucking love that fucking movie. Seriously, since I was twelve, it's been like maybe my number two or three fantasy to just wake up and not know who I am, but I'm able to, like, knife fight and scale walls and shit. It goes, number one, threesome with Daenerys and the girl who plays Wonder Woman, and then full-scale *Bourne*

Identity amnesia after that. I'm like, 'take my memories, dude. Take everything about my mom and dad and Lauren. I don't even care. I just want to wake up as Matt Damon in The Bourne Identity.'"

"You do know that the amnesia itself wouldn't give you your special assassin powers, right? You would have to have been an assassin first."

"Yeah, I do understand that, but I guess you are the amnesia expert, so thank you for your opinion, Dr. Girard."

She smiles faintly as she turns her head away to stare out at the ocean. Her cheeks darken, and I'm tempted to ask her what she's thinking, but she speaks before I get the chance. "It was unfair of me to tell you what you can and can't remember. I'm sorry I can be such a know-it-all sometimes. It must be annoying."

"Would you think I was weird if I said it actually kind of turns me on?"

She shuts her eyes, chuckling silently as she shakes her head.

I reach my hand out and run a finger along the inside of her thigh. "When you tell me I'm weak or have a dumb face or amnesia, I'm like, 'Tell me more, baby. Keep talking dirty.'"

Her eyes pop open wide. "You're insane!"

"Probably. Armaan always says I'm a pussy for it. I don't really care if I am. I like what I like."

She narrows her eyes. "Pussy! I'll have none of that patriarchy talk. I thought my boyfriend was a feminist."

My brows shoot to my forehead. "Am I your boyfriend now?"

She turns away to look at the water again. "For today," she says on a sigh.

"Good," I say with an effort at nonchalance, trying not to show how much that amendment deflated my buoyant hope. "Then, for today, I'll tell that I'm in love with you. In my case though, it will still be true tomorrow."

She twists her swing around slowly, giant brown eyes meeting mine.

"I'm in love with you. I'm not going to keep it from you just because it makes you uncomfortable." I shrug. "Sorry."

* * *

Leilani

"What's up?" Brenna asks. "You look like you're zoning out."

"I am sort of," I say.

As soon as I got back from the beach, I plopped down on this couch, and I've been lost in thought ever since. I'm barely even processing the episode of *Game of Thrones* we just started.

A notch forms on her brow. "What's going on?"

"Logan told me he's in love with me."

Brenna snorts. "Unsurprising."

"I know," I say, wishing I could be happier about his admission. Moments after he said it I wanted to burst with joy, but reality quickly hit. This is just a natural step in his rapid ascension to fevered, infatuated love. "He's quite predictable."

"Don't let it bum you out, though. Enjoy it. Armaan is the same way, even though he loves to make fun of Logan for it. He literally does exactly what I say. All the time. People think there's something wrong with that, but I honestly don't. I think that's how it should be. People with strong personalities like you and me need a subservient partner. And after thousands of years of patriarchy, is it so bad to have maybe a handful of years of matriarchy to even the score a little bit? I think not! I think it's justice."

I only smile faintly. I can't agree with her. My coldness is a big enough barrier to intimacy. I don't need the added distance of an unequal partnership.

She reaches her hand to my lap and grabs my own, delivering a tight squeeze before she says, "You're a queen and you deserve someone who worships you, and Logan definitely worships you."

For now, keeps playing over and over in my head. He loves me *for now*. He worships me *for now*, but just wait until the fevered infatuation breaks and his indifference becomes just as palpable as his adoration now, if only because its absence will so much harder to bear.

CHAPTER 7

Present Day

Logan

"Ugh," I groan, running my hands through my hair before gripping it tightly, sending tingles into my scalp. "Is this really necessary?"

I've never understood list makers. How does writing down things I'm determined to do make them any more likely to happen? I have zero desire to reach out to Leilani right now, even after five days of hearing nothing from her. Even knowing she's probably stewing in rage at what she perceives as my defection.

It's surprising. This separation from her feels nothing like I thought it would. I was certain I would worry about her, and especially about her Ativan consumption, given that I'm no longer around to make sure she's okay. I worried I would feel guilt even against my better judgment, knowing she's the one in the wrong. But I feel no anxiety, no guilt.

Only anger.

"Yes," Keira says firmly. When I look up at her, a smile plays at the edges of her full lips.

God, she's wonderful. She really wants to help me. I can't believe I almost felt guilty when I reached out to her a month ago.

Keira and I became friends when we lived on the same floor our first year in the dorms, though we'd only had occasional contact since then. But when things went to shit with Lani, I needed to talk to someone. I remembered that Keira's a Psych major, and her brother's a recovering alcoholic. She's a wealth of information about addiction and co-dependency.

I don't know what I would do without her.

I have no reason to feel guilty. I can't help that she's beautiful. It's certainly not why I sought her out.

Pleasure fills my chest as I smile back at her. I glance at the pen and notepad in her hands. "Alright. Hand them over."

She walks over to the desk and hands me the pen and notepad. "Okay," she starts, and on cue I set the notepad on my lap and write the number one at the top of the lined yellow paper. "It should go without saying that you can't have sex with her during your break."

She really thinks I would do that? Heat creeps into my cheeks. I drop the pen, frowning. "Well, obviously—" I begin, but she lifts a hand to halt me, a playful smile tugging at her lips.

"It doesn't need to be the first item on your list, but it needs to be on there. I know it's your greatest weakness with her."

"One of them," I say, my mind drifting back to those first few months. Talking is another. We'd lay in bed naked and I'd listen to her explain why *Jackie Brown* is objectively Quentin Tarantino's masterpiece, or something else off the wall and pretentious that only Lani would say. Then we'd have sex for the second time, and afterwards while she lay in my arms I'd tell her about the summer after my junior year of high school when my dad and I hiked Half Dome, and she'd listen intently—her brows drawn, her lips pursed—as if my inarticulate rambling was the most interesting story she'd ever heard. My chest aches at the memory of how things used to be before everything went to hell.

Once Lani found Ativan, she stopped giving a shit about me. She stopped talking. She stopped listening. She retreated so far into herself, it felt like there was nothing left for me anymore.

When I glance at Keira, she's frowning sympathetically. I sit up straight, schooling my face into a neutral expression. "It can be the *last* item on my list."

She nods. "I think the first one should be that you won't look at her Instagram."

I shake my head. "I have no desire to look at it."

"Right now, you don't." She points to the pad of paper in front of me, a challenging expression on her face. "This is about accountability."

My shoulders drop as I groan. "Fine... Whatever..." Next to the number one, I write, *Don't look at her Instagram.*

"You realize she's not going to let this 'break' slide, right? She's going to come after you with everything she's got to make you forget the boundaries you've set with her."

I lift my pen from the paper as I consider her words. I ought to feel ashamed that just the idea of that makes my dick stir. I imagine Leilani standing outside of my front door with a leather whip in her hand, a severe expression on her face as she tells me what she plans to do me for having the audacity to take charge in our relationship…

But she wouldn't do that. She's too fucking high all the time.

"I really don't think so. Ativan is all she needs right now." I hate how bitter I sound, like I'm jealous of a prescription drug.

"And this is part of addiction," she says. "You are a vital part of her relationship with Ativan, because you allowed her to use it without any consequences. You took care of her. You made excuses for her to all of her friends." She lifts a brow. "You took an online exam for her."

I laugh humorlessly. "That I did. Not one of my proudest moments. Thankfully I'm a lot dumber than her and got a C plus. She deserved it."

Keira rolls her eyes. "You're not dumb, and there's no need to dwell on the past. Setting boundaries with her was a big step for you, and you've stuck to it." She smiles faintly. "I'm proud of you."

And I would be proud of myself too if it was actually difficult, I'm about to say, but I stop myself. Something about it feels disloyal.

"Okay," I say, looking down at the single item on my list. "I think I've got it. Just give me a second." While I scribble away at the rest of my list, Keira turns away and starts walking around her room, as if to give me privacy—unnecessary given that it takes me about ten seconds to finish. I've known all along what needs to be done.

"What do you think?" I ask, lifting up the notepad. She walks over to me and takes it from my hands, her brow furrowing as her eyes scan the list. A smile hovering on her mouth, she looks up at me. "I like that you put the last one in all caps."

"Yeah well, given her erratic behavior lately, I can't be certain she won't show up at my doorstep naked."

Her smile falters, and I'm confused for a second before the reason behind it dawns on me.

Keira doesn't want to think about Lani showing up at my doorstep naked. She doesn't want to think about us having sex.

I look away, not wanting to send her any encouragement. Guilt gnaws at my conscience, and it shouldn't.

I didn't seek her out for this. I can't help it if she's attracted to me.

"I think you need to add something that says, if you do run into each other by 'chance'"—she makes air quotes, implying that Lani will force a meeting between us at some point—"you'll be polite but distant, and end the interaction as soon as you can."

I nod. "Fair enough."

"And here," she says, bending down and opening a drawer, grabbing a fresh, white printer paper. "Re-write it on this. Make it look nice. I want you to post it up somewhere in your room as soon as you get home."

I groan. "Armaan is going to give me so much shit."

She looks at me sternly. "Don't worry about Armaan. Don't worry about anyone else. This is about your recovery, and I do mean it when I say, 'recovery.' Co-dependency is just as much of a sickness as addiction."

Is it, though? I want to argue cynically, remembering the multitude of wrongs Lani's committed since she started taking Ativan, but I fight the urge to disagree with Keira after all the help she's given me.

"Done," I say, setting down the pen, looking over the completed list.

1. DON'T LOOK AT HER INSTAGRAM.
2. DON'T TEXT HER.
3. IF YOU RUN INTO HER, BE POLITE BUT DISTANT.
4. DON'T UNDER ANY CIRCUMSTANCES AGREE TO SEE HER IN PERSON.
5. DO NOT HAVE SEX WITH HER.

Keira nods once. "Good."

CHAPTER 8

Past—The Realization

Logan

The ocean breeze cools my sweat dampened face as I step outside. I feel like I can breathe again, though my ears are still pounding an echo of tribal drums from the blasting of "Shape of You" inside. Fuck, this bar sucks, and so does Ed Sheeran. We only came here because Brenna's douchebag older brother said it has the hottest girls.

How does he even know? He doesn't fucking live in Santa Barbara. Jesus, I hope I'm never that big of a loser to keep going to college bars long after I get a real job. And he keeps rubbing his career money in our face, as if we aren't all going to have real jobs too in less than a year. He's bought Lani two drinks already, and he got all specific about how to make her martini—"Only a splash of olive juice"—like he's fucking James Bond. The bar

77

tender looked at him like he's a dick.

Because he is.

And on top of that I had to listen to Leilani introduce me as Armaan's boyfriend. *Armaan's* boyfriend. You know, 'cause Armaan and I are so close, he's basically my boyfriend. Ha ha. God damn her. If I had been any drunker I would have pointed out that I haven't been fucking *Armaan* every night for the last three months.

I scan the patio for my *non*-girlfriend. She told me she was getting claustrophobic and needed to go outside. Her face was wan and she disappeared so quickly, I think she might have been getting sick. I was surprised. I didn't think she had that much to drink.

I catch sight of a bun of dark hair obscured by a swarm of people, so I start walking in that direction. As I inch closer—the bar patio is almost as crowded as the inside—I notice from her body language that she's talking to someone in front of her. Based on her bright smile and wild hand gestures—uncharacteristic of her—she must be talking to someone she really likes.

I take a deep breath, trying to calm the familiar feeling of jealousy. When it comes to Lani, I'm jealous of everyone. Anyone who has something of her that I don't. I'm jealous of Brenna for being the only non-family member Lani loves and trusts unconditionally. I'm jealous of all of her exes who at least had the privilege of being called "boyfriend." I can't let her see the full extent of what I feel because she would think I was crazy. Then again, how can she expect me to feel secure in her affection when she withholds it from me?

As if sensing my presence, Lani turns her head and our eyes meet. She reaches her hand to my arm and pulls me through the crowd. Once I'm flush with her body I look up and see Dean standing across from me.

That's who she was smiling at.

It takes everything within me to keep my facial muscles from scowling. Lani and Dean are close. She trusts him. All night it's been clear that she's much closer to him than she made it seem when she first mentioned he was visiting Brenna this weekend.

Lani and Dean stand in silence after I arrive, making me feel like an intruder.

Dean is the first one to speak. "We were just talking about horror movies."

"Big fan," I say blandly.

"This girl here's obsessed with *The Shining*." Dean smiles warmly. "I think it's kind of overrated."

"Great movie," I say.

Lani frowns. "It's your favorite too," she says, sounding a little defensive.

"Is it?" I ask, feeling less than enthusiastic about the whole world, let alone my favorite horror movie. "It was my first horror movie. I don't know if that automatically makes it my favorite."

"It's your second-favorite weed movie. A high honor." She purses her lips. I can't help but smile, even in the midst of my sour mood. It's amazing how much she remembers about what I say, especially since I rarely say anything worth remembering.

Dean intrudes on our moment. "Oh man! Remember that time you and Brenna stole the weed out of my sock drawer?"

Just like that, my mood plummets again. I can't even count the number of times tonight that Dean has started a sentence to Lani with "Remember that time." And I'd bet my first born child that he's saved all of his remember-that-times for when I'm around.

Dean looks at me. "They were like fifteen and had never smoked before. They made their own joints out of my mom's wrapping paper. Maybe one of the top five funniest moments of my life was coming home to them trying to smoke. This was before it was legal and it was, like, the shit you'd get in high school that came in a sandwich bag, you know? It probably didn't get you high, but they were acting crazy." He laughs loudly, almost a cackle. "Lani found this bag of stale pita chips in the pantry and she was practically having an orgasm every time she ate one." He turns to her with a lazy smile. "That was my favorite part."

Lani smiles wide at Dean, but she shoots me an apologetic look afterwards. It doesn't soothe me. I've just about reached my limit with Dean.

"He's had a lot," she mouths in my direction, as if to hide it from Dean, but it doesn't work. He takes a step forward—so close his stomach nearly grazes her tits—and looks down into her eyes. "What the fuck was that?" he asks with a smile that makes me want to punch him in the face. "What did you just whisper to him?"

"Nothing," she says, pouting her bottom lip. Dean narrows his eyes as he tilts his head down even lower, like he's about to kiss her. "I don't believe you," he whispers.

As if possessed by a demon, I find myself grabbing Lani's arm and yanking her away from him. I instantly regret it when she turns sharply to me, a look of genuine surprise on her face. Dean's glazed eyes also look confused, but neither call attention to my outburst. I'm left to stand in awkward silence.

Dean looks at Lani. "Are you okay now, or do you need me

to distract you more?"

"I'm okay," Lani says.

What the fuck are they talking about? I turn to Lani. "Were you sick?"

"In a way," she says.

"She was having an anxiety attack," Dean says. "She doesn't like crowds, especially smelly crowds."

"A panic attack," Lani corrects. "I get them periodically. It's not a big deal."

"Not a big deal" plays over and over again in my head as I stare at her, sensing an invisible wall rise between us. "Not a big deal" is just another way of saying, "you're not important enough to know this about me."

I'm not, but Dean is.

"Can we talk for a second?" She frowns in question before nodding. She turns to Dean. "I'm better now. You should go inside and find everyone." With that she grabs my arm and pulls me through the crowd.

After sifting through packed bodies, she pulls me to a small open space near the patio gate. "What's up with you tonight?" she asks. "I've never seen you this grumpy before."

I find I can't keep a filter on my mouth. "Why did you ask Dean to come with you during your panic attack and not me?"

She blinks once. "That's what you're upset about? I didn't ask him. He's known me for years. He could tell I was having a panic attack when I passed him on the way out, so he followed me."

"It seems like you guys are really close." I want to cringe at the surliness in my tone, but there's no going back now. I've made my jealousy embarrassingly obvious. Nothing to do now but plunge over the edge, even if it's to my death.

Her faint smile is almost piteous. "You don't have to worry about Dean. I've known him since I was five years old. He's like a brother."

"A brother who likes watching you eat pita chips when you're stoned."

"Well, my feelings for him are sisterly. I can't speak for Dean."

"He's super into you. It's obvious."

"He's just drunk." She reaches her hand out and places it on my shoulder. I close my eyes as she runs her fingers up my nape. When I open my eyes slowly, she's smiling wryly. "I think you are too, come to think of it."

I smile sheepishly. "A little."

Her smile widens.

"I also can't stand Dean. It's like he's been rubbing it in my face all night that he's closer to you than I am. I didn't even know you had panic attacks. You never told me that before… What?" I ask abruptly when she sucks in her lips, as if fighting laughter.

"You sound like a little kid."

My face heats. It's not the first time she's compared me to a child when I've pressed her for intimacy. "I love you!" I exclaim, my voice louder than I intended. "Is it childish that I want to know things about you?"

Her smile falters. She looks contrite, and something else that I can't quite decipher. She takes a step closer to me before wrapping her arms around my shoulder and pulling me down for a kiss. For the first time all night, tension eases from my shoulders. I pull her closer and deepen the kiss. When she pulls away, she stares deep into my eyes, as if trying to silently communicate with me.

I see love in her eyes, and I wish it didn't make me feel dizzy with elation. I wish it didn't make me want to lift her into my arms and carry her right home to my bed.

It's not fair that she won't say it. It's not fair that everything is always on me.

But it's enough, I tell myself, because I have no other choice. She's it. She's the end game for me, and if she still doesn't trust me enough then I have work to do.

I'll earn those words by proving to her day after day that I'm not going anywhere.

* * *

Leilani

Sleep eludes me long after Logan passes out with his head on my pillow, his soft breaths tickling my shoulder, his big arms wrapped around my waist. I may not like cuddling, but I love cuddling with him. I run his earlier words over and over again in my head. *Is it childish that I want to know things about you?* I can't figure out why they touched me so much.

I'm just starting to drift away when I'm startled awake by a sound. A moan. I lift my head from my pillow and turn to Logan. He moans again, a faint little hum at the back of his throat, and I know it's unpleasant from his slightly furrowed brow. I lift my hand and run my fingers through his hair, hoping to calm him.

His eyes pop open. "Lani," he whispers.

"Hi," I say softly.

His wide eyes locked on my face, he blinks rapidly. "I just had the craziest dream."

I smile. "Tell me about it."

His green eyes drift to the ceiling, growing unfocused as he speaks. "There was a huge earthquake. Everything was on fire. I could even smell the smoke. Lauren was with me, except for some reason she was a little kid, and I was so worried she was going to get crushed by all the debris. Things were falling from the sky, and I kept having to knock them away from her. We were at Coronado High School at first and then we ended up in downtown Santa Barbara. State Street was decimated. It was crazy…" Suddenly, his eyes lock with mine. "I was looking for you and I couldn't find you. I kept seeing girls who looked like you, but whenever I got close, it wasn't you."

He looks a little bewildered as he stares at me. Warmth fills my belly as I run my fingers through his soft hair. "You were whimpering."

"Was I?" An abashed smile tugs at his lips. "I was scared. I thought you were dead, and I'd feel so relieved when I thought I found you, and then want to scream when it wasn't you." His eyes narrow in indignation. "It *was* you too, but the faces would change into someone else when I got close. You know—that shitty dream trick. Oh man, I was so relieved when I woke up and saw your face."

He continues to stare at me with that rueful smile, as if his admission was silly and he's waiting for me to tease him, but I can't.

Something inside me shatters. My chest is gripped with an almost painful ache of longing. I hold my breath in an effort to keep the hovering tears from falling.

I've lost the battle of resisting him. I love him. How could I not fall in love with him when he's the opposite of what I most loathe in myself?

I don't want the kind of love that I'm able to give. I don't want the kind of love that's earned slowly over time—handed out in small, greedy doses—and withdrawn piece by piece for each mistake. I want love like Logan's—free and big-hearted and achingly sweet.

And I'll keep taking it without giving back because I'm terrified to compromise. Afraid that the moment I do, he'll flee.

I'm a coward, and there's only so much time before he realizes what a bad bargain he made.

"Are you crying?" he asks, sounding utterly incredulous. The look on his face would be comical under any other circumstances. His bewilderment is so visible I almost wonder if he thought I was incapable of tears.

"No, I'm not crying." I wipe the bottom of my eyes with the pads of my fingers. "You're crying."

The edges of his lips lift slightly. He waits a moment before asking, "What did I say to make you cry?"

The apprehension in his voice makes me hate myself. That he doesn't know these are tears of love only shows just how greedy I've been. Out of principle, I have to admit at least a part of what's in my heart.

"Nothing. You're just so wonderful I can't stand it sometimes."

When I see triumph ignite behind his green eyes, I know it was the right thing to say. His eyes locked on mine, he lifts his hand and tucks a strand of hair behind my ears, as if to give himself a better view of my face. "Really?"

"Yes!" I shout, several tears dripping down my cheeks.

The victorious gleam doesn't wane as his eyes roam all over my face. He's enjoying my tears and he can't hide it.

I forgive him. He deserves them after all I've put him through.

I want to tell him I love him but I just can't get the words out. Instead I just hold his stare with ugly tears running down my face. He smiles tenderly as he lifts a hand and wipes under my eyes with the pad of his thumb.

CHAPTER 9

Present Day

Leilani

Brenna takes a large gulp of her margarita before setting it firmly on the table, a splash of yellow liquid spilling over the edge. She grabs her cloth napkin and wipes the frosted glass. I glance at the small drop on the table she overlooked.

A waste.

If it were my margarita—if I had just one—I'd consume every sip, even the watery stuff at the bottom. I'd make sure my stomach was nice and empty and…

No. Because it wouldn't be *just one*. I'd need at least three to even come close to the mindless bliss of Ativan.

And I'm done with all of that.

"Alright," she says, thankfully pulling me out of my head. "Let's bang out this revenge plan."

The determination in her voice fills me with warmth. She's adopted the revenge list I wrote last night as if it were her own. The fact that she has her own relationship troubles hasn't dampened her enthusiasm.

"Before we get started on the list," I say, recalling myself, "what were you going to tell me about Armaan?"

Her expression changes. She lifts her margarita glass and takes three large gulps, as if to give herself sustenance before diving in. "Well," she starts, a little begrudgingly, "I was just looking through his phone, 'cause you know, I'm *super* trusting like that, and I—"

She halts when I snort. "No judgments over here. In the last month, I've read every text Logan has sent to a woman who wasn't me, his mom, or Lauren. Every. Single. One." And I died a little more each time I saw a new text from Keira. "I'm the Woodward and Bernstein of suspicious girlfriends."

She wrinkles her nose. "Who are they again?"

"The journalists who reported on Watergate."

An "o" forms on her lips as she nods thoughtfully. Narrowing her eyes, she looks at me. "I guess that makes me the Cersei Lannister of suspicious girlfriends, because I'd literally behead Armaan if I got the kind of phone call you did."

Ah, the dreaded phone call. Brenna looks away, not wanting to dwell on a memory she knows fills me with both a fiery rage and a cold, empty sadness.

I have to force my jaw to relax before saying, "I interrupted you. What did you find on his phone?"

She sighs heavily. "Nothing too incriminating. He was texting with"—she lowers her voice—"Logan's sister."

I can only nod slowly, wishing I could reassure her, but I've noticed Lauren and Armaan's affinity for each other every time she's visited Santa Barbara. I've often seen them hanging out— teasing each other, taking turns showing each other YouTube videos, laughing loud and obnoxiously. Basically, doing all the annoying things people who really like each other do.

"What were they texting?"

"Nothing bad, but I just know Armaan has a thing for her. I mean, she's literally the female version of Logan."

I shake my head. "She's nothing like Logan. I don't even think they look that much alike."

"No." She sighs. "But she's hot."

"You're hotter."

She smiles faintly before looking down at the hand clasped tightly around her glass tumbler. "I don't know... It's not just that. She's also...such a free spirit, you know? Or at least she seems like it. And I'm of course the raging, controlling bitch who annoys him even though..." She rolls her eyes. "Lani, I literally do everything for him. He would not survive without me. Would not attend a single morning class if I wasn't there to wake his ass up. He'd forget to turn in assignments. It's ridiculous."

"I know. It's like you adopted a teenager."

"Right? And the thing is, I can't even really blame him for it. I think a lot of it has to do with his ADHD. He never takes his medication, because he says weed works better, which...yeah, okay Armaan." She shakes her head. "It just goes to show that people who grow up with money are just as fucked up as the rest of us.

"Oh my god, speaking of which! Have I told you the latest in the Singh family drama?" When I shake my head, Brenna's eyes light up. "I shouldn't be laughing about it because it's really sad for Armaan, but oh man! Some shit just went down. His mom just told him flat out that she will not hire him at S. Singh because his grades are so shitty. He got turned down for a job by his own mother!"

When Brenna bursts into laughter, I give her a scolding look. She waves me off. "I know it's not funny. My heart really hurts for Armaan, especially since you know his mom could invent a fake job if she really wanted to. She basically *did* for Vik"—Armaan's older brother—"although it's a little different since Vik is basically a genius, and Armaan is…you know, Armaan."

When she giggles quietly, I send her pleading eyes, and this time she bites her lips to fight her smile. "I know I'm being an asshole, but the only reason I can laugh about all of this now is because I have full confidence that he'll figure everything out someday. He's a super smart guy, and I think he has drive in him somewhere deep, deep, *deep* down. He's just young for his years, you know? Both he and Logan are like that. They're babies in big masculine man bodies."

"Speaking of Logan," I say, hoping to sway her from the topic of Armaan's humiliation. "What did you need to tell me about him?"

When her face falls, my stomach sinks. I knew whatever she had to say would be bad news, and yet somehow I still find myself unprepared for it. "It's about Keira," she says.

My throat tightens. I swallow before saying, "I knew it was."

"She's been at their apartment a lot," Brenna says quietly.

An ache seizes my chest, but I try to manage a cynical smile. "Well, you know they are such great friends, Brenna."

She shuts her eyes, shaking her head. "God, he's the worst, Lani."

"I know."

"Do you remember that first night you met him? Remember how he and Armaan were going back and forth shit-talking Logan's ex for being crazy and then Logan basically admitted he was going after her best friend behind her back?"

That wasn't exactly what Logan had said, but I appreciated that Brenna was riled up in true girl-code fashion. I do remember doubting his innocence even back then. I almost want to laugh at how history has repeated itself. This is the nature of relationship amnesia, and Logan isn't even to blame. He can't help repeating his mistakes over and over again, but I knew better. I shouldn't have let him wear down my guard when I knew it would all eventually lead to this.

"He's such a fuckboy!" Brenna shouts.

I snort. "He should have kept it written on his car."

Brenna's eyes fill with laughter. "I forgot about that!" She bursts into a cackle. "Oh man! Logan's ex, whoever you are, you're my hero!"

"Brittani, remember? Brittani with an 'i.' We had it written on her Closure Cake. I felt a kinship with her even then. I could feel what it would be like to lose his adoration and become the 'crazy ex-girlfriend.'" I smile weakly. "Now I'm living it."

My eyes fixed on the wooden table, I see Brenna's hand slip into view as she wraps it around mine. "Honey," she says, delivering a tight squeeze.

I allow myself the comfort for a moment before pulling my hand away. I shake my head. "None of this. I'm sick of being sad. Let's plan my revenge."

Joyful wrath flashes across her face. "Yes!" she says through clenched teeth. "My mouth is literally watering thinking of making him cry."

A giggle bursts from my chest, even as I inwardly cringe at her words. I haven't quite reconciled myself to the last item on my list. It still feels a little cruel, even after rehashing his wrongs against me.

Maybe it's because I know deep down that I wronged him too.

"For starters," I say, stifling the rising panic at what I'm about to say, "we need to recruit his greatest weakness. Or rather…his greatest weakness where I'm concerned."

I suppress the rise of awful memories threatening to choke my throat. What I'm about to ask of Brenna is a low—very low—move. Underhanded and dirty. Logan hates her older brother probably even more than he loves me.

If he still even loves me at all.

At her intrigued stare, I tell her, "We need to recruit Dean."

Her eyes open wide. "Yes! Make him think you're fucking Dean. He'll go out of his mind!"

"No. Not that far." Even in my rage, I could never hurt him that much. "It's important to me that he never thinks I crossed that line, but I want him to think I'm considering it. It's the only thing he would care enough about to break his rule and reach out to me during our break. He may not want me anymore, but he definitely doesn't want Dean to have me."

When Brenna starts flapping her hands excitedly, a small laugh escapes my throat. "Dean said just the other day that he's been wanting to visit Santa Barbara before we graduate. I'll see if he can come next weekend, even."

"Okay, but we have to find a way to get him to do what we need without telling him anything. I don't want him blabbing to

Logan that I have a revenge plan."

That would mean the end of everything.

She rolls her eyes. "And he definitely would too. He's such a dumbass, which thankfully makes him really easy to manipulate. Leave it to me, girl! I have at least seven years under my belt of getting him to hook me up with booze. I'll come up with a plan. It helps that he *lo-o-oves* you." She winks at me.

"Right, which means we have to make sure he doesn't get any ideas. I don't want to lead him on…"

Brenna waves a dismissive hand. "Oh, he already knows you're way out of his league."

Biting my bottom lip, I nod slowly, surprised that I'm feeling so exhilarated over such a low, dirty move. I must be a sadist. When my eyes meet Brenna's, I say, "Let's do it."

CHAPTER 10

Past—The Compromise

Leilani

I loathe social obligations in general, but there is nothing I loathe more than the social obligation of meeting my boyfriend's parents.

Even when he's not technically my boyfriend.

I don't know what tonight entails, but since both John and Helen Henderson added me on Facebook this morning, I don't expect it to be pleasant. I expect a lot of questions. A lot of focus on me and my relationship with Logan.

I'm almost sick with dread.

I stare at my long, stringy damp hair in the mirror on my door, trying to decide what I should do with it. "Should I dress up?" I ask Logan as I look at him through the mirror. He glances up from his phone, his long body stretched across my bed.

He stares at me blankly for a few seconds as if processing my question. "No," he eventually scoffs. "My parents aren't like that. I'm surprised we're even going out. We usually just order pizza to their hotel. They must be trying to impress you."

Great. Which means they have high expectations of me too, and I'm destined to let them down. Parents don't like girls like me, and I can't blame them for it. I can't even fulfill their surprisingly low expectations. All parents really want is a girl who's an easy hang. Someone who smiles and tells stories. Someone who can tease grandpa when he cracks open his third Budweiser at Thanksgiving dinner. I've never been able to do any of that. I just sit and stare awkwardly at grandpa, and everyone else at the table, and parents secretly hate me for it. *Why can't our son just date a normal girl?* is what they're always thinking.

"What should I expect?" I ask, trying to make the question sound lighthearted, but I can't keep the strain from my voice.

Logan doesn't seem to notice my distress. He keeps his eyes fixed on his phone as he says, "My mom tells the same three stories every time she meets any of my friends. The one I hate the most is the story about how it was her dream to have children. She thinks it's so funny too. God, it's so stupid. She'll talk about how she had two failed rounds of IVF before she finally had Lauren and me. She was thirty-six and had waited her whole life to be a mom. She says when she held us in her arms she thanked God he chose her to be our mother. Until Lauren became a teenager and she said, 'Is it too late to send them back? Can I still safely surrender a fifteen-year-old at a fire station?' Ha ha."

Apprehension churns my stomach. "Will I be expected to laugh at that?"

He lifts his head, smiling warmly as he meets my eyes. "Only

95

you would ask that question. I love that you aren't even capable of laughing at something you don't find funny."

I swallow. "Logan, you only love it because we're alone. I don't think you want me to embarrass you in front of your parents."

My social awkwardness won't be cute anymore. He'll see the real consequences—the never-ending pauses and blank stares.

I dread his disappointment the most.

He smiles fully, his bare abs flexing as he leans forward and hops from the bed. His eyes meet mine in the mirror as he walks behind me and wraps his arms around my waist. He plants a kiss on my cheek before meeting my eyes again. "Nope. I'm actually looking forward to the moment you annihilate her with your intense eye contact and give-zero-fucks bluntness. It will make my night. And Lauren's too. Seriously."

I try to smile back but I can't muster it. He doesn't know what he's saying.

He lifts his hands to my shoulders and gives them a tight squeeze. "You're so tense! I've never seen you this nervous before. It's kind of cute." His pale green eyes grow intent. "You must really like me if you want to impress my parents this much."

"I won't impress them. I can guarantee that. I'm awkward with parents and kids. So, I'll fail with Cadence too."

"You seriously have no reason to be nervous. My dad is the chillest guy ever." Under his breath, he adds, "He has no choice being married to my mom."

When I bite the inside of my lip, he smiles sympathetically. "She's fine though. She's only an asshole to her children. And Lauren much more so than me. And no one will notice if you aren't good with kids, because they aren't either. Not even

Lauren. I'm the only one who ever actually talks to Cadence or plays with her, but I'll make it a point not to show you up tonight if it worries you."

I give him a small smile. "You're being really sweet."

He smiles back, holding my stare in the mirror. Suddenly, his face grows serious. "Oh, and I guess I should tell you now… My parents think you're my girlfriend." He must see the change in my face when he raises his hands from my shoulders in a gesture of defense. "I didn't tell them you were my girlfriend. They just assumed it."

At my skeptical look, his dark brows snap together. "Why wouldn't they? You're with me almost every time my mom calls, even at night. And I didn't correct her because I barely ever get a word in during her rants—as I'm sure you've noticed. Don't look at me like I'm being sneaky. You're the weird one. It's weird that we spend this much time together and you're not my girlfriend."

"I don't want to get into this argument again."

"Of course you don't." The words are clipped.

"Logan," I say, my voice pleading. "I'm really nervous about meeting your parents, and especially your mom. Can you just give me a break?"

His eyes soften. "Sure. And you have nothing to worry about. She's not nearly as bad as I've made it sound. When she's in a good mood, she's totally fine. And she's a legitimately fun hang when she's drunk. That reminds me—we need to keep her wine glass full tonight."

"And mine," I add with a strangled voice.

"Oh yeah. Drink those fears away. Seriously." He lifts his hands to my shoulders and gives them a squeeze. "My parents are totally cool with drinking. And weed too since it's been legal." He glances around the room. "Shit, that reminds me. Armaan got Lauren some dark chocolate from the dispensary. He was really adamant about me not forgetting to give it to her. We're going to have to swing by my apartment first."

* * *

Logan

She's so quiet on the drive to the restaurant, I can almost feel her nervousness radiating from the passenger seat.

I've never understood social anxiety. There are plenty of real things to worry about, like going on academic probation or Trump starting a nuclear war. Why focus your anxiety on something as trivial as a dinner date? What's the worst thing that can happen? I could never say these things to Lani without sounding like an asshole, so I've tried my best to be empathetic.

But when you look at it, I have much more at stake than she does. I don't give a shit what my parents think of her, so she has nothing to lose if she fails to impress them, but what will I do if she announces to the table with her usual bluntness that she isn't my girlfriend? And more importantly, what will it mean?

That she doesn't love you, an inner voice whispers.

We park on the fourth floor of the parking garage. She's distracted on our long walk to the restaurant, giving me only half-smiles when I try to tease her out of her nervousness. Just as we approach the gated patio, Lauren bursts through the restaurant door. Squealing as she wraps her arms around me.

"Y'all are late," she scolds as she pulls away. Without any

warning, she wraps her arms around Lani, whose eyes go wide with surprise. "I'm already two mojitos deep, so you'll have to play catch up," she says without even thinking to introduce herself to Lani. She looks at me pointedly. "I assume you told her that booze is necessary for a night with Mom."

"She knows."

"Good." She nods sagely, grabbing both of our arms as she guides us into the restaurant. "Aunt Lisa volunteered to watch Cadence last minute, so things are going to get crazy this weekend. I won't let you be all couply and have a quiet night at home tonight. We're going out on the town!"

Lani shoots apprehensive eyes at me, and I give her a brief shake of the head to reassure her.

When we get to our table, Lauren strokes the side of Lani's face as she presents her to my parents, and I'm torn between laughing and cringing at her lack of boundaries. "Look at her! Isn't she so naturally beautiful?" She turns to Lani, who looks almost dazed. "Logan usually goes for a really flashy kind of pretty"—she lowers her voice to a half-whisper—"which basically just means lots and lots of makeup."

Inwardly I wince, but I know better than to intervene about something so minor, especially by Lauren's standards. Lani's seen my full Instagram already. She knows what several of my ex-girlfriends look like.

"Lauren, none of that," my mom says as we all take our seats. "But she's right that you're a very pretty girl, Leilani." She reaches out her palm across the table, as she introduces herself and my dad, shooting me a knowing smile afterward. "Logan's told us a lot about you."

A lie of course, though I'm not even sure if my mom realizes it. I couldn't tell her a lot about anything when I almost never talk about myself when she calls.

"It's nice to meet you as well," Lani answers, and even that small response seems to take tremendous effort.

My dad smiles at Lani. "So Logan tells us you're a fellow Bay Area native."

"Yes," she answers tightly.

When my dad just stares at her, expecting her to elaborate, Lani grabs her water glass and takes several rapid sips.

Damn, she really is nervous. I've never seen her at a loss for words before. "She grew up in Palo Alto," I say. "Her parents' house is only a few streets down from Aunt Carrie and Uncle Jack's." I turn to Lani with a smile, hoping she doesn't mind that I stepped in for her. I'm relieved when she gives me a small smile back.

"Born and raised in Oakland," my dad says, lifting a hand. "So I've got to ask, even though I might not like the answer, are you a Giants or an A's fan?"

Lani lifts her head to look at my dad, her brows drawing together thoughtfully. "Neither. I don't care much for sports in general, but I can confidently say I'm against baseball. On principle. No source of entertainment has the right to be that aggressively boring."

My dad's wide-eyed smile is fixed as he nods, but he looks like he doesn't quite know what to do with Lani's response. A smile rises to my lips, but I clench my teeth to suppress it. Lani wouldn't want me laughing at her right now, but damn if she isn't cute when she does that.

I'm about to express my support—which everyone will know is a lie because I fucking love baseball—when Lauren interrupts.

"How long have you guys officially been together? It's been, like, since March, right? Logan, I think that might be your longest relationship ever."

I fight the urge to shut my eyes in exasperation. Leave it to Lauren to bring everything out into the open on a complete tangent. "Brittani and I were together for eight months," I say, though I don't know why I'm defending myself. I should have just let it go.

"Yes, but you were fully checked out for at least two of them."

I turn to her, lowering my voice, "Can you not right now?"

"I agree," my mom says. "I don't like this conversation, Lauren."

Lauren visibly bristles at my mom's tone and I search my brain for a way to keep peace between them, at least long enough to get through dinner.

I'm surprised when Lani jumps in. "We've been together five months. So, I guess Brittani still has me beat by a month, if we're only counting those six months when Logan *wasn't* checked out."

Relief overwhelms me, a warm smile spreading across my face. I stare at Lani in an attempt to show her my gratitude, but she keeps her eyes fixed on the glass of water in front of her. I reach my hand under the table and place it over hers. When she interlocks her fingers with mine, I give her hand a tight squeeze. Only belatedly do I recognize how the table went quiet with her reply.

"She was teasing," I say, realizing that my family might have mistaken her comment about Brittani for passive aggression. "She doesn't smile when she teases, so it can be hard to tell."

At that, my mom releases a brief, forced chuckle. Lani lifts her eyes to mine, scolding me with them.

I shrug. "My family needs things spelled out for them. I'm sorry we're not as smart as you."

She blinks slowly in irritation, but a small smile forms on her lips.

Feeling triumphant, I lean in and plant a hard kiss on that smile.

* * *

Leilani

This dinner feels interminable, and we've only just finished appetizers. I hate being forced to recite boring autobiographical details like I'm telling a riveting story. Thank god Logan seems to have taken on the role of my social buffer.

I don't know how someone so perceptive and attentive could have come from this family. John barely seems aware of anything, and Helen's entirely focused on herself. Lauren, at least, seems to be interested in other people, however little she cares about embarrassing them with her candor.

"I know exactly what you're thinking right now," Lauren says, apparently sensing my gaze on her face. "Logan is the better-looking twin, huh? It's okay. I've come to terms with it."

I force a smile, not having any idea how to answer such a question.

"There's always a better-looking twin," she continues. "And it's a tragedy, really, because it's the first thing on everyone's mind when they meet you. Their eyes go straight to my nose and they're always thinking, 'Oh, you poor thing!'"

I glance at Logan for help, but he doesn't seem to think that anything is amiss with this conversation. Looking back at Lauren, I force a friendly smile. "I thought fraternal twins didn't share any more DNA than regular siblings."

Lauren's mouth opens in surprise. "She's smart, Logan!" Immediately turning back to me, she adds, "It's not that I'm surprised, but we have met a wide spectrum of women over the years. Every time we visit Santa Barbara, he has a new girlfriend—"

"Hey!" Logan shouts. "Stop what you're doing right now."

Lauren waves a dismissive hand in Logan's direction, but she keeps her eyes on me. "Oh, like she hasn't heard it a million times from every single person who knows you. Am I right, Lani?"

I smirk, looking apologetically at Logan before saying, "Yes, I've heard some things."

"I don't care what she's heard! Keep your mouth shut. This isn't story time."

Her eyes grow wide as she leans in closer to me, lowering her voice. "Oh my god! I have so many stories! When we go to the bathroom together, I'll tell you some."

"No you won't," Logan says.

Lauren ignores him. "Since our time will be limited, I need to think of some of the best ones." She lowers her voice. "Did you hear about how Brittani keyed 'fuckboy' into his Prius? It was actually my dad's Prius, which just makes it so much better—"

Lauren stops when Helen interrupts. "Leilani," she says

with a mischievous smile, "if you want stories about Logan, you should ask me."

My smile planted on my face, I turn to Helen. "I'd love to hear about when Logan was little." It's not a total lie either. I do want to know what he was like as a little boy. I just wish I wasn't in the position of having to laugh if her story isn't funny. When I glance at Logan's face, he has a smile of such warmth, my heart clenches. Guilt gnaws over my lack of total sincerity.

"He was a beautiful little boy," Helen says. "You think he's cute now, you should have seen him when he was little. Everywhere we went—the grocery store, Disneyland—people were always commenting on it. One time someone even asked to take a picture of him, which of course I said 'no,' because…" She cringes, and yet that ghost of a smile still plays at her lips. "That's weird." After swirling her wine in front of her, she takes a small sip. "My friends were always hounding me to get a modeling agent for him, but I don't believe in doing that to my children. When they're that little they can't really give you their consent. Plus, I didn't want to exclude Lauren. She never could have modeled with the Henderson nose."

"Thanks, Mom," Lauren says, clearly annoyed but also underwhelmed enough that this is likely the kind of thing that Helen says regularly.

"Maybe I made the wrong decision though. Who knows?" Helen looks at Logan, smiling affectionately. "Maybe you'd be an actor now. Or something."

"Probably not, Mom," Logan says.

Helen only smiles and takes a sip of her wine. I stare at her, waiting for the punch line of her "story." When it doesn't come, I speak without thinking. "That wasn't really a story."

When the table goes quiet, I recognize my rudeness. Heat creeps into my neck, and my armpits start to tingle from the gathering sweat. I take a deep breath before speaking again. "I just mean I wanted to hear what he was like when he was little."

Helen nods profusely, obviously feeling awkward for me by proxy. "Sure, sure, sure. Um…" She purses her lips to the side, narrowing her eyes as she stares out into space. The look reminds me of Logan. He favors her more than his dad. I wonder if Helen was once as beautiful as Logan, and that's why she seems so vain about beauty that isn't her own.

"He's always been my mama's boy. Always a good kid. I could tell you about a thousand stories about Lauren getting into trouble, but not a single story about Logan. He could definitely talk our ears off though, right, John?" She doesn't wait for John to answer. "He used to follow me around the house talking about everything under the sun. His comic books. Things that happened with his little friends at school. Whatever episode of *SpongeBob* he just watched. You know, things that adults find *super* interesting. Headphones were a necessity if I needed to get anything done around the house." And with that she breaks off into a light chuckle.

She looks at Logan, who's smiling abashedly. "Obviously, I should have started a podcast."

I'm not sure if it's just my predisposition to dislike Helen, but even knowing her "story" was told in jest, I hate it. I hate it so much that in the moment I feel like I hate her too, and Logan's deprecating response only fans my fire.

Indignation loosening my tongue, I make an impulsive move. "That's kind of mean," I say. "I think kids are boring too, but I hope I'll actually listen to my own when they talk. Instead of tuning them out with headphones."

Silence fills the table again, and this time I try not to let it bother me. What do I care what these people think anyway? My relationship with Logan is destined to fail.

Though that thought isn't nearly as palatable as it once was.

Not wanting to see Helen's face—or anyone's for that matter—I keep my eyes fixed on the wine glass in front of me. My ears are drawn to a quiet snorting sound, which I assume is Lauren's barely concealed laughter.

"Well…" Helen starts after what feels like an eternity. Her icy tone makes me nervous, but I try to be brave. I brought this on myself. I lift my eyes to meet hers squarely. Though her expression is pleasant enough, I see steel in her eyes. "When I was your age, I said a lot of things like that too. 'When I have kids, I'll never do this…' But when you actually have kids, you realize it's much harder than you ever expected. Being a mom is the most rewarding job I've ever had, but it's also the most challenging, and the least glamorous. If you become a mom someday, you'll find that no one ever notices the things you do right. John, on the other hand, would get praised to high heaven for doing even the simplest job, like changing a diaper. As a woman, you have to be the one to give yourself grace for your mistakes, because no one else will. Especially not your children." With that she sends a pointed but somewhat cheeky look at Lauren.

I nod slowly, my face growing hot with shame. I should have just kept my mouth shut. Logan probably hates me right now, but I don't dare look in his direction.

"You're right," I say when I feel like I have my voice. "I have no idea what it's like to be a parent. What I said was rude—

and anti-feminist, now that I think about it. I apologize. Logan should have warned you that I have no social skills."

"It's alright," Helen says, her tone notably softened. "You were defending Logan. You love my son. That's all any mom wants." With that she smiles. I smile back, though it takes effort.

This dinner can't end soon enough.

When I feel a pinch on my thigh, I realize that Logan is warning me to keep my mouth shut, and I can't believe he thinks I'd be so petty as to correct Helen's assumption that I love him.

But my own assumption is dispelled as soon as I look at his face. I'm arrested by what I see. There's so much love in his eyes I can almost feel it, like the warm morning sunlight that stirs you from sleep.

"Thank you," he mouths, before leaning in and pressing his lips against mine.

* * *

"Oh my god!" Lauren exclaims as we walk into the bathroom.

She stood up abruptly a few minutes ago and asked me to come with her. Logan warned her not to stay in here too long, clearly anxious about what stories she might tell me.

"Isn't my mom a delight?" she asks.

"She's not as bad as I expected, actually."

"You were a-mazing! Seriously, Logan didn't build you up enough. I love how you were like, 'Shut the fuck up, Helen. No wants to hear your god damn stupid stories about Logan's non-existent modeling career or about what a shitty mom you were using headphones to ignore you kids.' You are my hero. Seriously."

"It has nothing to do with heroism and everything to do with my lack of social skills. Trust me. And what your mom said was actually very true. I have no idea what it's like to be a parent, so I have no right to be judgmental."

Lauren waves me off as she steps into a bathroom stall. "Oh, she's so good at doing that—switching from bitch mode to Perfectly Reasonable Helen. Don't let it fool you. She's one of those people who will go from being your friend to being a dictator like that." I hear the snapping of fingers. "Like, literally she could end this night so furious with me that she threatens to kick me out of the house. She'd dump me off here with you and Logan and have my dad drive her wined-out ass home. That's how unpredictable she is."

My eyes widen. "Really?"

"Oh, yeah. Kicking me out of the house or taking my daughter away are daily threats, and for Logan the threat is his college tuition. One time she needed a date for a wedding because my dad was out of town and Logan refused to come home from Santa Barbara for the weekend—because he had a final, by the way—so she literally threatened to stop paying his tuition and rent."

My jaw drops. "You can't be serious. That's psychotic."

"Yes! But then she'll switch to Reasonable Helen and make it seems like she's not psychotic. She'll say, 'You know Dad and I want you to learn life skills,' or some bullshit like that." The toilet flushes and Lauren emerges from the stall, still buttoning and zipping her jeans as she walks to the sink. "Poor Logan too. You know she's the reason he always has a girlfriend."

I freeze at the offhand statement. Sweat starts to break out in my armpits and on my forehead. Lauren doesn't seem to sense my unease as she continues to talk while she washes her hands. "It's so sad. I'm sure you've noticed he's not the sharpest tool in the shed when it comes to his feelings. Most men aren't, but Logan's such a softy, you know?" She pouts her lips as she grabs paper towels from the silver wall mount. "He's on an eternal quest for love. That's what happens when you have a mom who makes you earn her love by bowing down to her."

My face feels like it's drained of blood. My mouth has gone dry. The words *earn her love* play over and over again in my mind.

"Oh my god!" Lauren releases a loud cackle that grates on my nerves in my present turmoil. I think I might have even flinched. "Logan would hate me for telling you this! I promise you he's the absolute best. He's so kind and such a good listener. He's, like, probably my best friend…"

She continues to gush about Logan's good qualities, as if I needed to hear them. I force a smile, but I'm too sick with self-loathing to really listen, wondering what I could possibly do to fix this.

* * *

Logan

Lauren told her something. I know she did. Lani barely said a word at dinner after they came back from the bathroom, and she's been completely silent since we started our drive home.

Seriously, fuck Lauren! And here I was on cloud nine after the showdown between Lani and my mom. I can't remember ever being happier than when I watched Lani jump to my defense—her eyes sparking, her jaw set. She was furious, and I didn't even think what my mom said was all that bad. It was a balm to every insecurity I've felt since we started dating.

And my mom assumed she loves me, and she didn't correct her. I've been trying not to read too much into it, but I couldn't quite stifle the rising hope.

And then she returned from the bathroom, and all of my hopes sunk.

"What did she say?" I ask. She doesn't answer right away, and I know she's thinking about what she should tell me, not wanting to betray Lauren. "She won't care if you tell me. She's a fucking loudmouth. She does this all the time." In my anger, I'm unable to stop myself from adding, "Most people have the common sense not to believe everything she says."

Lani sighs heavily. "She didn't say anything bad."

"Sure she didn't. You've barely said a word since you came back from the bathroom."

She goes quiet again, and I can't stop anxiety from clawing my insides. What is she thinking about? What could Lauren have told her? I'm no saint. I've had a lot of ugly breakups, and Lauren wouldn't hesitate to tell her about one of my less than stellar moments. On the contrary, she'd talk about it with glee and shameless laughter.

God damn it, I'm so pissed off. I'm calling Lauren the second I get home and bitching her out.

"Logan…" Lani begins, her tone hesitant. "I want to…" She breaks off. "I want to make a compromise."

I grip the steering wheel harder, curiosity making me tense. "What do you mean?"

"Well…" When out of the corner of my eye I see her licking her lips and blinking rapidly, I nearly drop my jaw. I've never seen her speak with such uncertainty. "I need you to realize," she restarts with a steadier voice, "that I still have the same reservations I've always had about you. I'm still not okay with how easily you fall in love and how many relationships you've had."

I shut my eyes briefly in disappointment, reminding myself to keep my eyes on the road. "Okay," I say tonelessly.

"But I won't let that… I don't want to be selfish anymore."

My curiosity is piqued again. "Okay."

"It's not fair what I've been doing."

"Okay…"

"I'll be your girlfriend."

She says the words so quickly, I'm not sure if I heard them correctly. Making a snap decision, I click the turn signal and pull the car off to the side of the road. After shifting the gear into park, I turn to Lani. "Can you repeat that?"

"I said I'll be your girlfriend."

I frown, unwilling to trust it just yet. "Are you being serious?"

"Of course."

My eyes roam her face. She means it. Of course she does. She never says things she doesn't mean. Elation courses through my veins as I unbuckle my seat belt and pat my lap. "Get over here." She smiles mischievously before unbuckling hers and sliding her butt from her seat to my thighs.

What follows is a lot of contorted limbs, bumped heads, and laughter, because car sex isn't easy when you're six-three, even when your girlfriend is tiny. When it's over she rests her forehead against mine, straddling my hips while I stroke her back.

"I love you," I tell her.

"I know," she says, like she's Han Solo, but I try not to let it bother me. I try to embrace today's victory.

I'll save her "I love you" for another day.

CHAPTER 11

Present Day

Leilani

Item 1-Makeover

"What do you think?" I ask Brenna as I walk out of the dressing room. She emerges from behind a rack of clothes. "I love it!" she shouts. "You look like a slutty Audrey Hepburn!"

A smile spreads across my face as I stare into the mirror, running my hands over the black, elastic fabric hugging my hips. The dress shows off my long legs. Logan loves my legs. The last time I wore a short dress, he told me he wanted to lick them.

"You think so?" I ask while I run my eyes over my reflection.

"Absolutely. You just need a pair of sunglasses and a long cigarette. Armaan, what do you think of her dress?"

Armaan's eyelids flutter as he lifts his eyes from his phone.

He's been sitting in a chair near the dressing room for the entire forty-five minutes we've been in this boutique. Once, he mentioned walking to a pub a few blocks away and waiting for Dean to arrive, but Brenna threatened to castrate him. His presence is essential this afternoon after all our careful planning.

Everything has to be executed perfectly. Everything from my new dress to Dean and Armaan's unknowing cooperation to Logan's whereabouts. If anything goes wrong, it will be back to the drawing board for Brenna and me.

Armaan sighs heavily as his eyes roam my body, making it clear to both of us that he finds his assigned task of fashion judge onerous. "She's too skinny for a dress that tight."

"Fuck you!" Brenna shouts. "*You're* too skinny."

Armaan returns his gaze to his phone, not even flinching at Brenna's tone.

Something about the contempt in Brenna's voice causes a memory to surface. The memory I often try to suppress, of the horrible things I said to Logan on that wretched night. The memory I don't remember, thanks to Ativan, and the shame that comes with it makes my throat tight.

Brenna walks over to me, holding a deep burgundy maxi dress high in the air to keep it from brushing the ground. "I want you to try this on. Red for *the meeting* this afternoon," she enunciates with a raised brow, "and Slutty Audrey for later tonight." When her phone rings, she glances down at her purse. She pulls it out and looks at the screen before looking back at Armaan. "Your mom is calling me. Can you please call her back? I'm sick of making excuses for you."

He keeps his eyes fixed on his phone. "No," is all he says.

Clenching her teeth, she turns back to me and mutters under

her breath, "Fucking worthless, piece of shit son. I wish I was fucking his brother instead of him." I widen my eyes at Brenna to silently scold her, but she only waves me off. "Next time his family visits, I'm switching. No joke."

I glance at Armaan just before walking back to my dressing room. He doesn't look at all offended, and he must have heard her. She meant for him to hear her. She knows his older brother's academic and career success is a sore spot for him, and she used it to hurt him.

The memory of that night threatens to choke me as I unzip the black dress and let it drop from my body to the floor. I can't even be angry at Brenna for being cruel, because that's exactly what I did to Logan. I shut my eyes, lifting the burgundy dress from the hanger and clutching it to my chest.

Don't think about it. Think about that god-awful phone call instead.

He paid me back for my sins.

By the time I open my eyes, I feel significantly calmer. I can't let shame and guilt interfere with our plan for today.

* * *

Item 2-Lure him back

By the time we arrive at *bouchon*, Dean is already sitting at a back table. He waves an arm high in the air as we walk through the front entrance. "Look at you, Lani!" he says as we approach the table. "That color looks great on you."

I glance down at my burgundy dress, smiling. "Thank you."

I'm about to ask Dean about his drive from the Bay Area

when our server comes, handing out menus and asking if we want anything to drink. Dean orders a pitcher of beer and four mugs. Heat creeps into my cheeks as I correct him, telling him we only need three mugs, but thankfully he doesn't ask for details.

Belatedly, I realize I wasn't even tempted to let his mistake slide, to have *just one* beer because, *what's just one beer going to do?*

It gets easier every day.

Granted, I still long for Ativan. Sometimes I catch myself fantasizing about what it was like when that warmth descended over me, when my mind went quiet and my heart grew light. Sometimes I even think about running outside in the middle of a rain storm, dodging pedestrians as I rush down a busy sidewalk, and bursting into an Upper West Side apartment in my soaking clothes so that I can tell Ativan what I fool I was for ever letting it go.

But it gets easier.

"So, what are your plans after graduation?" Dean asks, drawing my attention to his golden-brown eyes.

Ugh. The dreaded question. I force a smile. "I'll probably move back home for a bit and apply to graduate schools in the fall."

Apply to graduate schools for the second time you conveniently left off, Leilani—is what everyone at the table is probably thinking but won't say.

Dean grins. "So, you'll be a deadbeat just like Brenna? That'll be awesome. Seriously!" he exclaims when he sees my doubtful expression. "You guys can watch Netflix all day and go out to clubs in the city on a weeknight with no lines. It'll be like college life but without classes. I would seriously kill for a year of that. Being an adult fucking sucks. Don't let anyone tell you otherwise."

I smile sympathetically, but I can't help feeling a little jealous of him. Dean may be a frat boy grown up, but he has his shit together. He has a real job at a big accounting firm in San Jose and his own apartment in Mountain View. He only misses the limited responsibility of being a college student because he has no idea what it feels like to be aimless.

Dean would never miss out on graduate school because he couldn't do an interview without having a panic attack.

"Armaan, what are your plans?" Dean asks. My gaze automatically shifts to Brenna. She doesn't lift her eyes from her menu, but I know she's bracing herself for Armaan's answer. He's never even given her a direct answer on this subject, and I know she's had her heart set on moving with him, though she's never said so out load.

"I don't know," Armaan answers, grabbing a menu from the center of the table and laying it out in front of him. "I'll just be happy to graduate."

Brenna smiles sarcastically. "He has a 2.1 GPA."

"That's right! Which means I'm no longer on academic probation!" Armaan lifts his hand and gives Dean a high-five.

"His brother graduated *summa cum laude*," Brenna adds. "From Stanford."

I sigh heavily as I look down at my menu, wondering if this is what I sound like when I talk about Logan. I hope not. I hope my hurt hasn't made me quite this spiteful.

Though I suppose I did write a revenge list.

"And he tells literally everyone who ever talks to him about anything," Armaan says. "If he was here, he would tell our server."

Brenna glares at Armaan. "I've literally never once heard Vik mention that he graduated *summa cum laude*. Not once."

Armaan keeps his eyes fixed on the menu. "Well," he says quietly. "He's always thinking about it."

"So, Lani," Dean starts, thankfully changing the subject. "Brenna told me you and Logan are on the outs."

I try to seem unmoved when I say, "That's right."

"So obviously that means you and I are going to finally take this rampant sexual tension to the next level."

"This will be her first post-breakup lay," Brenna says. "You're crazy if you think she would settle for you."

"Nah." Dean shakes his head. "She needs to slum it the first few times. That's how rebounds work. She needs to pick a guy who's so into her, he's okay doing all the work. She can just lay there if she wants." He turns to me. "I'd be honored to do all the work for you."

I wrinkle my nose as I smile at Dean in gratitude. This is a good sign. If his thoughts are already in this direction after ten minutes of social chatter, I can only imagine what he'll be like at the bars tonight. "I'll think about it."

"You and Logan are *not* broken up."

The statement startles me, mostly because of the icy tone rather than the words themselves. I jerk to face Armaan. I'm confused by his hard eyes and tight jaw, and I realize it's because I've never seen him angry before.

"It's not really clear what we are right now," I say.

Armaan tilts his head to the side sarcastically, pursing his lips. "Hmm, no, it's perfectly clear actually. You're on a break.

You're not broken up."

"They're on a break?" Dean nearly shouts. "You've got to be kidding me! God, Logan's a fucking douche, Lani. You need a real man." Wincing, Dean turns to Armaan. "No offense to your boy. I've just never been a fan. He's one of those people who pretends like he's the nicest guy ever, but deep down he's a dick. In his heart. Where it counts." He gestures in my direction. "Who in their right mind would want to go on a break from Lani?"

"Who, indeed." I smile at Dean, relieved that Logan's dislike of him is mutual. It will only aid my scheme. Maybe Dean will intentionally make him jealous today.

As we finish our meals, I shoot Brenna a look. She nods faintly and mouths what looks like, "I got you, girl." Turning to Armaan she says, "I have three more stores I need to hit before we go home. You're coming with me."

"Absolutely not. I've put in my time today. Have Lani go with you. You can take my car. Dean will take me home."

Brenna shakes her head. "Lani has a meeting with a professor at two o'clock, and I'm not going shopping alone."

Armaan groans. "Dean can go with you, and I'll take Lani."

Dean helpfully interjects. "Nah man, I call dibs on Lani."

Brenna and I send small smiles to each other. We can always count on Dean.

"Can we leave soon?" I ask him. "It will be a long walk from wherever you drop me off."

"Yeah, let's head out now." He reaches into his pants pocket and pulls out his wallet. "And I'm not dropping you off. I'll walk with you."

Even without looking in her direction, I can feel Brenna's

smile. "That's sweet of you," I say.

"It's a huge hardship for me since I have so many things to do right now. I'll expect payment later." He winks.

Just before Dean and I stand up from our seats Brenna looks at me pointedly, her smile slow, her eyes menacing. "Make him cry," she mouths.

I strain my facial muscles to fight my smile as we walk away.

CHAPTER 12

Past—The Plan

Logan

"You loved it," I say, though I'm not really sure. She looks lost in thought as she lifts the remote from the lump of blankets and turns off the TV.

Watching a movie before bed has become our nightly ritual. We take turns choosing the movie—usually something important to us now or when we were kids—and then we talk about it afterwards. I love it. I love everything I do with my girlfriend.

My girlfriend my girlfriend my girlfriend.

I say it as often as I can, taking every possible opportunity to announce to the world that she's my girlfriend, and mostly when it's completely unnecessary. "Does my girlfriend want a beer?" "Can you tell my girlfriend her phone is ringing?" I make it seem like I'm just trying to annoy her, but really I love saying it. Every time I do it feels like a victory.

Except somehow it's not quite enough.

I don't know what it is about her that makes me so greedy, why I can't ever seem to get enough. Sometimes I feel like I won't be fully satisfied until she has a ring on her finger and a big, pregnant belly.

It's insane. She makes me insane.

"No," she says, without any hint of apology. "I kind of hated it actually."

Leave it to my girlfriend to give me her honest opinion. She'd never tell me she likes a movie just because she knows I love it. A smile rises to my lips. "Liar. You were laughing."

"It was funny, but I still hated it. I hate it on principle, and I don't understand why you love it. Especially since you genuinely love superhero movies. I hate any piece of art that's disdainful of its own genre. *Deadpool* thinks it's so much smarter than superhero movies in general. The whole movie is your pretentious, hipster friend who likes superhero movies ironically."

"Wait. So it's you?"

She blinks once before she seems to catch my meaning. She responds by rolling her eyes with a small smile.

"Are you saying that you—Leilani Girard—are actually Deadpool, and I'm only just now finding out about it?"

"Go fuck yourself, Henderson."

I turn over until my body is flush with hers. "I'd rather fuck you."

She shoots me a playful glare. "Do you think I fuck people who call me pretentious? Absolutely not. Also, I don't like anything ironically. I only ever love things earnestly." Under her breath, she adds, "like you, for example."

My body grows very, very still. "Wait… What?"

Her eyes move away from mine. "I mean when I say I love a movie like *Showgirls*, it's because I think it's a well-made movie and I genuinely enjoy the experience of watching it. I don't believe in ironic love. It's mean-spirited."

If it wasn't for the way her speech sped up with that answer, I might actually think she misunderstood my question. I pat her shoulder. "Can we back up a bit?"

She swallows as she nods. "I don't actually mind that you called me pretentious. I like that you see my flaws so clearly and don't seem particularly bothered by them."

"You're right," I begin, amused by her evasiveness. "I'm not particularly bothered by you. I love you actually, as I've told you many times. And I think you just tried to say that you love me too. Except you buried it in that long…*way too long* explanation of…I'm not really sure what. Oh, and I'm in the same category as *Showgirls*, apparently."

Her eyes fixed on my shoulder, she gives me a small smile. "High praise."

I exhale a shaky breath, caught on the frustrating verge between disappointment and euphoria. "I'm not letting you off the hook here."

As if recognizing her position of power for the first time, she smiles coyly up at me. "What else needs to be said?"

"A lot more than 'like you for example.'"

"I made it clear enough."

"I know you won't make me ask you to say it. You can't be that much of an asshole."

She grins. "Are you sure about that?"

"Oh my god! Fucking say it, Girard."

She stares at me for a moment, that playful smile fixed on her face, but then her expression begins to soften. I hold my breath waiting for her to say the words, my stomach rolling over in anticipation.

"I love you, Logan."

I shut my eyes, taking in her words over and over again. I love you. I love you. I love you. An electrical current flows through my body—so powerful that I feel almost lightheaded. But when the wave of euphoria recedes, I'm left with something stronger in its wake. Certainty.

This is it. It's her. It will only ever be her. Even if it doesn't work out between us. Even if she rejects me someday. For me, it will only ever be her.

I open my eyes and give her a hard stare. "I want to move with you after college."

In a flash, her tender expression transforms into what looks like shock. "What now?"

"If you get into University of Chicago or Indiana or wherever, I want to come with you."

"It seems a little precipitous after six months—"

"No it's not. I'm not even totally sure what precipitous means, but I know that I've never been more certain about anything in my life. I've never felt this strongly before about anyone."

"Love isn't just about feelings. And it's very like you to have strong feelings about this kind of thing, but it doesn't mean—"

"Oh. Fuck. No. It's not fair for you to always throw my past in my face. This is different. I've never told a girl I want to follow her to graduate school before—"

"Because it's crazy!"

"I disagree."

"What about your own career? You're basing one of the most important decisions of your life on a girl you kind of like."

"Haven't we just been through the fact that I more than kind of like you? And we must have different priorities, because I consider you more important than my career."

Her lips part before closing again. Brown unfocused eyes drift over the ceiling. It looks like I've stunned her. I bite the inside of my lip while I wait for what she's going to say next.

"What about Armaan?" she eventually asks. "What about your plan to travel together for a year?"

I make a deep snorting sound at the back of my throat. "That's never going to happen. That was his mom's ploy to get his GPA up to a 3.0, which is a mathematical impossibility at this point. Besides, if I'm going to travel Europe, I'd rather do it with you. We could spend a summer backpacking and do the whole hostel thing. It would be cheaper, and you wouldn't even have to take a break from school."

Her eyes lose focus again. She looks torn by indecision, and I can barely take a breath wondering what is going on inside her head. "I can't believe we're having this conversation," she mumbles, but without any disdain. She almost sounds like she's talking to herself, like she's stunned by her own participation in this conversation—the fact that she's even willing to think about all of this without trying to pull away.

"Sometimes you just know when it's right."

When she glances at me warily, I realize it was the wrong thing to say. She doesn't like that I rely on my gut instincts.

She's much more cerebral in her decision making. "We get along really well on a day-to-day basis," I say, in an effort to be more pragmatic. "People romanticize long-term relationships, but that's all they really are—being with someone day after day and not wanting to kill them."

She lifts a brow. "You've never gotten to that place with anyone."

"Nope," I respond instantly. "Not until you."

She looks surprised, as if she expected to goad me with her repeated reference to my past. "You've never seen my anxiety at its worst. You might be speaking too soon."

I snort. "Considering I once had my car vandalized, I think I can handle a little anxiety."

She doesn't believe me—I can see it all over her face—but it doesn't matter. I can prove it to her. Now that she seems willing to give me a chance, all it takes is time. Time to prove that I'm not going anywhere.

"Would we live together?" she asks.

My stomach flips when her question registers. We're in the hypothetical now. She's moments away from giving in entirely. In an effort to conceal my eagerness, I say calmly, "It would make sense financially, but I'm open to whatever you're comfortable with."

She looks at me sternly. "If I sign a lease with you, you're not allowed to dump me and head back to California a month in. I'll hunt you down if you do try something like that. I'll find a way to punish you, and I'll make sure it hurts."

I feel almost hysterical in my giddiness. Involuntary laughter erupts from my chest. "Well…you know I like it when you punish me, so…"

With that she lifts her hand to my nape and claws her nails into my skin, holding my head in place. She lifts her mouth to my cheek first, but that's not her final destination. I know what's coming. Her lips graze my skin, but the warmth of her breath trails from my cheek to my neck. She nips lightly at first, but then she sinks her teeth into the elastic skin and gives it a tug. I groan as she pulls away.

"I left a mark this time," she says quietly. "You might want to start buying concealer. You'll be getting at least five years of those."

Five years.

Euphoria comes in a rush. I have to concentrate to keep my eyelids from falling shut. I have her for five years. It doesn't even seem possible.

She looks startled when I press my lips against hers. After devouring her mouth, I trail kisses from her jaw to her neck.

I love her neck. I have five years of her neck.

I kiss her collarbone just before setting my mouth on her nipple. She sucks in a breath as I lick the smooth skin. Her nipples taste like her pussy. Is that true of all women? I never paid attention before. I feel like these are the only nipples I've ever licked. As I pull away, I stare at the brown, glistening skin, wet from my saliva.

I have five years of her tiny, perfect tits.

Five years of *her*.

I lift my head to meet her eyes. "I love you."

Her expression softens. "I love you too."

She really means it, and somehow I know in my gut that she felt it long before now.

But I needed this. I needed her to say it.

Relief washes over my body like a drug, turning my arms and legs into jelly. I collapse against her small body and rest my head on her shoulder.

I don't have to worry anymore, and somehow I'm transported back to that first time I hiked Half Dome. Standing at the top and looking down, after a year of preparation. I'm not even sure if I saw Yosemite Valley. My reward was inward, a mixture of exhilaration and relief, and maybe even something more primal, like I'd conquered something.

After months and months of anguishing uncertainty, she's finally mine.

CHAPTER 13

Present Day

Leilani

My heart pounds in a mixture of anticipation and nerves. Even with careful planning, there are a lot of unknowns, especially since I no longer have contact with Logan. Maybe class was canceled today. Maybe he was let out early. Maybe, god forbid, he's so caught in his fevered infatuation with Keira that he'll do irresponsible things like miss class.

Which brings me to the biggest unknown—the one I've tried not to think about since I wrote my revenge list. Maybe none of it will work. Maybe even if I execute the plan perfectly, and he sees me with Dean, talking and flirting and wearing this low-cut dress, he won't care.

Maybe he's in love with her already.

My heart still racing, I pace a hallway of the Social Sciences building and hope Dean's still waiting for me outside. My nerves are so frazzled I keep checking my phone. I don't have enough time to pretend like I actually met with Dr. Graves. Parking and walking over here took too long, so now I'm forced to improvise. How much time would be reasonable? Two minutes, I decide.

When I open the heavy industrial front door, Dean is still leaning against the concrete planter where I left him. He looks up from the phone in his hand. "That was fast."

I try my best to look annoyed. "He wasn't even there. He ditched me."

Dean frowns. "And you had this scheduled? What a dick."

"I know." I shrug. "Oh well."

I start to walk in the direction of the Engineering Science building, hoping I don't seem in a hurry. Dean follows my lead. In an effort to distract him from our circuitous route back to his car, I give him a beaming smile. "It's so good to have you in town."

It has the desired effect. He beams back at me. "I wish I could come more often. Being an adult sucks."

"You've said that already. Is your job awful, or what?"

He shrugs. "The money's awesome. Like, I make hella money. Not to brag. And my job is fine, it's just boring, you know? Boring and monotonous. Every day the same."

I smile wide. "You just said 'hella.' God, I miss the Bay! You never hear 'hella' in Santa Barbara."

"Dude, people are assholes here, and the line starts here too. It goes, people north of Santa Barbara—chill. People south of Santa Barbara—assholes. It's a scientific fact."

"I can't argue with science."

"Isn't your boyfriend from Coronado?" he asks with a hint

130

of disdain.

His mention of Logan makes me even more aware of our surroundings. Ambient voices around me grow sharper as we approach Engineering Science. I hear a few muffled male voices that could be his. We could run into him at any moment.

If the universe is on my side.

When I only nod in response, Dean says, "People from the San Diego area are the worst kind of assholes, because they're assholes who think they're chill."

For the first time, I feel the urge to defend Logan, but just as I open my mouth to speak, the universe intervenes.

"Lani!"

Logan's deep shout fills my belly with heat.

I did it.

Schooling my face to look confused, I turn in the direction of the voice. He's standing in a group of three girls—friends of his that I recognize. He tells them something I can't make out before jogging in our direction. As soon as he approaches, his eyes lock on Dean, his expression a combination of surprise and irritation. "What are you doing here?" He glances at me briefly but then returns his gaze to Dean.

"I had a meeting with Dr. Graves."

"And Dean came with you?"

When he doesn't even bother to greet Dean, I know he's rattled. Eventually his gaze fixes on me, and he runs his eyes up and down my body, settling on the low cut of my bodice.

"Why are you dressed like you're going out to the bars?"

"We just came from lunch, and we went to *bouchon*. I had to look fancy."

What could almost be described as horror spreads over

Logan's face as he looks from me to Dean. When his gaze returns to me, all of his earlier surprise is gone. He looks only angry. "You and Dean went out to lunch at *bouchon*?" It sounds like an accusation.

I try to stifle my triumph, straining for nonchalance. "Yes," I say. "With Armaan and Brenna. Dean treated us."

"Yep, I paid the tab for this deadbeat," Dean adds with a smile, not seeming to feel any of the awkwardness from Logan's incivility.

Dean's comment seems to make Logan even angrier, which sends a thrill down my spine, but I remind myself that the longer I stay, the more suspicious this "chance" meeting will seem. Plus, I can't trust Dean not to blab something that might make our walk over here seem calculated.

Just as I'm about to tell Logan we have to leave, he takes a step closer and grips my arm. "Can I talk to you for a minute?"

I look at Dean and shoot him a conspiring look, as if to say "back me up." "We're already late picking up Brenna from downtown. Can we talk another time?"

Logan doesn't remove his grip from my arm. He looks a little desperate as his eyes dart side to side, as if he's thinking of an excuse to keep me here.

"Yeah, man," Dean says. "We got to go."

He places a hand on my shoulder and gently guides me away from Logan, who looks a little bewildered as I drift away from him.

Both Dean and I start to back away, and Logan's eyes fix on the spot where Dean's hand still touches my shoulder.

As we turn around and continue our walk, Dean starts to talk about how awkward it was running into Logan and how he's

SKYLER MASON

glad he was there to "cover for me" with the lie about picking up Brenna, but I'm too distracted. My ears strain to hear the sound I know should be coming any moment.

Less than a minute later my phone buzzes. Smiling, I lift my phone from my purse and open the text.

Logan: What the hell was that?

I quickly put my phone back into my purse. I won't answer this one.

Let him stew for a while.

* * *

I'm on pins and needles for the rest of the day, waiting for the second text that will tell me the plan worked.

I hope that it was enough. I hope that Logan still hates Dean enough that he'll act impulsively.

But a voice from somewhere deep down whispers that nothing could ever be enough, that the whole list was written in vain, that I can make myself as hot and aloof as a femme fatale, but I can't make him care for me again. Not when he's already found someone he cares about more.

To snuff out the voice, I distract myself by giving my bedroom a deep clean.

To make room in my closet for my new makeover clothes, I grab every piece of clothing in a drab color like gray or cream and toss them into a bag meant for Goodwill. As I sift through my closet, I half-consciously wonder where that single bright color went. The red "My Boyfriend is a Feminist" T-shirt.

Oh, that's right. I took it off and tossed it onto his floor that morning in his apartment. "You are unhinged right now," he said. An involuntary giggle bursts from my chest, but my attention is immediately drawn to a buzzing sound on my desk.

When I turn around, my phone is lit up. Even from this distance, I recognize the name on the screen. I rush to my desk.

Logan: I think we need to talk about the parameters of our break. I thought I made it clear but you must have misunderstood.

A malicious smile spreads over my face. His tone may be neutral, but I know him better. I know it took him great effort to make this text sound reasonable. I know he sat and seethed over it. I know the first text he wrote—then promptly deleted— was much more inflammatory.

He's furious, and I need to capitalize on it.

I set my phone back on the desk and start to pace the room while I think of my next move. If I agree right away, he'll want to "talk about the parameters of our break" over the phone, and I can't have that. If I want to really lure him back, I need to see him in person again, preferably tonight at the bars.

I grab my phone and type out a text.

Me: No, I understood everything fine. Dean and I were just hanging out as friends. He's been my rock this past week. I don't know what I would do without him.

I snort after I type the last sentence and press send. Anyone with half a brain would know that I'm goading him with it, but hopefully Logan's over the top possessiveness will blind him to my wiles.

The "…" appears and then vanishes before appearing again.

I shut my eyes as I giggle, giddy at the evidence that my strategy worked, that I flustered him, but the text that appears shortly after is beyond my wildest expectations.

I squeal when I see it.

Logan: Are you home right now? I'm coming over.

CHAPTER 14

Past—The Bliss

Logan

I unzip my hoody to let the autumn breeze sweep over me, still not used to the way the Santa Ana winds can make Novembers warm in Santa Barbara even though I've lived here three years now. When I look up, I catch sight of her fancy grey dress, so out of place in the middle of the Old Town Farmer's Market. Our eyes meet and she smiles at me. My breath catches. It's my favorite smile—the one that brightens her whole face, like she's delighted to find that I'm here waiting for her. As if she wasn't just with me two minutes ago when she walked over to that booth to buy her oatmeal pancake mix.

"How much time do we have?" she asks as she approaches me.

I glance at my phone. "Shit. We should probably start

walking over there now."

We're celebrating tonight. She submitted her last graduate school application this morning. I was planning to take her all the way to a fancy restaurant in Malibu, but I ended up making a reservation at *bouchon* instead. Lani insisted on staying local because she didn't want to miss our weekly farmer's market trip.

I love how she does this. I love how she treats our everyday routines like they're sacred.

The last few months have been absolute perfection. I finally feel like she's lowered the invisible wall. She tells me she loves me all the time, with almost religious diligence. It doesn't even sound natural coming out of her mouth. It's stilted and awkward, almost robotic, but that just makes it all the more special, because I know why she's doing it.

She's trying. She's making the effort because she knows it matters to me.

She hasn't given in on everything. She still won't commit to living with me after we move, but she insists it's because I wouldn't like living with her. "I'm a nightmare to live with, Logan. I'm a neat freak and I never sleep and I constantly have a TV running in the background to block out my anxious thoughts." As if I didn't know all that stuff about her already, when we're practically living together now.

I can let it pass. If she's willing to meet me halfway, the least I can do is the same for her.

As we start walking toward *bouchon*, I glance at the bag in her hand. "Why didn't you get the oatmeal kind?"

She takes a deep breath, squaring her shoulders. "I'm attempting your Grandma Louise's chocolate chip banana pancakes again, and this time, I'm getting them right. I'm determined."

I smile as I grab her hand. "They were delicious the first time."

She shakes her head sharply as she interlocks her fingers with mine. "They weren't right."

"Yeah, because you're a much better cook than Grandma Louise. She made hers out of the just-add-water stuff. I never should have told you they weren't the same. Now the perfectionist in you is obsessing over it."

"I only obsess when I'm on the cusp of innovation, and *this*," she lifts the pancake mix in the air, "is a just-add-water mix. I'm getting them right this time. And so help me god, when you try these, you'll be transported back to your Grandma Louise's giant, cold basement with the old-school Nintendo."

The warmth that spreads through me makes me feel almost lightheaded. How the fuck does she remember every single trivial thing I've ever said to her? I ought to be embarrassed that it makes me feel like the king of the universe, but I'm too happy to care.

"I think it's my turn," Lani says, startling me out of my reverie.

Oh, that's right. I forgot about our game. "Truth or dare?" I ask her.

When I glance her way, her eyes are narrowed and she's pursing her lips to the side, like she's mulling over her choice. I look away so she doesn't see my smile. Lani takes everything seriously, even the silly kid games we play sometimes to pass the time. I'd bet my last dime that she was the kid who played every game of Monopoly from start to finish, diligently putting houses on all of her properties and calling out her friends when they tried to steal from the bank.

"Dare," she says.

Now that we're on State Street, I glance around to make sure I don't see anyone we know. When the coast is clear, I look back at her. "I dare you to take off your underwear and hand it to me. You've got to do it right here too."

"Easy. I can even do it while I walk." Just as she reaches toward the skirt of her dress, she frowns up at me. "I'm not wearing underwear. I forgot."

I narrow my eyes. "I feel like there should be some kind of penalty for reneging on a dare."

She bites her lip for a moment before looking up at me with that steady, brown gaze. "What if instead I stuck my finger in my pussy and put it in your mouth so you could lick it?"

I inhale sharply. I don't know why I'm not accustomed to this by now, how even after spending almost every waking moment with her, she still manages to shock me. My already half-mast dick grows fully erect. "Lani, don't do this to me, please. I'm still a little hard from when you flashed me. I don't want to have blue balls the whole time we eat."

"Why would that give you blue balls?" She sounds genuinely baffled. "You lick my vagina all the time. This is just a finger."

I shut my eyes tight. "Please stop talking about your vagina."

"Aww, I'm sorry. You're so susceptible to dirty talk. I love that about you." She sets her hand on my nape and runs her fingers up my scalp. "Don't worry, I'll take care of you as soon as I can. I'll blow you on our way home, and I'll make it nice and sloppy too. You can even come on my face, if you don't mind getting your car a little dirty."

My stomach clenches so tight, it's almost painful. With

effort, I smile at her. "I know you're trying to be sweet right now, and I really appreciate it, but as usual when you try to do normal human things like be sweet or affectionate, you're just making it a lot worse. No more Truth or Dare. And can we please try to make this dinner last less than three hours? No asking the server a million questions about the charcuterie board. I can tell you right now it's got cheese on it, and that's the only part you ever eat anyway, and you leave me all the shitty stuff, like the almonds and the pickled asparagus. And please just eat your god damn food. Fast. Without talking between every bite, because while I'm sure the oral history of the invention of crab cakes is riveting, I'm so hard right now I think I might die."

She bursts into laughter. "Oh my god, am I really that annoying?"

"Yes," I answer right away. "You are a nightmare at a restaurant. Well actually, I take that back. I like the oral history thing, just not when I'm hard."

She shakes her head, smiling. "I was never able to deal with teasing before you. I was always too sensitive. You tease me all the time, and I'm fine with it."

I grimace. "That makes me sound like a dick."

She shakes her head sharply. "No. That's the whole point. You're so sweet when you do it." She pauses for a moment, looking thoughtful. When she starts talking again, her tone is somber. "You're just wonderful all the time. I can't ever remember being so happy."

"Hey," I say softly, squeezing her hand. "That's a good thing."

"I know."

I can't tell if I've reassured her because her eyes stay downcast. Her lips twist, as if she's biting them from the inside.

Abruptly, she stops walking. She turns toward me with an expression of such vulnerability, I have to fight the urge to take her into my arms, knowing she probably wants to tell me something first. "Can we do one more Truth or Dare?" she asks.

Caught off guard, I frown. "Um… sure." When she looks at me probingly, I say, "Truth, I guess."

She sucks in her bottom lip before pulling it out slowly. "No. Say, 'dare.'"

I smile. "Okay. Dare."

She straightens her posture, lowering her chin, as if she's steeling herself for something. I can barely take a breath wondering what she's about to say.

"I dare you to live with me. In Chicago or Bloomington or wherever I end up going. In a one bedroom or studio apartment. With one bed."

My jaw drops.

"And it really is a dare," she says, "because you're going to hate it. I'm a terrible roommate. I like everything my way. I won't let you organize a single cupboard. You'll do it all wrong. The cupboards in your apartment are an absolute disaster, and it ruins my whole baking experience."

My throat tightens with emotion, but I swallow to ease it away. "I don't know how I'll survive. You know how I love organizing cupboards." I smile warmly at her, but she doesn't see it. She's staring down at the sidewalk.

I grab both of her hands and squeeze them tight. "You don't have to do this. I'm not going to pressure you, I promise. If you need your space, you can have it."

She lifts her head and settles hard eyes on me. "No. This is what I want. This is how normal human beings behave in a relationship. They don't move across the country together to live in separate apartments. It's high time for me to get off my bullshit. And you need to hold me accountable."

With those last words, her stern expression softens into something I can't quite interpret. She almost looks…afraid.

She *doesn't* want to do this, despite her insistence. I can see it all over her face.

But she's doing it anyway.

The tenderness that flows through me makes it hard to take a breath. I run my thumbs along the soft skin at the back of her hands. "I just want you to know that I'm happy. Just as we are right now. You don't have to do anything more for me."

I mean it too, surprisingly. I don't need her to give me everything. I'm so happy with what I already have, I feel like my heart might explode.

It's terrifying to be this happy, because I know I could lose it all in an instant.

But I'm finding I hardly even think that way anymore. The more she compromises, the more she does things that scare her because she knows they're important to me, the more certain I become.

I have her.

She's mine.

CHAPTER 15

Present Day

Logan

1. DON'T LOOK AT HER INSTAGRAM.
2. ~~DON'T TEXT HER.~~
3. ~~IF YOU RUN INTO HER, BE POLITE BUT DISTANT.~~
4. DON'T UNDER ANY CIRCUMSTANCES AGREE TO SEE HER IN PERSON.
5. DO NOT HAVE SEX WITH HER.

"Talk me out of driving to Leilani's right now."

Keira exhales heavily, sending a rush of feedback through the phone speaker. "What did she do?"

"I'm not really sure if she's done anything yet, but I'm suspicious. I ran into her on campus today. She was with Dean."

There's no need to say more than that. Keira knows

everything about my justified hatred of Brenna's older brother.

"Do you think that was a coincidence?"

"It does seem suspicious, but he does…'get her.'" My teeth clench over the words.

"Right," Keira says. "And I'm sure she had a perfectly reasonable excuse to bring him to campus today. And how strange that they just happened to run into you."

"Yeah, I don't really think it was a coincidence either, but I can't just let it go."

She's silent for several seconds, and I can feel her disappointment through the phone. "Logan…" Her tone is pleading. "This is why you made your list."

"I know."

"And I told you she would go after you with everything she's got."

"I know."

She sighs again. "I can tell there's no convincing you. I hear it in your voice."

"You're right," I admit right away. "And I'm sorry."

"Don't say sorry to me. The list was about you."

I don't respond right away, because she and I both know that's not true. Maybe the nobler intentions of the list were about me and my boundaries, but we both also knew that it was about what happened that night and our mutual guilt. The list was meant to soothe it.

After hanging up with Keira, I walk into the kitchen and grab my keys from the counter.

As I walk to my car, I stifle the guilt gnawing my conscience by reminding myself that it's just going to be a conversation. I'm just going to make it clear that neither of us is single right now—despite our separation—and then I'll leave.

By the time I pull up to the Blue House, I still have no idea what to say to Lani. I hear my pulse pounding like a tribal drum as I walk up the stairs to her porch. I knock once before walking into the house.

I immediately head in the direction of her room—where she's spent most of her time since she started taking Ativan—but I'm startled when my eye catches a petite figure leaning against the kitchen counter, cradling a mug to her chest.

"You got here fast," she says.

Unable to comment, I stare at her dumbly for several seconds, taking in her appearance.

Her long hair hangs in damp waves down her back. She's wearing a baggy T-shirt that just barely covers her butt, exposing her long, lean legs, and even though I've spent hours memorizing every inch of her body, I'm overwhelmed with the curiosity of what I would find if I lifted up that black material. Is she wearing shorts? Underwear? Nothing?

She doesn't look like she's wearing makeup, but somehow her face looks bright. Bright and healthy. It occurs to me that I didn't take in much of her appearance earlier today, besides her fancy dress and the douchebag standing next to her.

Frowning, I stare at her head. "Did you do something to your hair?"

"I washed it." She smiles, and even though it's just a small quirk of the lips, the sight of it freezes me in place. I can barely take in a breath. I haven't seen that smile in months.

And it turns out that part of this ache in my chest is from missing her.

Missing her even when she's been in the same room.

The old Leilani went somewhere else when she started taking Ativan, somewhere faraway. I was angry with her for it, yes, but also sad. And I didn't recognize the sadness until now as I stand here looking at the old Leilani, smiling as if these last few miserable months never happened. As if she only left for a weekend retreat and came back rested and fresh.

I come back to earth when I see that smile falter, a notch forming between her brows. "What did you want to talk about?"

Recalling myself, I look away from her. "Dean," I say sternly.

"He's here, so keep your voice down." She quirks her head toward the hallway.

Horror grips me for an agonizing moment before I realize that she's gesturing in the direction of Brenna's room.

Of course. He's here because he's visiting Brenna. I exhale in relief, but my ire only cools for a moment when my attention is drawn once again to her exposed legs. "Why are you standing in the kitchen in your underwear if Dean is here?"

She lifts the bottom of her T-shirt and exposes her hips. "I'm wearing volley ball shorts," she says, revealing the tight black shorts.

She's looking at me as if I've lost my god damn mind, and for the first time, I question my impetuosity in coming here.

Still, I can't leave here without saying my piece. "I don't feel good about you hanging out with Dean."

She narrows her eyes. "What do you expect me to do? Send him home? Tell him he can't visit Brenna?"

Irritated by her lack of remorse, I take a fortifying breath. "Okay, fine. You can't help that he's here, but I'd feel better if you didn't hang out alone with him."

"We're not hanging out alone."

I frown. "Where's Brenna?"

"Grocery shopping with Mia."

I'm about to ask why Dean didn't go with her, when a hallway door opens and Lani turns away from me. Her smile softens as Dean walks into the kitchen, and for the millionth time since I met him, I want to punch him in the face.

He smiles intimately at her before glancing my way, and when he does, his face instantly changes. He looks at me suspiciously, as if I'm the intruder here. As if it's completely out of line for me to be hanging out with my girlfriend at eight p.m. on a Friday night but perfectly normal for him.

"Hey, Logan," he says, but it sounds like a question, like, "Hey, Logan, what the fuck are you doing here?"

I can't even force a smile. "Hey, Dean."

"How did you like *Phantom Thread*?" Lani asks him.

"Well…like every other time I've watched a Paul Thomas Anderson movie, it was…" he pauses as if for effect, "nap time."

When Lani giggles, it takes all of my willpower not to scowl at her. If I ever said anything like that she would give me the longest, most pretentious lecture ever about the value of auteur filmmaking and how our generation is snuffing it out with our pedestrian taste in billion dollar franchises like *The Avengers*. She already did, actually, when we watched *Phantom Thread* in bed a few months ago.

"PTA isn't for everyone," she says.

"Can we go to your room?" I ask her abruptly. I look at Dean. "We're kind of in the middle of something."

Not waiting for Dean to make an awkward apology, I start in the direction of Lani's room. I'm almost out of the kitchen when I'm halted by her voice.

"No," she says. When I turn around, she standing in the same place she was before. "We're done talking. We understand each other perfectly, and anyway, I don't have time to talk right now." She picks up a chunk of her damp hair and runs her fingers through it. "I need to get ready. We're going out as soon as Brenna gets home."

"Going out?" I ask, unable to hide my dismay.

When I said I wanted a break, I meant I wanted her to seek help. To increase her sessions with Dr. Scott. To start going to NA meetings. And that was the best-case scenario. Worst case, I worried she'd lay around all day crying, start taking even more Ativan, call me and beg me to end our separation…

Never in my wildest dreams did I imagine she'd be going out to clubs with Brenna and her fuckboy older brother.

"Yeah," she says, as if it's the most natural thing in the world. "Dean is only here for the weekend and we want to make the most of his time."

I stare at her in stunned indecision, clenching my teeth in an effort to keep my shit together. The idea of her spending the night out with Dean makes me want to hit something, but what could I possibly say? If Brenna is going, then she won't be alone with him, and will technically be fulfilling what I asked of her. I can't tell her I'm going with her because that violates everything I'm trying to do, and Keira would kill me.

A questioning frown mars her brow, like she's waiting for me to say something. "Where are you guys going?" I ask, trying to sound nonchalant.

The corners of her lips lift marginally. She opens her mouth to speak, but Dean interrupts. "Hipster bars. Or…I'm guessing we are, knowing my sister."

I don't look his way. "So, Test Pilot?" I ask Lani.

"Why do you want to know?"

"Just wondering if we'll run into each other. Armaan and I are going out too."

Her eyes narrow. "Armaan said he has a midterm in the morning. Brenna wanted him to come with us, and he said he wouldn't."

Shit. With effort, I keep my face blank as I shrug. "We're not staying out long."

She nods slowly, clearly not believing me, but I don't care. I have just as much of a right to go out tonight as she has. "Well, I'm heading out. Maybe I'll see you later." I make pointed eye contact with Dean just before turning around and walking to the front door.

As soon as I get into my car, I pull out my phone and call Armaan. "Change of plans. We're going out tonight."

"Oh my god! I have a fucking midterm tomorrow and I just got off of academic probation." He sighs heavily. "What did she do to you?"

"I just can't stand by and let her go out with Dean. I'll be thinking about it all night. You know she's going to get super drunk and take Ativan and get all sloppy…" My knuckles go white as I clench the steering wheel. "He'll probably use it as an excuse to help her undress at the end of the night."

"Oh my god, Logan," Armaan groans. "Dean's not a rapist. You need to find your chill."

"You would be the same way if it were Brenna."

"No," he says immediately. "I wouldn't."

"I can't let her go out with Dean."

"Ugh," he groans again. "Fine."

149

CHAPTER 16

Past—The Spiral

Leilani

At two o'clock today I have my first graduate school interview at USC.

I didn't sleep last night. Not for a single moment. For the entire six hours I spent in my bed, thoughts raced in a buzzing hum while my heart pounded in my ears, and any moment my exhausted mind drifted off, my body jolted as violently as if I'd been hit in the face.

I'd spent all of winter break obsessively prepping for this interview. I'd even bailed on going to visit my parents for Christmas so that I could have some rare alone time at home.

Everything was riding on my grad school interviews, on my ability to pretend to be normal. It wasn't just my future on the line, but Logan's future too. *Our* future.

It was too much pressure.

I could tell I was headed for a panic spiral if I kept obsessing, so I'd changed tack. I skipped three classes the first week back to try and find my chill. I baked. I watched movies. I even got a massage.

Nothing worked.

I look at the mirror on my bedroom door, wondering how I'm going to use makeup to mask the wraith staring back at me. My sunken eyes and pale lips are a giveaway that I've lost more than a single night's sleep.

Suddenly, the otherworldly aura descends, and the area around me starts to buzz.

Oh, no. No, not this. Please not this.

The furniture in my room looks bright. Electric. Menacing— as if the whole universe is against me, everything from the relentless sun in the sky to my cheap IKEA desk.

It's happening. There's no going back now.

The spiral has begun.

I could have a panic attack for any reason at all, something as small as a first date to as big as a ballet solo in a packed auditorium. Sometimes I'd even have one over something I'd done dozens of times before, like a class presentation. There's no rhyme or reason to it, but once it begins, there's no stopping it.

I know it in my gut.

This won't be my only panic attack.

I'll have one tomorrow, and the day after that, and probably another one that night, and then I won't sleep, and I'll live in a simmering state of panic for the next three days until I finally pass out from exhaustion for a few hours, but then, of course, panic will haunt my dreams in order to keep my body from fully resting, a reminder that no matter what I do or where I go, I can't escape it.

As if out of acceptance, my chest rises and falls in a shallow pant and the muscles in my hands and feet starting twitching.

In an attempt to pull myself out of my head, I frantically reach for the phone sitting face up on my desk.

Me: Can you come over?

As if he's a magical antidote to anxiety, my body immediately starts to relax after I press send. I think of his kind, smiling face. Logan. My shelter from the storm.

I hear Bob Dylan's voice singing a similar line in my head.

Jesus Christ, has there ever been a worse singer than Bob Dylan? It reminds me of the endless, claustrophobic drives to Malibu in the back seat of our family Honda Accord with my brother's feet in my face as shitty classic rock played on my dad's Satellite radio. I remember wondering if we had all died in a car accident that we didn't remember, and hell was just a slow torture of monotony. That I would spend eternity in a limbo of the present, with a window view of cars against a smog-pink sky in the start-and-stop LA traffic. My brother farting and then extending his long arm into the front seat to press the child window lock. My parents gossiping like teenagers about the uncle and aunt we're on our way to visit—"How much do you want to bet they're going to order a two-hundred-dollar bottle of wine tonight?"—all but forgetting my brother's and my existence in the back seat.

I wonder if I'm still in that Honda Accord right now, only starting to wake from a dream designed specifically by the devil to make the monotony more unbearable.

I find myself walking in circles as if the ritual could stifle Bob Dylan's raspy voice. "Shut up, Bob!"

I halt when I hear my phone vibrate.

Logan: Is everything ok?

Me: I'm just nervous about my interview.

Logan: I have to stay after for a bit to ask my professor a question, but I can come right after that.

I imagine Logan in a flannel plaid shirt sitting at a desk, rapt by a lecture about god knows what. Engineering shit. I love the black square glasses he wears only for class, and the way they make his green eyes look large and vulnerable. "I can't see the lecture notes without them," he says, with that self-deprecating half-smile.

Somehow the thought makes me sad, like I'm an unhappily married sixty-year-old lady wistfully remembering her perfect college boyfriend. The best she ever had.

No, no, no. Negative thoughts. Self-loathing. None of this is good. I'm starting to unravel.

It's only when I see Logan's startled face as he stands in my doorway that I realize how long I've been pacing in tiny circles in my cramped bedroom. "Hey…" he says softly. He approaches me slowly as if afraid to startle me. A hysterical giggle bubbles from my chest as I realize how insane I must look. "Are you that worried?" He sets a hand on my forearm as if to steady me.

Immediately the tears come in streams. I giggle again out of embarrassment, but it sounds more like a sob. "I'm a mess right now."

He pulls me into his arms and I cry silently against his chest, loathing myself for doing it, but having no willpower to stop.

"Lani," he says into my ear. "How could you of all people be worried about this? I don't think I've ever asked you a question that you didn't have an answer to." I hear a smile in his voice. "It's shocking sometimes what you come up with, like you've had a year to think about it."

"That's not what I'm worried about."

Lightly, he grips my upper arms to shift my body back, as if to give himself a better view of my face. "What then?"

I move away from him to collect my thoughts. "It's all the other stuff. Talking about my drive from Santa Barbara, as if I don't want to die of boredom just thinking about it. Looking at the pictures on their desk and telling them their ugly children are cute. Laughing if they tell stupid jokes. I didn't sleep at all last night worrying about this interview. I'm too exhausted to fake social graces. I'm not good at them as it is."

His concerned smile makes me realize that I'm pacing again. I stop and fold my hands stiffly in front of me, as if I can force them to keep still.

"You should just give them the 'I'm awkward manifesto' you gave me the first night we went out. I thought it was pretty cute."

"They don't want cute! This is a fucking PhD program. I'll be their peer when it's over. They're picking a future research colleague. They're picking someone they have to spend hundreds of hours with over the next five to seven years. They want someone they could go get a beer with after class."

He frowns. "Are you out of your mind? Who wouldn't want to get a beer with you? People get PhDs in fields like yours mostly because they wanted to have interesting conversations with interesting people. You might be bad at laughing at dumb jokes, but you're a magician at interesting conversation." His smile is so kind, I wish I could find it comforting. "You're being too hard on yourself."

I shake my head.

"Okay, I'll help you. We'll practice having small talk right now."

I fight the urge to groan. That is so how someone without anxiety tries to fix anxiety. "Just do this," they always say. Oh, so you're saying I should just calm down? Excellent advice. I don't know why I never thought of it before.

"Fine." I turn toward him, taking an inventory of his appearance. "I would tell you I like your shirt, except I don't think I could say it with a straight face."

His brow furrows before he looks down at the *Iron Man* logo on his chest, as if he forgot what he was wearing. As he lifts up his head, he grins. "That's my girl. Maybe you should just be yourself. It always works on me."

Anxiety makes me two people. A girl deep within me feels comfort at his gentle acceptance of my shortcomings, but her voice is silenced by the raving lunatic pacing this room right now.

I'm calling our campus health services tomorrow. I need a therapist. I can't stand for him to see me like this.

Suddenly, I need him gone. I can't handle having him see me like this. I stop in my tracks to face him and take a deep, steadying breath. "I won't need you to drive me today."

His eyes widen as he steps into a straighter posture. "I thought we were going to the beer garden at California

Adventure afterward to celebrate."

I shake my head. "I'm too exhausted to do anything fun. Plus, I doubt that there will be anything to celebrate, and I don't need the extra pressure. I'll just go by myself."

His tone is much more serious when he says, "We don't have to go anywhere after, but you should let me drive you. If you go alone you're going to torture yourself with these thoughts. If I go with you I can distract you, or better yet, you can sleep in the car."

I meet his eyes, resolved. "No. I'd rather go alone."

As he crosses his arms over his chest, I can see that he's angry. He thinks that I'm purposely putting distance between us, closing myself off yet again. Partially, he's right.

Mostly though, I'm not ready to admit out loud even to myself that I'm bailing on a graduate school interview today.

CHAPTER 17

Present Day

Leilani

~~Item 1 Makeover~~
Item 2-Lure him back

An icy breeze stirs the branches of the sidewalk trees. I hug my arms to fight the cold as we walk to the entrance of Test Pilot. Dean's hand lingers on my shoulder as we step inside, and the thought that Logan might be watching it sends a delightful chill down my spine. Brenna guides us to a small open couch in the back of the bar. We cram so tight I'm practically sitting on Dean's lap. Brenna smiles wickedly as she leans into my shoulder. "He's going to die," she whispers.

I certainly hope so.

The plan for tonight is rather fluid. I just need to look hot, remain aloof, and leave abruptly. I need to stimulate his curiosity enough to leave him wanting more. The lure is a slow burn. It doesn't happen in one night.

The first part was easy thanks to my makeover. My slutty Audrey Hepburn dress barely covers my ass now that we're sitting down. If I feel brazen enough later, I might open my thighs for Logan like Sharon Stone in *Basic Instinct*.

Leaving abruptly won't be difficult either. I've always hated muggy bars, and I hate them even more now without the dulling balm of alcohol and Ativan.

And I absolutely will not be drinking tonight.

Which brings me to the difficult part. Staying aloof might be hard. Logan knows me well, and he's always been attentive to my moods. If panic comes on, he'll know. I won't be able to feign indifference.

"I hope so," I whisper to Brenna. "Have you heard from Armaan yet?"

"Yes." She reaches for her purse, pulling her phone out. "Logan is such a liar. Armaan had no intention of going out tonight."

"He didn't even make much of an effort to hide that he was lying. That's Logan Henderson in a nutshell. He even knows that I know he's lying, and he doesn't care. Absolutely shameless. If I confront him on it he'll just smile and be like—" I imitate Logan's playful half-smile and lazy speaking style, the way he draws out the vowels and talks out of the side of his mouth— "'And I'm not really sorry.'"

"That's so Logan! You sound exactly like him."

My chest aches. I smile, turning away to hide my sudden

rush of overwhelming nostalgia. It's true that I know him well. I know him well enough that I have his exact replica in my mind, capturing everything from his voice to his movements to his mannerisms. I've used it to anticipate arguments—if I say this, then he'll say that, and so on.

It makes me wonder what will happen to this replica of Logan when the real Logan is gone. Will I still hear his voice and see that beautiful smile ten years from now?

God, I hope not. I want to forget him.

"Shit," Brenna says. "They're here."

Her exclamation startles me from my reverie, but the melancholy is only momentarily suspended, plummeting into an agonizing ache at the center of my chest when I see what she means by "they."

Keira.

How could I have forgotten? Of course she would come tonight. Probably to keep Logan in line. After all, his "boundary setting" intervention was her idea. I can only admire her cleverness. She wanted Logan, and found a healthy, rational way to overcome the pathetic, pill-popping obstacle that stood in her way.

My only comfort is her obvious irritation in having to be here tonight. Her jaw is set and her face expressionless as the three of them make their way through the crowd. Armaan approaches first with a cocktail in each hand. He places one of them in front of Brenna just as Logan sits on the ottoman directly across from me. I don't look his way, but I sense his attention on my right hip as it presses against Dean's thigh. I fight the urge to lean back into Dean's shoulder.

Too obvious.

Brenna takes a big gulp of her yellow cocktail before setting it down on the table in front of us. She grabs the pineapple garnish and takes a bite. "Armaan, I'm drinking yours too."

"Whatever," Armaan says, long accustomed to Brenna's high-handedness. "I don't like this tiki shit anyway." He looks around the misty bar with a frown on his face. "Like, just give me a normal fucking drink, dude. Don't make me pay fifteen dollars for a tiny umbrella."

I turn to Dean, smiling wide. "I love the tiny umbrellas."

He smiles back. "Do you want me to get you something? I'm sure they could make any drink on their menu virgin."

I shake my head. I'm about to tell him that I'm against virgin cocktails in principle when Logan's voice booms through the ambient bar noise. "Why would you order a *virgin* drink?"

His tone says it all. He's both frantically curious and grimly suspicious, wondering why I'm not drinking, and more importantly, why Dean knows and he doesn't. With effort, I keep my face blank as I turn to him. "I'm not consuming any mood-altering substances for the time being." His brow furrows in question, but I don't acknowledge it as I turn back to Dean. It's crucial that I stimulate Logan's curiosity without satisfying it.

I frantically search my brain for a topic to bring up with Dean, when Logan's voice booms once again. "Does that include Ativan?"

The disdain in his voice combined with his obvious disbelief leaves me momentarily frozen. In Logan's mind, the chances of my quitting Ativan are so slim that he doesn't even bother to hide his sarcasm. The realization leaves me stunned.

I was right. When he told me he wanted to go on a break so that I could figure things out, he didn't think there was a chance in hell that I actually would. The one-month break was only Part I of our breakup.

Tears threaten behind my eyes, but I strain my facial muscles to keep them in place. Why does it all still hurt so much when I already knew it to be the truth?

I take a deep breath through my nose and release it slowly through my mouth. I turn to him and give him the direct, unblinking stare he said made him hard on the night we met. For added effect, I wait a few seconds before answering him. It works. The sternness in his face softens into uncertainty. "Yes," I say. "I stopped taking Ativan. It's been thirteen days and…" I glance at my watch, "seven hours."

His eyes grow contrite as he leans forward in the chair. "That's great." His lips close as if he's considering his next words. "I'm proud of you."

His words make me shudder, the kindness and sincerity in his tone having no effect. I'm propelled into action. This overwhelming self-disgust is a precursor to panic, and I don't want to be tempted to grab that tropical drink on the table and down every last drop. I turn away from Logan and grab Dean's arm, leaning in and whispering, "Do you want to go outside with me for a minute? I need some air." He nods once before standing up. As I turn to Brenna to let her know where we're going, I catch the look on Logan's face, the wide frantic eyes at my sudden flight, but I'm too far gone to feel any sort of satisfaction. My heart is already pounding, my breathing shallow as I try to take gulps of the wet, Tiki air. If I don't get out of here soon, panic will take over, and I'll make a fool of myself.

Brenna mouths something about coming with me, but I shake my head. While I could use her comforting presence, I would look foolish and weak. At least having Dean with me will have the desired effect on Logan.

Dean grips my arm as we sift through the crowd. I try my best to avoid bumping into people, feeling even slight contact might suffocate me. After what feels like an endless maze, we've finally made it to the sidewalk outside.

My sharp intake of wet ocean air is an instant relief, but not enough to halt the steady rise of panic. The aura has now fully descended, the world around me electric with menace. Even Dean's sympathetic face looks vicious.

"Are you having an anxiety attack?" he asks.

I shut my eyes, nodding. I can't see him but I know he's nodding back. "You've been getting them for a long time. Remember that time you ran off at Disneyland and my dad had to chase you?"

Even in the midst of panic, a smile rises to my lips at the memory. I was ten years old and we were all standing in line at Splash Mountain when suddenly I felt like I couldn't breathe. It was always the symptoms themselves that scared me back then. When my breathing was shallow, I really thought I couldn't breathe. When my heart raced, I thought I was having a heart attack. Only years later did the true fear settle in—*Will I go crazy and, if so, will the people I love abandon me?*

"I remember my parents were like, 'Hol-ly. Shit.'" Dean says. "'Did the child we were trusted to watch really just jump the turnstile and disappear into the crowd, at fucking Disneyland? They just stared after you at first, like they had no idea what the fuck just happened."

A giggle bubbles out of my chest. "Your poor dad."

"Watching him run after you made it all worth it. I don't

think I've ever seen him that sweaty."

Feeling calmer, I open my eyes. Dean's smiling face looks as benevolent as I've known it to be. The aura has receded, leaving me almost giddy in its wake.

"I think only bottled up people have panic attacks," I say in a rush. "People who are so terrified of vulnerability that they eventually explode with all of their pent-up emotions."

His smile falters, his brow wrinkling into a questioning frown. "Are you saying that's you?"

"I don't know. For some reason I've never been able to be completely vulnerable with people I haven't known since I was five years old. It's been especially true with boyfriends."

Dean narrows his eyes as they drift away from my face. "Do you think maybe it's just that your boyfriend's an asshole and he made you feel insecure?"

I choke out a laugh at his unexpected question.

Dean smiles. "Seriously. Why the fuck is he here tonight? He told you he wants you to stay away from him and then he just shows up here ready to hang out. What's up with that?"

I smile sheepishly, averting my gaze from his face.

"What?" His tone is suspicious.

"Brenna and I may or may not have used you to make him jealous…"

I feel better after admitting it. What's the use in hiding it now? Logan isn't stupid. He knows I'm trying to make him jealous.

When I look back at Dean's face, his eyelids flutter in an exaggerated eye-roll. I laugh at the sight.

"That's so something you and Brenna would do. You guys haven't grown up at all since high school."

I take a step closer to him, lifting my head and fluttering my lashes. "Don't be mad," I say silkily.

He leans in, grinning. "I'm not mad. It should go without saying that you can use me anytime you want. Preferably when we're..." he trails off as though distracted.

It takes me a beat to understand why he didn't finish that thought.

* * *

Logan

Oh, hell no. Don't you dare finish that sentence.

As I march toward them, his smile falters. Lani's slower on the uptake, frowning at Dean in question before turning her head in my direction. I don't waste a moment. "Can I talk to you?"

Though she agrees, she's noticeably annoyed. She asks Dean to join the others inside, telling him she'll only be out here a few more minutes. She softens her dismissal by thanking him for coming out with her, emphasizing her words by gripping his forearm and giving it a squeeze.

I look away, certain that if I witness even one more sign of their obvious intimacy and affection for each other I'll be compelled to do something truly stupid. Like finally giving Dean the punch in the face he's been begging for since I met him eleven months ago.

When Dean is gone, I walk up to Lani, stopping within inches of her chest so that I have to tilt my chin down to look into her eyes. When her unblinking gaze meets mine, her face is as placid as a porcelain doll's, without a trace of guilt for having spent the last five minutes flirting with Dean and trash-talking our relationship.

"Why are you looking at me like that?" she asks. When I don't answer, she narrows her eyes. "You're angry because I was *talking to Dean*?" She emphasizes the last few words disdainfully. As if they were really only talking. As if Dean wasn't just about to say, "Let's fuck," right before I interrupted him.

"No," I say, trying to keep my voice cool. "I'm just an asshole, and I want to make you feel insecure."

Her eyes grow wide. "You were listening to our conversation?" Her eyes dart to the entrance of the bar and back again. "How long have you been out here?"

She finally looks a little guilty, thank fuck, but it does nothing to cool my temper.

"For like two minutes!" I shout. "It's not like I was hiding. I was standing right there"—I gesture to the side—"but you guys didn't even notice. I didn't want to interrupt your cute little heart to heart, but it was hard to just stand by and let him shit-talk our whole relationship." I shake my head. "And you didn't even stop him. How could you let him say all those things after everything? How could you *use him to make me jealous* after everything?"

Since she shuts her eyes and lifts a hand to her brow, I'm unable to see if she's contrite or not. I look away for a moment to fight the urge to start shouting at her again.

When I finally look back at her, her hand is lowered and I can fully see her face. Relief rushes through me. The invisible wall has lowered. I can feel it in the air between us.

"I'm sorry. I can be so petty sometimes. Such a child…" Her

voice is just above a whisper. She shakes her head, as if to clear it. "But can't you at least sympathize with the desire to show off how great you're doing to your ex?"

The relief is short-lived.

My brows shoot to my forehead. "I am *not* your ex! I asked for one month away from you, and you agreed to it. Then you use Dean to make me jealous… To break my rules and come out with you tonight…" I trail off to get control of my emotions. I take a deep, shaky breath as I run a hand through my hair.

"Logan," she says calmly. "You did this. You texted me, showed up at my house, and came out to the bars uninvited. You can't blame me that you're here. Yes, I tried to make you jealous, but I didn't make you do all of this."

I sigh heavily, weary of this conversation and even more so of her repetition of clichés she learned in therapy. "Let's just go. Let's just mutually agree to stop being childish. I didn't even want to go out tonight, and Armaan is annoyed with me for making him come. Let me take you home."

"No."

My stomach flips over in surprise. "No?"

"No. I came out because I needed a distraction, and I was having fun before you showed up. I think just you should leave."

I exhale. "Okay…"

"I think Keira's annoyed with you too. For coming here, I mean."

Something about the way she says Keira's name makes me uneasy, but I don't have time to figure out why when she starts talking again.

"We can agree to stop being childish, but I won't change my plans tonight just because you want me to. It was…unkind of me to use Dean to make you jealous, but that doesn't mean I don't fully enjoy having him in Santa Barbara. I know you hate him, but it doesn't change the fact that he's a close friend, and hanging out with friends is good for me right now. This is all part of my recovery, which you asked for by the way. This is all part of me learning to live without you."

A chill runs down my spine at her word choice. "I never asked you to learn to live without me—"

"Well I'm doing it just the same. So please let me. Go home." With that, she turns around and walks away.

Lani loves having the last word, and out of expediency, I usually let her have it, but that's not what's keeping me from running after her this time.

For the first time since I asked for time apart, I realize that I'm not the only one with a say. Just because she's the one with the drug problem, and I'm the wronged party, doesn't mean everything is within my control.

And I'm frozen in fear that I might lose her.

CHAPTER 18

Past—The Shift

Leilani

"What are we doing here?" I ask, hating that I sound so churlish.

I can't let him see how I'm feeling. He can't know how desolate I feel at just the thought of losing him. He would think I'm pathetic.

"I thought it would help distract you," he says, but I know it's not that. That doesn't explain the nostalgic bent to his impulsive choice in taking me here. The weather is warm for February and the sky is clear, casting a metallic glow over the ocean. The beach is nearly empty, so like that evening after the Women's March. He even guided me over here to the swing set, as if we could laugh about that stupid T-shirt and reminisce about the first time he told me he loved me, in the middle of my fucking panic attack.

Bringing me here was a statement, whether he knows it or not. Even as he tells me he loves me—which he has on an almost hourly basis over the last month of my constant panic attacks— he can't hide that a part of him is screaming inside. I see it in his eyes when he watches me pace the floor. I hear it in his voice when he tells me to breathe in through my nose and out through my mouth. "I didn't sign up for this!" is what he would shout if he could. "Go back to who you were before!"

The problem is that this is who I've always been.

And he's retreating, but only on the inside. He can't admit what he's really feeling because he knows how poorly that would reflect on his character after months of insisting on the constancy of his love. He's in a bind, which explains that look on his face. Even as he relaxes into the swing, he looks like a trapped animal, his unseeing eyes darting around the beach, his lips pursing and releasing, over and over again.

"So…" he begins, and I hold my breath for what he's about to say. Is this it? Has he figured out a way to back himself out of his trap? "You have panic attacks because you're afraid of having panic attacks?"

I exhale in relief, though annoyance prickles at the disbelief in the question. He didn't say anything the first time I explained this to him, and I knew why. He thinks it's absurd.

"Yes," I say, my tone churlish again. "It's a vicious cycle."

He nods slowly. Suddenly he frowns. "I mean can't you just…" He trails off, clearly doubting the wisdom of what he's about to ask, but he doesn't need to finish. I already know what he's going to ask. I've heard this question before.

"Can't I just not be afraid?" I ask. "What a great idea. I should just not be afraid. Then I won't have panic attacks.

Problem solved. Are you sure you chose the right field? You'd make a brilliant psychologist."

I shut my eyes briefly at the end of my statement, hating myself for being so nasty, but I'm surprised when I open them to see a faint smile on Logan's face. "That was pretty brilliant, huh?"

My chest aches at his self-deprecating warmth. I'll miss it desperately when he's gone. I shut my eyes, knowing I need to apologize. "It's okay if you don't understand panic disorder. Most people don't. Not even my parents, and they've watched me have panic attacks my whole life."

He frowns. "Why didn't you tell me about this?"

I bristle at the question. *Why didn't you warn me what I was getting into?* is what he's really asking.

I try to sound calm when I say, "I told you I have anxiety."

"Yeah, but this is *next level* anxiety."

I stiffen. "You're not entitled to know every detail of my life."

He grunts, shaking his head. "This is a pretty relevant detail for someone who loves you and wants to follow you across the country."

My chest aches at his declaration, a mixture of pleasure and pain. A part of me knows he's saying that mostly to himself, trying to convince himself that he didn't make an epic mistake that night in my bed when we made all of our plans.

"Relevant because it would give you time to back out?" I ask, unable to help myself, wanting two contradictory things at once. Wanting him to admit that he made a mistake. Wanting to know with certainty that his words sound just the slightest bit hollow because he doesn't even believe them himself. But also wanting him to insist that it's still true. To prove that he loves me against all odds.

"What the fuck kind of question is that?"

"Maybe you're having second thoughts after experiencing the full spectrum of my mental illness."

He grabs my chin, twisting my head to face him. His eyes are hard. "Your panic attacks don't change how I feel about you. I still love you more than I've ever loved anything in my life, and I love everything about you. I love that you're weird and socially awkward, and I love that you told me I was weak on the night we met—"

I pull away from him, unable to take it. I can't sit here and listen to him tell me that he loves the little crinkle above my nose when I'm looking at him like he's nuts. Words like that are empty coming from a boy who's in love with being in love.

After gripping the metal chains, I launch up from the swing and walk toward the ocean. I hiss when my toes hit the cold water, sending a rolling shiver up my spine. I hate that he brought me here. I hate that I'm forced to remember our beautiful beginning as we're nearing the end.

Without seeing him, I sense his presence. I hug my arms around myself. "If you tell me you love my panic attacks, I might scream."

He snorts so loud it echoes through the wind. "No worries there."

My head jerks to face him.

"Oh, that's right. I said I loved everything about you. My bad. I don't love your panic attacks. You're an epically bad hang when you have a panic attack."

Incomprehension gripping me, I stare at him for several seconds. He has that faint side-smile. Suddenly, I'm overcome with relief. So overwhelmed I can't even gauge its source, but I feel almost lightheaded with it. Laughter bubbles from my chest.

Logan's smile grows. "Would you like me to list some people I'd rather hang out with than you when you have a panic attack?"

When I nod eagerly, his eyes flash in delight. He gestures a *one*. "Lord Voldemort."

"Naturally."

"Right. It should go without saying. Another would be the little girl from *The Exorcist*... And now that I think of it, she kind of reminds me of you when you have a panic attack. Except, you know, a lot more fun."

I choke out a laugh at the apt comparison. Panic attacks often feel like a demonic possession.

He lifts his hand again to gesture a three. "Thanos."

I draw a blank. I stare at him as I search my brain for whatever stupid super-villain he thinks I should understand implicitly, as if superhero lore is a national religion.

"Thanos!" he shouts, his dark brows drawn together. "From the last two *Avengers* movies."

"All of those movies are the same to me."

"Oh my god. I don't believe this. You had a whole fucking theory about Thanos after we watched *Infinity War*. And you said it in your whole Leilani way too, like, 'Even though I've never seen these movies before, I'm right because I'm Leilani and I know everything,' and now you can't even remember who Thanos is! You're so full of shit, Girard. I'm never going to believe anything you say ever again."

I purse my lips, fighting my smile.

"Don't laugh, you asshole! *The Avengers* are some of the most important movies of the twenty-first century, if not *the* most."

I nod solemnly, though I can't hide my smile.

"They are!"

I straighten my posture, meeting his eyes squarely. "I refuse to accept your cartoon books as sacred texts just because you rule the world."

"I don't even know what the fuck that means." When my smile returns, he glares at me. "You're a dick."

"I'm sorry to break your heart."

"You stomped all over my heart!"

I cover my face, my shoulders shaking from laughter at his genuine distress. I'm still almost hysterical with relief, but suddenly the source of it dawns on me.

I forgot about my panic attack.

Somehow in the midst of his gentle teasing, he pulled me out of my head. I forgot about my agonizing fear that he'll leave me. He made me laugh at myself.

I *never* laugh at myself.

I feel my face contort as tears trickle into my palms in rapid succession. I couldn't stop them if I tried. Knowing there's no way to hide it, I remove my hands from my face.

In a flash, Logan's smiling face transforms into shock. "Hey…" he says gently, stepping closer and reaching out to touch my shoulder. I back away from him, waving him off with a hand.

"What's wrong?"

I lower my hands, shaking my head jerkily. "It's nothing. I was just thinking about my past."

"Tell me about it." His voice is gentle.

I turn away to stare out at the crashing waves, not wanting to see his face while I embarrass myself. "When I was little, I used to think I was dead. It happened all the time, and usually out of nowhere. I could be on the playground at school or sitting at the kitchen table eating breakfast, and suddenly I would be convinced that I was dead. I was so certain, my dad would sometimes spend hours trying to convince me otherwise. And he usually wasn't successful. 'You can't be dead if I'm talking to you.' He'd usually say something like that, but then I'd ask how he knew I wasn't in a coffin somewhere dreaming that I was alive, and dreaming that he was talking to me. 'Dead people don't dream.' 'How do you know they don't dream?' 'Your brain stops working when you die.' 'How do you know?' And it would go on and on like that."

I pause, keeping my eyes fixed on the water, feeling silly and ghoulish.

"Man, that's fucked up," Logan says, sounding genuinely dismayed.

A faint smile rises to my lips. I'm reminded again why he's perfect for me.

"You know...I mean it's fucked up for a kid to think something like that," he says, perhaps feeling that his original comment was silly. He can't know how much silly comments like that make scary things feel small and manageable.

"I was having a panic attack. I know that now. I can't even really remember what it felt like back then, but I'm certain it was the same feeling that I have now. This out-of-body, detached feeling, like I'm completely alone, and no one can help me."

He gives me a sympathetic frown. "That must suck."

I smile. "It does."

I look away, not wanting to see his reaction to what I say next. "You make it better."

In my periphery, I see his head jerk back in surprise. "You mean like…I make your panic attacks better?"

The hint of pleasure in his voice gives me courage to say more. "You're perfect for me. I think I've known it all along." I wrap my arms around myself. "It scares me."

I look back at the ocean, not wanting to see his reaction. This conversation makes my skin prickle with uncomfortable heat. I feel the pressure of his hand on my shoulder. "It's okay. That's how relationships are supposed to be. We're supposed to rely on each other, and make each other better."

I shake my head sharply. "No. I've never subscribed to that theory. It's antiquated and rooted in patriarchy. We should all be just fine on our own."

I hear a smile in his voice when he says, "Noted. In the future, I'll try to be a little shittier to you, so you won't rely on me as much."

He doesn't get it. Even after everything, he still doesn't get it. I jerk away from his hold as I turn around to face him. Suddenly, I want to test him. I feel almost possessed with the desire to scare him off. "I need you right now! That's what I'm trying to say. This is a dark time in my life, and it isn't the first. It won't be the last. If I come to rely on you, you're going to see some dark shit. Do you know one time Brenna called 911 when I was having a panic attack? It was two in the morning and I had my arms wrapped around myself, rocking back and forth muttering to myself like a fucking lunatic and she got scared. I was too in my head to realize what she was doing and stop her. Talk about an awkward conversation with the paramedic. He was hot too. It was fucking humiliating. Do you want to be around for shit like that?"

He only stares at me, a mixture of emotions in his eyes. I won't try to decipher them yet. I'm not done. "I don't think you've really heard anything I've said to you. I was the creepy little kid who was obsessed with death. Do you remember that kid? I'll bet you didn't invite her to your twelfth birthday party at Disneyland."

"I don't care what you were like when you were twelve."

"Maybe you should. Maybe you'll realize…" I lower my voice to a whisper, "that we're not right for each other."

He's long since looked away from me, his jaw set, but at this he turns to face me. His eyes are blazing in what looks like contempt.

There. I've done it. It didn't take much.

"Let's just get the fuck out of here," he says. "You're really starting to piss me off."

My heart sinks. Why did I push him so far? He was already starting to feel trapped. Did I have to press for disgust as well?

As we walk back to his car, I feel empty and hollow, almost sick to my stomach. I can't even muster the angry triumph of getting him to prove what I've known along.

When we get back to my house, he doesn't walk to my room. I turn to him, fearful that he's going to leave. Out of desperation, I try to sound nonchalant when I say, "Let's just chill and watch *The Office* or something—"

"No. I'm going home."

I clench my teeth in an effort to look expressionless as I lift my eyes to meet his.

Then I see it.

Everything I've feared over the last eleven months since I met this perfect boy is there in his eyes. Disgust. Contempt. And maybe a little fear.

Like he's afraid of *me*.

My chest seizes. I feel like I can hardly breathe. I'm going to lose him. It's just a matter of time. "Logan, please…" I say, loathing how pathetic I sound.

"No," he says right away. "I'm pissed off and I want to go home. We'll talk in the morning. Ask Brenna to help you if you're having a panic attack. Maybe she can call another hot paramedic for you. I don't care. I just need some time to myself."

I nod forlornly. If he senses my anguish, he doesn't show it. Without saying goodbye, he turns around and walks out the door, almost, but not quite, slamming it shut.

Later that night, I cry on Brenna's lap after telling her the whole of what happened today. "I'm seeing Dr. Scott tomorrow," I say. "I need to get something for this. Some kind of medication. I just can't live like this anymore."

I can't watch him run away from me without something to dull the pain a little.

CHAPTER 19

Present Day

Logan

1. DON'T LOOK AT HER INSTAGRAM.
2. ~~DON'T TEXT HER.~~
3. ~~IF YOU RUN INTO HER, BE POLITE BUT DISTANT.~~
4. ~~DON'T UNDER ANY CIRCUMSTANCES AGREE TO SEE HER IN PERSON.~~
5. DO NOT HAVE SEX WITH HER.

"You should have checked her Instagram," Keira says. "You would have broken four of your boundaries in the span of six hours, instead of just three."

I smile, trying not to show that I'm irritated. "I thought about it, but it wouldn't really be worth it unless I broke all five.

It would be like the Warriors in 2016. Going 73–9 is meaningless if you can't win the championship too."

"Agreed," Armaan says, but he seems like he's only half-listening. He lifts his beer to his mouth, his eyes locked on the TV screen to our right. Ostensibly Keira invited us out to happy hour to watch the NBA playoffs, but we all knew what she was really asking for. She wanted to lecture me, but needed an opportunity to do it.

As if I need a lecture. As if I don't already hate myself enough for my weakness. Just three days ago, I was certain I would stick to my list. The Lani who once held me hypnotized under her unblinking stare was long gone. I was in charge now. She wronged me, and it was time for her to pay for it, and no power on heaven or earth would compel me to let her off the hook.

Except the very earthly power of jealousy, it turns out.

"I'm starting over with my list," I say in a lowered voice, making up for my earlier sarcasm. "I haven't seen or heard from Lani in three days."

And I've been going out of my fucking mind, especially after her parting words Friday night, but of course I can't tell Keira that.

"And what happens if she shows up on campus in lingerie next time? Will you break all five of your rules?" She shakes her head. "It was a pretty epic failure, Logan."

Her continued roasting rubs me the wrong way. The list may have been her idea, but the boundaries were mine. I'm the only person who has a right to be angry here, and I'm already furious with myself. I don't need her to beat me over the head with my "epic failure."

"I know," I say. "And I feel like we should not only talk

about it in even more detail, but we should also discuss the time my high school lacrosse team lost in the last round of the playoffs, because I had a fever and I let Torrey Pines score when I was literally staring out into space. I was exactly like Michael Jordan in the Flu Game. Except in reverse. Armaan, do you have anything you want to add to my list of epic failures?"

When he doesn't shift his gaze from the TV, I wonder if he's listening at all anymore, but he eventually speaks. "Let's talk about that night at Delta Tau when you got so drunk, you took a piss in the drawer of your nightstand thinking it was a toilet."

I nod once. "I also fell asleep in a puddle of my own vomit that same night. We should discuss that in detail too. It was purple. My vomit, I mean. I have no idea why. I don't remember much from that night." I smile lazily at Keira, but she only stares at me blankly. I glance down at the table, having no clue what to do with her stern mood. *This isn't about you, Keira,* I want to say. Instead I turn to Armaan. "Can you go to the bar and get me another beer?"

An indignant frown starts to form on his face as he turns to me, but it's quickly gone when he sees the look on my face. His eyes dart to Keira and back to me again. "Sure," he says as he slides out of our booth.

After several uncomfortable minutes of silence, Keira speaks, and the disappointment in her voice fills me with guilt. "You don't really care about any of this, do you?"

"I do," I say, my tone softened. "But you were right. I failed epically. What else can I do? I can't go back in time."

"Why did you even write it in the first place? Did you even mean any of it, or was it just to please me?"

"I meant all of it, I promise. I planned on staying as far away from Lani as possible. I never would have thought I would fail so epically a week ago."

At my answer, she exhales, her shoulders slumping. "Is she just that hard for you to resist?"

The scornful disbelief in the question surprises me, rendering me momentarily unable to answer. She's never been petty like this before. On the contrary, I've never heard a single catty remark in Lani's direction. Since that moment on campus when I impulsively confessed my misery, Keira assumed an almost inhuman objectivity in helping me navigate my mess of a relationship.

It's surprising considering the truth we both know and can't say. She clearly has feelings for me. It's evident in everything from her body's awareness of me to her vested interested in my relationship with Lani. I've admired her self-control. It went a long way in assuaging the guilt over what happened between us that night before I called a break with Lani.

"I take it from your lack of response that the answer is 'yes'?"

My eyes dart to her face. "No. You were right from the beginning. She manipulated me. I should have seen it coming, but unfortunately I'm dumb and I make bad decisions." I shoot her a half-smile. "I'm an easy target for her."

She smiles warmly. "You certainly are that."

"Thanks, Keira."

She rolls her eyes playfully. "You're not dumb, but you need to be careful with her. Leilani may look like Dawnstar, but she's actually Lex Luther."

I smile affectionately back at her. Comic book references are part of our bond, something unique to my relationship with Keira. Lani would probably think Dawnstar is a brand of dish soap. "Can we pick a Marvel villain instead? Can she be Thanos?"

Keira responds, and it's something playful, but I don't hear the words.

I'm seized by a memory.

That day on the beach, when Lani confessed all the ugly details about panic disorder… Everything changed after that day. I don't even know what brought it to memory, but something about that day is the answer to everything. The answer to my misery. The answer to the crumbling mess of our relationship.

"…you'll be careful?" I'm summoned to the present by the lilt of her question.

"Yes," I answer decisively, though I'm not totally sure what I'm agreeing to. "I won't fuck up again. I promise."

* * *

Leilani

I stare at the packet on my desk. I pulled it out from my file cabinet yesterday so that its visual presence would prepare me for what I plan to do today. The thought alone would have made my palms sweat a few weeks ago.

I'm still not entirely at ease, but it has to be done. It's crucial for my next move with Logan.

I haven't heard from him in four days now, and I know he's going to resist me even harder the next time I reach out.

I need something with an impact.

When the packet arrived a month ago—clearly an acceptance

letter, since rejections always come in much smaller form—I shoved it into the drawer the second I walked into my room, trying not to even think about what was inside.

How could I go to graduate school when panic disorder was so crippling that I couldn't even attend an interview in person? The hurdle felt insurmountable.

Indiana University was the one grad school that allowed me to do an interview over Skype. All of the others canceled my applications after I turned down their in-person interviews. One even offered to hold the interview at a later date if I changed my mind and they still had an open space—a sign that my application was strong—but I had no faith I'd be any better by the time that date rolled around. Plus, I didn't want the added pressure, so I turned it down as well. The whole miserable process made me sick to my stomach. I felt like a dying woman making preparations for a world that would continue without her.

But I was able to do that one Skype interview after taking three Ativan. Since it was the most I had ever taken up to that point and I felt so relaxed during the interview that my eyes were half shut, I remember it mostly as a low point. I have a few hazy memories of perplexed stares from the professors conducting the interview, and one instance of dulled, distant panic after forgetting a question in the middle of my wordy, repetitive answer.

In essence, it was a shitshow, and I never thought anything good would come out of it. In fact, I vowed to forget it the moment those faces disappeared from my iPad screen. Thanks to my blessed Ativan, the vow was easy to keep.

I can feel the pulse in my neck as I pick up the packet. After a swooshing sound, the envelope is on the floor, the packet of paper exposed in my hand.

There's no doubting the "I am pleased to inform you" at the opening of the letter placed conspicuously at the front.

I've been accepted.

I take a deep breath in through my nose and release it out of my mouth slowly, knowing it will take at least ten more of these to slow my pulse.

I'll never forget Logan's resigned pity on that overcast morning when I told him the application process was over, that I no longer had a plan. "You can always apply again next year," he said, but I could hear the doubt in his voice. I knew what he was really thinking. *I've been with you more than a year, and I'm only just now realizing how weak and pathetic you are.* My chest ached as I watched all of his delusions about me crumble behind those perplexed eyes.

The memory propels me into action. Before I talk myself out of it, I sign into my account on the university website. I click through the prompts so impulsively I'm not even sure that I'm doing it correctly, but when it's over I see "Welcome to the Indiana University Sociology PhD program!" on the screen in front of me.

It's done.

CHAPTER 20

Past—The Confession

Logan

To say the last two months have been rough would be an understatement. It's incredible how something that seemed so untouchably perfect could crash and burn in a flash. Just two months ago I had her.

Now she's gone.

Oh, she's there in body, but the Lani I met and fell in love with is somewhere faraway, buried in a vessel that barely resembles her. She even looks and talks different. That blunt, self-assured voice is a whisper now. Her almost unnaturally straight dancer posture and intense eye contact are now a distant memory. She hunches, and her eyes seem vacant.

Just this morning she confessed that she's not even going to graduate school next fall, that she canceled all of her interviews. I could hardly believe it. She's been talking about graduate school since we met, as if it's a sure thing, as if she wasn't even nervous about getting accepted. Why would she be nervous? She's Leilani Girard. A mortal graduate school would never have the audacity to turn down an all-knowing goddess.

Where did my brash, know-it-all girl go?

I need to fix it. I just wish I knew how.

"Are you okay?" Keira asks. I jerk my gaze up from the grass, realizing I almost forgot her presence. We've been meeting here between classes for the past week or so, alternating buying each other coffee. She even has my order memorized. We don't usually talk about serious stuff, but her presence calms me.

I'm hesitant in answering her question, caught by a gnawing fear that it might start something from which there's no going back. But what do I have to lose? Things couldn't be worse between Lani and me, and Keira might actually be able to help, which is the whole point of why I called her last week. "I've been kind of having a tough time lately." I chuckle humorlessly. "Not that you probably want to hear it. It's not a fun story."

She stares at me steadily. "I didn't ask you if you were okay because I wanted to hear a fun story."

She means it. I know she does, and somehow knowing that her "are you okay" was not just a social nicety opens the floodgates. I start talking and I find I can't stop. I tell her everything. All of the ugly details. Even some of the dark, embarrassing things that I didn't even want to admit to myself, like that Lani is different when we have sex now, as if she's doing it just to please me, and how it makes me want to hit something. I can't even believe that I'm telling her things like this, but it's amazing how good it feels, akin to the first time I was able to stretch and twist my ankle under the sun after I removed the cast from my lacrosse injury.

And Keira is so perfect the way she just sits there in silence. She doesn't react. I don't see judgment or pity or even sympathy, and it keeps my mouth flowing freely. By the time I'm done, I've left out no detail. She even knows about the gnawing anxiety I've felt all day since I left Lani this morning, how she was still sleeping and she never sleeps in. How she was snoring, and she never snores.

"I think it was the Ativan. Do you know much about that?" I ask, hoping that since Keira is a psych major, she might know at least a little about anxiety medication. "It doesn't seem like it could be good for her. Sure, it makes her panic go away, but it also changes her. It's like she's in her own world. Is that normal?"

Keira narrows her eyes as she thinks about it, and I'm amazed anew at the lack of judgment in her eyes. She almost looks like she's puzzling out a math problem. "Do you know how much she's taking?"

I'm stunned for a second. This is the first time it's occurred to me that Lani might be taking more than she's supposed to. "Is there a way I could tell?"

She opens her mouth and closes it again before eventually speaking. "I would say that if she seems out of it, she's probably taking too much."

I nod slowly, my whole understanding of everything changing, everything starting to fix into place. "It's like I'm not even there most of the time," I say almost to myself. "When we hang out, like... She almost looks through me. And it's so different from how things used to be. She and I used to talk all the time. It was one of my favorite things about her. She could have a conversation about literally anything." A smile rises to my lips. "Like, I could ask if she felt like taco truck burritos for dinner, and she'd launch into the history of the burrito and how she's against rice on burritos in principle and how even distribution of burrito ingredients is the low key defining feature of a good burrito…"

I trail off at the knowing smile on Keira's face, feeling embarrassed over the grin on my face. "That really happened," I say. "She really said all that."

Keira's smile spreads into a toothy grin. "I can tell. You're cute, Logan."

My smile turns rueful.

"It's obvious you really like her."

"Yeah, well… I don't like how she is right now." I swallow. "I love her," I say, feeling guilty. "But I don't like her right now."

CHAPTER 21

Present Day

Leilani

~~Item 1-Makeover~~
Item 2-Lure him back

In principle, I'm against posting passive aggressive memes to my Instagram Story.

Almost everyone I know does it after a breakup, and the intention is usually embarrassingly obvious. They want to announce to their ex that they're doing just fine on their own, but know that sending a direct message or text would convey the opposite. If their ex is perceptive enough, they might be able to get away with something as subtle as an inspirational quote, like "And then she became her own source of happiness." If he's dense like Logan, they'd have to choose something with a little more of a punch, something like "That moment you realize you dodged a bullet" on a picture of Meryl Streep accepting her third Oscar.

I'm against the practice as a whole, because breaking up should never be about the other person. It should be only ever be about you.

And I would never violate my principles with such a petty vengeance. With such little reward! What's the fun in posting a meme when you can't even see his reaction to it?

No, revenge is only worth it if it's grand and spectacular. Revenge should be the steadily growing shock in his pretty green eyes when you break up with him while he's still inside you.

I lift my Indiana University acceptance letter into the morning sunlight before snapping a picture with my phone.

I snort out a laugh just before I press the button to post it to my Story. This is so much better than a breakup meme.

I should have my entire list accomplished by end of day.

* * *

Logan

It's been five days since my last conversation with Leilani.

I've stuck to my list, resisting all urges to contact her. I even taped it on my bedroom wall like Keira originally suggested as a reminder of the commitment I made, and Keira has been sending me daily encouragement, reminding me that the list is not only good for me but good for Lani too. If I want her to get healthy, I have to stick to my boundaries.

I might find that comforting if I wasn't dying inside.

I can't do this for one more day. I need to know what she meant when she said she's learning to live without me. Was she just trying to unnerve me, or is she actually feeling so much better that she doesn't need me anymore?

I haven't checked her Instagram once since I made my list. Then again, it wasn't difficult. Lani hasn't posted to her Story at all since the start of our break.

Until this morning.

I felt like a saint for not pressing on it the moment it appeared at the top of my feed, but my self-congratulatory high has waned in the hours since then. I'm dying of curiosity, but is it really worth violating my list when it might just be a picture of her morning coffee?

Yes, I quickly decide. It will be worth it to know that's it's only a picture of her morning coffee—maybe with one of those heart or leaf designs she likes to make with the foam—and not a picture of her holding her morning coffee with Dean laying in her bed in the background.

I open the Instagram app while I'm driving, blaming my lapse in judgment on the distraction of my mind. Without giving myself a chance to reflect, I press on Lani's Story. I'm perplexed when I see what looks like some kind of university letter. Lani wrote a caption underneath that says, "So this happened." I squint to read the small writing on the top of the letter, my eyes skimming the text frantically from top to bottom and back again, over and over before the picture quickly disappears. I only really caught two important things. "I am pleased to inform you" and "Indiana University."

"I am pleased to inform you" means she was accepted.

To graduate school.

I drop my phone on my lap. "What the fuck?" I shout.

And maybe I can also blame the distraction of driving on my next decision. I pick up my phone, pull up Leilani's name, and send her a text.

Me: I'm coming over.

I expel a quivering breath, self-loathing and relief flooding me all at once. Yes, I've backslid again. But what's done is done, and now I have to see her. I put on my signal and make an illegal U-turn.

CHAPTER 22

Past—The Night Lines Were Crossed

Logan

"Hey, stranger." When I whip around, beer splashes out of the bottle in my hand, a cold stream running down my arm. I lift my hand to my mouth and lick from my wrist to my thumb.

"Classy," Keira says with a wide smile.

My answering grin is so big, I must look like an idiot. Jesus, she's gorgeous, with her pale blue eyes and dark hair. Such a contrast, just like the rest of her. She looks so sharp with her prominent cheekbones and square jaw, but she's so soft on the inside. The complete opposite of Leilani, who looks so soft with her full cheeks and big brown eyes, but she's...

No. I can't go there.

Things have only gotten worse between us. I'm now one-hundred percent convinced that she's taking way too much

Ativan. I've barely spoken to her in the last month, even though we're almost constantly together, and we haven't had sex in two.

I have no idea how to fix it, and I'm starting to wonder if it even can be fixed.

No. Don't go there. You love her. Things are just tough right now.

Thank god I've had Keira to talk me through all of this. We still meet regularly on campus, and we've been texting a lot too.

"It's too good to waste," I say. "Armaan's older brother brewed them in his garage. There was only one left last I checked. Should I grab it for you?"

Her nose wrinkles. "Would you think less of me if I said I don't like beer?"

"Yes."

I wince when she punches me on the shoulder. "You're the worst!" she shouts.

"Yeah, but you love me anyway." I feel a pang of guilt when she smiles affectionately. Half-consciously, I take a step back and scan my eyes around the crowd. I shouldn't have left Leilani alone, but fuck if I don't deserve a moment of peace. A break from babysitting her.

I don't spot her, but that doesn't mean she isn't somewhere nearby. She disappears at parties, shrinking into crowds and hiding in plain sight. Even before she started taking so much Ativan, she seemed faraway in a crowd, staring instead of smiling, looking at her phone instead of talking. The complete opposite of the girl in front of me.

"You never told me what you thought of *Aquaman*," Keira says. My cheeks heat. She's always asking me about what I think about things, always interested in my opinions. I would feel like a fraud if she didn't seem so riveted by my inarticulate answers. I ought to feel guilty for how much that eager smile makes me want to…

But I don't. I haven't had a real conversation with Leilani in months. It's perfectly natural that I would be drawn to this beautiful girl who hangs on to my every word. I'd be crazy if I wasn't.

"I loved it!" I yell over the murmur of voices around me. "Like, it's campy as shit, but it owns it, you know?" She grins as she nods frantically, like she knows exactly what I mean. "I fucking love movies like that. It reminds me of the old school superhero movies, like Tim Burton's *Batman*. Have you ever—"

"Yikes." Keira winces, leaning to the side to look at something. The shriek of a familiar giggle sends a chill down my spine. When I jerk around, I finally see her. She's only a few feet away, wiping red liquid from some dude's stomach with the sleeve of her cream-colored sweater, laughing like a maniac. When I glance back at Keira, she's frowning sympathetically.

Without any prelude, I march over to Leilani. She looks startled when I grip her arm, but then she smiles lazily, her eyelids heavy. "Jeffrey, here, wanted to try my Merlot, but I decided to give him a more complete sensory experience."

More than anything else, I'm shocked she was able to say such a long sentence. Her speech is so thick, the words should have all slushed together. I glance at the dude next to us, who's smiling uncomfortably. Jeffrey. I would bet that last home-brewed IPA that he introduced himself as Jeff. "I don't think Jeffrey appreciates you ruining his shirt."

She shakes her head slowly. "It's postmodern. I've made him my palette." She turns to Jeffrey, smiling up at him from under her long lashes. "He feels honored. Right, Jeffrey?"

When I glance back at Jeffrey, I'm surprised to see that he's looking at me. And that awkward smile... I know what it means. The *sorry, bro* smile. *I'm sorry your girlfriend is such a hot mess that she's flirting with me right in front of you.* Just another confirmation that she doesn't see me anymore. She can flirt sloppily with this douchey looking frat boy, but she'll give nothing to me. Within minutes after we walk through her front door, she'll be passed out and snoring, and I'll be left to entertain myself with porn on my phone and my right hand, resisting the urge to slip my left under the blankets for just one brief touch of the soft, warm flesh of her bare ass, feeling like a fucking creep for even thinking of it.

Suddenly, Leilani stumbles into Jeffrey. He wraps his arms around her to keep her from falling to the ground, shooting me another apologetic look afterward. I only roll my eyes as I reach my arms out and grip her by the waist. Just as I start to pull her away, she wraps her arms around Jeffrey and presses her head into his chest. She slurs something so quiet and imprecise, I'm surprised I'm even able to make out the words, but I can, and the rage that flares makes my ears ring.

"Take me home," she said. I know she did.

I tighten my grip on her waist and yank her away. She stumbles and giggles while I drag her around the house, searching for a private place. By the time I pull her into the empty bedroom, she's barely able to stand.

She sways as she stares at me. "Are you going to spank me?" she slurs.

"No. Wait here while I go find Armaan, and by that I mean don't fucking leave this room."

She smiles lazily. "I like it when you take charge."

The look in her eyes makes me cringe in revulsion. She doesn't even look drunk. This look is different. Frightening somehow. Her eyes are faraway, even as they focus on my face, like a ghost inhabiting two worlds at once.

"We're leaving *now*."

She nods, but it looks like it takes effort. I turn and walk toward the door, but then stop. When I turn back, she's swaying even more than before. "You're a fucking shitshow."

Her head shoots up, and her body straightens, as if my words summoned her from the other world into this one. She must have heard the disgust in my voice. I couldn't hide it. She looks sad and a little disillusioned, but it doesn't stop me from turning around and walking out the door.

My conscience is clean by the time I find Keira. "So, turns out I'm going to have to leave early," I say. "I don't know if you noticed, but I think my girlfriend's a little drunk."

Her sad, caring smile almost makes me forget what I'll have to deal with later.

CHAPTER 23

Present Day

Leilani

~~Item 1 Makeover~~
~~Item 2 Lure him back~~
Item 3-Seduce him

Logan: I'm coming over.

I smile wide as I set my phone down on my counter, resisting the urge to squeal in delight.

I did it.

I'm a master.

I'm so confident in my success today, I already started baking the Closure Cake: a two-tiered chocolate cake with a smooth custard filling and bittersweet chocolate buttercream frosting. A perfect representation of our failed relationship. A soft, gooey, and ultimately insubstantial core encased in a bittersweet tomb—bitter because he fucked me over with Keira, sweet because at least I'm making him pay for it.

And I'm dressed like a whore, like the femme fatale of Logan's wildest fantasy and worst nightmare. I applied just enough makeup to make my skin glow without looking like I'm wearing any at all. I spritzed so much beach spray into my carefully unkempt hair, I smell like a god damn Pina Colada. My short white sundress is practically lingerie, barely covering the tan skin I lathered with enough lotion to make me look— just a little—sweaty. Like I need a bath after working in this hot kitchen.

I'm so dirty, Logan. Wash me.

I smile as I touch my cakes to test their temperatures. No, still too warm. They need another five minutes.

And in just five more minutes, Logan James Henderson will walk through that door, just as I start to frost his own Closure Cake.

It's poetry.

I'm so giddy, I need occupation. I take the custard out of the fridge and give it an unnecessary stir. I check the cake more often than I should, and ultimately remove them from their tins too soon out of impatience, as if I can get him here faster by speeding up the clock.

After what feels like an eternity, I check my phone. Eight minutes have past. I bite my bottom lip, wondering if he's sitting in his car right now debating whether or not he should come in.

Or maybe he called *her* to talk him out of his impulsive decision.

I try not to think about it as I start to assemble the cake.

But trying not to think about it is futile. I'm practically counting the seconds as I spread the gooey custard across the bottom layer. Just when I'm about to check my phone again, I hear a knock at the door, and I feel almost drunk with relief.

If he did call her, she wasn't able to convince him.

I ignore the knock, knowing he'll let himself in. I walk to the fridge and pull out the glass bowl of frosting, making sure I bend over far enough to show off my freshly shaved legs. Footsteps pound over the living room carpet. In my periphery, I see a dark figure appear at the entrance of the kitchen.

"I guess congratulations are in order," he says, not sounding congratulatory in the least.

"Thank you."

As I plunge the wooden spoon into the dark brown lump of frosting, I set my other hand on my hip to make my short dress ride up my thigh.

"When were you planning on telling me?"

I grit my teeth, annoyed that he hasn't seemed to notice my dress yet. "I'm not supposed to contact you."

"And this doesn't seem like it would be an exception to you?"

"Why would it be an exception?"

"Because it affects my future!" he shouts. "I might be moving to Indiana with you. I could at least use a heads-up to start looking for jobs."

I can't respond to that. Not yet. Instead I talk around it. "I don't imagine they have good Mexican food in Indiana."

Out of the corner of my eye, I see him smile at the memory of that first night we spent in his bed.

"You're baking," he says with a delighted lilt, apparently just now becoming aware of his surroundings.

"Yes," I say, still not looking in his direction.

"I fucking love your chocolate cakes."

I smile. "I made this one just for you."

"Did you really?"

The innocent delight in his voice gives me pause. Am I really doing this? Am I really going to feed him his own Closure Cake before I seduce him?

Yes. I've come this far. I'll finish the job now and think about my integrity later.

I lift my head over my shoulder, planning to give him a sultry smile, but as soon as I see his face my mouth freezes.

He's so beautiful. His hair still wet from the shower. His tight workout shirt hugging his chest. And, oh god, that smile. That sincere half-smile I never could resist.

Unable to stand it, I turn back to my cake. I gently lift the top layer and place it on the custard covered bottom. After I remove my hands from the cake, I lift my index finger to my mouth and slowly suck off the non-existent drop of custard. When I glance back at Logan, he's still looking at the cake. I turn away, rolling my eyes dramatically as soon as my face is out of his view. Was this dress even worth eighty dollars of my god damn student loan money?

"Can I frost it?" he asks.

My hands freeze in place. Why does he have to be so cute?

Every time I bake, he asks to "help" me by doing his favorite tasks—the easy things, like running the stand mixer or frosting the cake—with the unguarded enthusiasm of a six-year-old boy. That guilty pang in my chest grows heavier.

"Sure," I say, but I take no pleasure watching him reach for the frosting bowl, his broad shoulders bracing as he gives it a stir. He stares at it thoughtfully as if he has any clue about the desired consistency. He knows nothing about baking.

Clenching his fingers around the wooden spoon, he takes a large glob of frosting and plops it on the top layer. I wince. "That's too much. You need much smaller spoonfuls if you want it to smooth out properly…"

He whips around, shooting me a playful glare. "I know what I'm doing, Girard." Turning back to the cake, he presses at the frosting with the wooden spoon. "I like the frosting to be thick," he mumbles.

"It's buttercream. It's very rich, and…" I trail off when he scoops another giant lump of frosting from the bowl. "Oh my god, Logan. That's way too much!"

Keeping his eyes fixed on the cake, he smiles to himself, clearly amused by my outburst. In an obvious effort to annoy me, he scoops another lump of frosting, this one nearly double the size of the last.

Standing up straighter, I lower my chin to give him my death stare. "Don't move another inch."

He stills at the command, the spoon hovering above the cake. Mischief lurks in his eyes.

"Hand that spoon over now." The words are a hiss though my clenched teeth.

He turns to me slowly, a faint smile quirking one side of his mouth. Not trusting him for a second, I narrow my eyes as he slowly extends the full spoon in my direction. Just as I reach my hand up to grab it, he jerks forward, ramming it into my chest. I gasp as the cool frosting drips down the crevice between my boobs. My lips part as I glance down at the spoon just before it falls to the floor, leaving behind a glob of brown sludge on my chest. "Are you fucking kidding me?"

His smile grows. He shrugs as he says, "You were asking for it."

I look at the glob as it seeps into the white fabric of my brand-new seduction dress and then back at him. "And you're asking to be punished."

His wicked grin falters. He stares at me for several seconds in a look I can't quite decipher.

A sad look.

"Oh god, Lani. I've missed you so much."

I'm perplexed by the longing in his eyes until full understanding hits. He doesn't miss Lani of two weeks ago—the girl who took Ativan with alcohol and spilled wine over random guys' shirts. He misses the Lani who called him weak on the night she met him. The Lani who mauled him in the stairwell.

In a sudden motion, he yanks me against his chest, his face crushing mine. My eyes pop open when his tongue plunges deep into my mouth. His own eyes are clenched shut, looking almost pained. His desperation leaves me breathless. I've never seen him like this before. Like he might die if he doesn't kiss me.

Without warning, he pulls away, and I moan at the loss of him. His face inches from mine, his breath coming in pants, he searches my face. "Can we go to your room?"

In a daze, I stare into his eyes. I'm confused by the uncertainty I find in them until I recall that, of course, he doesn't know I planned to seduce him today.

"Okay," I say softly.

He smiles in what looks like relief. When he bends his knees and reaches for my body, I realize he's planning to lift me into his arms.

"Stop right there," I say. He halts before standing back up, his eyes filling with apprehension, as if he thinks I'm going to call it off altogether. I stare at him quietly for a few seconds, fighting the rising guilt. "Did you forget that I have fucking chocolate between my boobs?"

He smiles wide.

"It's all over your shirt now too." I point to his chest. "I don't want to get it on my bed."

"No worries." He grips my waist and pulls me closer to him. "I'll lick it off."

He bends down, his breath heating my chest. He extends his tongue and takes a quick lick, the slippery warmth sending a tickling sensation into my belly. He pulls away quickly, frowning. "I'm going to be totally honest, this frosting is not your best work. It's... I don't know. Too strong or something." He wrinkles his nose. "Kind of bitter."

"I made it that way intentionally."

He smiles warmly. "Sure you did, my know-it-all."

He steps away and grabs a dish towel near the sink. He turns on the faucet, testing the temperature with his fingers before soaking the towel. "Come here," he says.

"No."

His eyes lift to mine, a questioning frown forming on his brow.

"I don't want to be clean. I want to be dirty. None of my roommates are home. Who needs a bedroom?"

His eyes spark just before his eyelids grow heavy again. He steps closer, lifting his hand to my thigh and slowly trailing it up under my dress. I suck in a breath when his finger slips between my lips. His heavy lids drift even lower, nearly shutting. "You're wet already." The whisper is breathless. "And you're not wearing underwear. You were planning this." It doesn't sound like an accusation. On the contrary, his tone is almost reverent, like he's thanking the heavens for his good fortune.

I don't deny it. He seems lost in thought as he stares down at my hips. Suddenly, he grips my butt with his palms. I squeal as he lifts me into the air and plops me onto the counter. My eyes level with his, he stares at me steadily. "You won't regret this."

I stare back at him, keeping my face blank in an effort to hide my thoughts. *I won't, but you probably will.* Without looking away from me, he reaches his arm to the side. In confusion, my eyes dart to his hand. My eyes widen when he sinks his fingers into the sparsely frosted cake. He lifts a dark brown chunk up to my face, and I open my mouth at his cue. He lowers his hand slowly as if to feed me, but then abruptly smashes it into my face, rubbing his thumb into my mouth and across my tongue. When he removes his hand, he stares at my face for a moment, a tender smile in his eyes.

As if satisfied with his work, he leans in and kisses me hard, sifting his tongue across my lower lip before pulling away. He reaches his hand out and grabs another chunk of cake. This time he holds it in the air for a few seconds, as if to heighten the suspense of what he plans to do with it. He lowers his eyes to my parted legs. I resist the urge to pull them together. *He wouldn't do that. No way.* As if reading my thoughts, he lifts his eyes to mine, his smile growing. He lifts one brow just before plunging the lump of cake into my crotch. "Is that dirty enough for you?"

My lips part as I stare at him. I glance down at the splattered mess between my legs and back up at him. His shoulders shake in silent laughter as he watches my consternation grow. "Too dirty!" My voice is shrill. "As in *unhygienic* dirty."

At my outburst, he gasp out a laugh. Lowering his head, his shoulders continue to shake.

"What the fuck is wrong with you? I'll probably get a yeast infection."

His head jerks up, his lips parting. "You mean like from cake yeast? Does it really work like that?"

I shut my eyes tight. "No, Logan. I mean from having something on my vagina that isn't supposed to be there. From having a *dirty* vagina. That's how you get yeast infections."

He grins. "Well, I'll make sure it gets all...*cleaned up*." With that he lowers his head between my legs. The heat of his mouth makes me cry out in a whimper. It's been so long, and the last time he did this I was in such an Ativan haze, I was hardly there, sensing his touch as if from a distance. This time I feel every warm, slippery sweep of his tongue as he licks the smashed cake from my inner thigh to my clit.

By the time he settles into the rhythm his tongue seems to have memorized, I'm almost over the edge. Seeking more of it, I rock my hips into his head, nearly tipping off the counter. I lean back to catch my balance. The motion makes me cry out, my legs involuntarily clenching around his head. I feel large hands part my thighs as he pulls away. "Not yet. I want to torture you more before I let you come."

Feeling bereft from the loss of his tongue, I lower my head to glare at him. "You're the one who needs to be punished!"

He makes a deep sound at the back of his throat before he launches upward, grabbing my face and pulling me in for a kiss. When his tongue brushes mine, I catch the metallic, faintly sweet taste of cake and my own pussy. He pulls away abruptly and stares into my face, his palms still bracing my jaw. "God, I've missed you," he says with an aching tenderness that almost steers me from my purpose.

I summon the memory to fight the rising guilt.

Even in my erotic haze, it makes my bones chill.

The phone call. The phone call that changed everything.

When I overheard him with Keira.

I clench my teeth, narrowing my eyes. "Take off your pants now! I'm sick of waiting."

His eyelids grow heavier.

"I'm also going to make you lick me again when we're done." I spread my legs wider and roll my hips back to give him a full-frontal view of my pussy. I wrinkle my nose in disdain. "You missed a few spots."

His shuts his eyes, groaning. "You're going to kill me," he mumbles, stepping away to pull down his joggers and toss them on the linoleum tile. When he yanks down his boxers, his cock springs out, bouncing a little before settling into its usual leftish tilt. My eyes pop open. "It looks like it's grown two inches since I last saw it."

He smiles faintly as he walks into the arch of my spread open legs. "I'm so *fucking* turned on right now." He says "fucking" with almost angry emphasis. "It's been too long. It feels like that first time in the stairwell. You need to stop talking or I'm seriously going to explode all over you before we even start."

I lower my chin. "Maybe I'll make you lick that up too."

His head jerks up, his lips parting as he stares at me with that look of wonder I remember from that night in the stairwell. I fight the urge to smile.

He's adorable.

For someone with forty-plus ex-girlfriends, Logan's sexual taste was remarkably vanilla before I corrupted him. Teaching him my deviant ways was like opening a closet door with Narnia inside. He was dazzled.

And this is *nothing*.

He startles me by reaching forward and grabbing my face. "I'm going to last two minutes, and I'm not even sorry. It's your fault!" he says through clenched teeth.

When I giggle, he glares at me. He grips my waist and squeezes so hard I gasp. His eyes on his dick, he drags my butt across the counter until I tip over the edge, falling into his hips. I shriek as he pierces into me, pleasure clenching my stomach. I glance at his face to see his eyes are shut tight, his jaw clenched. Unable to suspend my pleasure any longer, I start to rock my hips against his. "Oh." My moan is low and guttural. "I've missed your cock, Logan."

His eyes pop open. "No, you can't do that this time. No talking. Save it for round two."

At my glare, he says, "I'm serious, Lani. I want it to last."

"Well, I don't want it to last. I want you to slam your cock—"

He grits his teeth, looking almost pained as he interrupts me. "Shut. The. Holy. Fuck. Up. I'm not even kidding." But just after he says it his lips lift into a smile.

I lift a brow. "What will you do if I don't?"

"This!" he shouts just before pulling out and thrusting so hard he lifts my hips into the air, sending an explosive wave of pleasure through my core. "Oh my god," I gasp. "Do that again." He shuts his eyes tightly. "*Please* stop talking," he says, but still he obeys my command by thrusting again. I'm lost in a fog of pleasure, only distantly recognizing the growing tension in the muscles of his back under my palm as he thrusts again and again. Suddenly, his thrusts become rapid, jerking bursts and I'm just on the verge of coming when I feel that hot liquid filling my insides. Remembering how much I love to watch him when he comes, I open my eyes and stare at his anguished, jaw-clenched face. "Oh, god!" I scream as I reach my own peak, heat radiating throughout my body in wave after wave after wave.

Why didn't I quit Ativan sooner? I must have forgotten I could feel this good without it.

Long after the last spasm, he lowers his forehead to rest on my shoulder, pulling me into a tight embrace. "I love you, Lani," he whispers.

I can't say it back. I just can't, but luckily he's still too far away to notice.

CHAPTER 24

Past—The Betrayal

Leilani

I wake up.

I'm confused.

I'm sitting up on the couch in the living room and… I start to pant when I realize I don't remember how I got here.

Oh, please. Please say I didn't do anything terrible.

Yet, somehow I know that I did. Some deep, primitive part of my brain knows what happened tonight, even if it refuses to tell my consciousness.

It isn't the first time I've blacked out since I started taking Ativan. *You can't drink, Lani. You know you can't drink. This is why.*

My heart beats faster. What happened? What happened tonight?

My brain strains to see through a fog of scattered memories, but I can't piece them together to figure out how I got here. The last thing I remember was… Logan and Keira talking.

The memory sends a cold shiver through my body. He was riveted by whatever she was saying. I couldn't hear, standing where I was, but he stared at her with that affectionate smile once reserved for me.

My chest starts to heave. I gasp, unable to take in enough air. My eyes dart around the room to look for…

I see him. His tall form hovers in the hallway entrance, like a dark figure of peril. "How are you feeling?" he asks, his voice almost shrill with malice.

The look on his face makes me want to dry heave. It lifts an instinctive memory, though the details continue to elude my hazy mind. Like a forgotten dream, they hover at the edge of consciousness, just out of reach, but I feel them in my gut.

I was terrible tonight. I did something really, really bad.

"Not good."

His half-smile doesn't reach his eyes. "I wouldn't think so."

Tears start to prickle behind my eyes, but I can't cry. He won't like that. He won't feel any sympathy.

"I'm sorry," I say weakly.

"Sorry for what?" he asks, and I flinch, knowing I can't answer. He knows it too. "Sorry for embarrassing both of us in front of all our friends? Or did you not realize you were the only drunk person there? Everyone else did. I can tell you that. Cam's girlfriend asked me if we were day drinking before. If only she knew you took pills every day."

My lips start to twitch downward, and it takes everything within me to keep the sob stored within my chest.

"Sorry for pouring wine all over some guy's shirt? And then asking him to fucking *take you home?*"

I can't stop my face from contorting. A sob heaves forth, but I hold it back, making it sound more like a gag.

"Sorry for making me leave a party when I was actually enjoying myself for the first time in months?"

Logan walks over to the couch and kneels in front of me. His eyes are nearly level with mine, and they look frightening, a blazing green like the fire from the dragon's mouth at the end of *Sleeping Beauty*. I've never seen him this angry before.

"Sorry that you passed out during the five minutes I left you alone? Sorry that I had to carry you out to the Uber in front of everyone? Sorry that you made our Uber driver pull over when you were pissed off at me? Sorry that I had to chase you down State Street and practically carry your wasted ass the last mile home, while you squirmed and kicked and screamed that you hated me?"

I stare at him in a daze, unable to believe all of that could have happened without sparking a single memory, like I wasn't even there for it. Like an automaton of Lani acted in my place.

"Sorry that you told me you're 'thoroughly bored with me?' That you've always thought I was boring and can't believe I managed to hold your interest this long? That you've secretly always known you'll end up with Dean someday because he quote-unquote 'gets you' and I don't?"

For the first time, I hear something other than anger in his voice. I hear something that sounds like pain, and I want to curl into a ball and die.

He pauses, as if momentarily unable to speak. He stares at me with his chest rising and falling in rapid breaths. Seeming to collect himself, he continues in a slightly smoother voice. "Sorry that you told me in excruciating detail about a time you and Dean went to a Warriors game and he fingered you under your sundress in public, and how much you liked it? How it was *the best orgasm you've ever had in your life?*"

Oh, god. How could I have said all that? How could I have said something so patently untrue? And yet it's so in line with my vindictive streak, I can't deny it. I can't deny this dark, childish impulse to lash out in revenge whenever I'm hurt or rejected. Even though I still can't remember, it feels true in my gut. I would say that. I would make up a story with the sole intention of hurting him.

He hurt me first.

That day on the beach when he confirmed my deepest, most secret fear. When he abandoned me after he learned about my mental illness.

My chest heaves as I launch from the couch and run to the bathroom. I barely make it in time. Vomit scatters my vision. I wretch out the entire contents of my stomach, which isn't much. Mostly red liquid.

Still hunched over the toilet, I wipe my face with a nearby towel. In my periphery, I see Logan's tall form in the doorway. "I don't feel sorry for you," he says. My chest heaves again. I open my mouth, but nothing comes out.

He laughs humorlessly. "You're a fucking mess, do you know that? You were such a shitshow tonight, it was almost impressive. Like, there seriously should be some kind of sloppy drunk girl championship ring for your performance. Although, I guess it would be a sloppy, pill-popping drunk girl in your case."

A sob wrenches from my chest. "Can you please stop being

so mean?" I say, unable to take a moment more of this.

He doesn't answer, and I can sense the clenching of his teeth. "I might have been able to forgive you if it wasn't for all that shit you said. It's really making me question everything…"

"No!" I shout, breaking into another sob. "No, Logan. I didn't mean any of that. I don't know why I said it. I don't remember any of it, but it feels like I was possessed by a demon. Like you were describing someone else. I don't know why I said all that."

He shrugs jerkily. "Maybe because you've been thinking it all along. You know people tell the truth when they're drunk—"

"No!" I shout. "I wasn't telling the truth. I was probably just angry and trying to hurt you. I already knew you were jealous of Dean. I chose the meanest thing I could think of to get to you. That's the only way to explain it."

Logan cringes. "That's almost worse."

I sob. "I know. I'm so sorry."

"I don't care," he says tonelessly. "I'm going home."

"No!" I shout, but he's unmoved. "Please! Please…" My chest heaves with another sob. "Please don't leave me."

We both know what I mean. Not just here tonight. Don't leave me forever.

"Logan…" My chest heaves in another sob. "I love you. You're my everything. I would crumble without you."

It was the wrong thing to say. In my agony, I lost my filter. Yes, I love him, but I also need him. I can't survive without him. Not as this shell of a person I've become.

And he doesn't find that flattering.

"I'm glad you're awake," he says almost lightly. "I couldn't leave before because I was worried you might be in actual danger." His nostrils flare. "You know, because you took Ativan with booze. A typical Saturday night with you."

I hunch over, despair gripping my chest like a vice. He's going to leave me, and this time it will be for good.

"We'll talk tomorrow," he says.

Through my daze, I hear his loud footsteps and the slamming of the front door. I can't even cry anymore. I'm too empty. Too lost. Sitting in front of a toilet with little memory of how I got here. And not just tonight. What has happened these last three months?

How did I get *here*?

CHAPTER 25

Present Day

Logan

1. ~~DON'T LOOK AT HER INSTAGRAM.~~
2. ~~DON'T TEXT HER.~~
3. ~~IF YOU RUN INTO HER, BE POLITE BUT DISTANT.~~
4. ~~DON'T UNDER ANY CIRCUMSTANCES AGREE TO SEE HER IN PERSON.~~
5. ~~DO NOT HAVE SEX WITH HER.~~

Oh shit.

Fucking, fucking shit.

It's amazing how quickly reality hits after the sublime pleasure starts to fade. When you realize you're standing in the middle of your girlfriend's kitchen with no pants on, your dick still inside her while she straddles you on the counter, both of you covered in sweat and chocolate frosting, and finally fully accept that you have no self-control. That even after everything she's done to you, she still owns you.

The worst part is that I committed the cardinal sin this time, and all it took was…

What? What did Lani even do to make me devour her like a maniac, smashing cake onto her face and pussy just so I could lick it off?

Jesus. What a disaster, and there's no one to blame but myself.

I lift my head from Lani's shoulder to look her in the eyes. I'm about to tell her this can't happen again, when I'm momentarily arrested by the look on her face. Her eyelids are lazy. Her expression is blank. Something about the look makes me uneasy. She looks resigned somehow.

"You're about to tell me this can't happen again," she says in an empty voice.

"Yes, but I'm not blaming you."

"It doesn't matter either way." She sets her hands on my shoulders and pushes me back. I grunt as my dick slips out of her. She lowers her head to look at her body and then mine. "We're filthy. I'll go get us some rags."

After slipping down from the counter, she turns around and walks out of the kitchen, her movement as slow and steady as a ghost. My eyes fix on her butt as she disappears into the hallway.

Even the way her body moves seems strange. But why? How would I expect her to look, move, and behave right now? I consider it as I pick up my pants from the floor and slip them back on.

I still haven't figured it out by the time she emerges from the hallway with a large towel in hand. She walks back to the kitchen sink and turns on the faucet. She places the maroon towel in the sink, creating a blood-red spot under the running water. "I know what you're thinking," I say, hoping it will prompt her to tell me.

After turning off the sink, she turns around to face me. "What am I thinking?" She tosses the towel in my direction.

I grab it and run the warm, wet spot along the front of my chest. "That I put on this big show of setting boundaries with you, and now I'm the one violating them." A nostalgic smile rises to my lips. "You think I'm weak."

She doesn't smile back. She seems to consider my words. "I've since revised that opinion. I think you have trouble accepting other peoples' weaknesses. And you like new love. A lethal combination."

I expel a frustrated breath before meeting her eyes. "If you're implying I set boundaries with you because I had trouble with your 'weaknesses,'" I emphasize the word, thinking it not quite adequate to describe her Ativan addiction, "I don't think that's really fair."

"It doesn't matter."

"Actually it does matter. I set boundaries with you for both of our sakes. We couldn't go on like that any longer, not if we wanted to make it long-term. For the sake of our relationship, we should both agree to stick to the break. We'll start over with it. Right now. No trying to make me jealous, and I won't keep showing up here when the mood strikes me."

Her jaw clenches. "Agreed."

Though I'm still perplexed by her strange mood, I accept her agreement. "Okay, at least now we can be on the same page.

We won't see each other. We won't text or talk at all, and just keep doing whatever you're doing because you really seem like the old Leilani, so it must be working. A month from now we'll re-evaluate—"

"That won't be necessary."

The uneasiness at the back of my mind rises to the fore. "I don't understand…"

Her expression doesn't change. "We won't need to re-evaluate in a month if we end everything now."

I stare at her dumbly, sickness stirring in my stomach, even though I know she couldn't have meant what her words implied. Taking an unsteady breath, I run her words again through my mind. "End everything…" I trail off, unable to form the question rising to my mind. "You mean… I don't understand what you mean by 'end everything.' Do you mean we shouldn't go on a break?"

Something that looks like sympathy flashes into her eyes, but it's quickly gone. "Logan, why draw this out? Let's just end it now so we can both enjoy our last month of college."

My heart jumps into my throat, my pulse pounding like a hammer. "Draw this out? What do you mean draw this out? We're talking about making things better so that we can be together after college. So I can move with you to Indiana—"

"No we're not." Her tone is final. "And you know it. You've done this before. Think about it. This is what you did with Brittani. You let your relationship drag out long after you'd already emotionally checked out. You waited until she *vandalized your car,* for Christ's sake. And even then, you still went to her house at night to comfort her after you broke up—"

"This is nothing like that!" I shout.

"It's exactly like that, and I knew it right away. I knew exactly what Brittani must have felt like on her slow, humiliating descent from adored girlfriend to crazy bitch—"

"No!" I shout, taking a step closer to her, clenching my fists in almost unbearable frustration. "This is a completely different situation. I didn't want to be with Brittani... Or Harper... Or Ashley, or any of my other crazy as fuck ex-girlfriends, so you can't even compare..."

A chill runs down my spine at the sound of her laughter, my hands growing cold and numb. I stare at her in bewilderment as she leans her head back, her shoulders shaking. She looks joyful—her eyes squinting, her full cheeks dimpling. Who is this person? Who is this person laughing gleefully while she destroys me?

"Why are you laughing?" I ask, my voice unsteady.

She leans forward, pursing her lips as if to hold back laughter. With the pads of her index fingers, she wipes invisible tears from the corners of her eyes. "I shouldn't find it funny," she says, her words strained from laughter. "But I'm hearing my future." Her voice becomes hushed, almost wistful. "Someday Logan, you'll be fighting with a girlfriend and you'll bring up 'crazy as fuck Leilani,' the Ativan addict with panic disorder. I can hear it now." She ends her speech with a soft chuckle, shaking her head.

"Who the fuck are you?" I shout. "How can you say things like that and laugh about it?"

She doesn't answer, but continues to shake her head wistfully.

Panic seizes my chest so tight that it takes effort to breathe. I finally understand why her behavior seems so strange. She should be crying. The idea of breaking up with me should devastate her. It should be like that night when she begged me not to leave her.

She should be telling me she'd crumble without me. Not this.

"Have you ever seen *The Stepford Wives*?" I ask, my voice strained. "That old seventies horror movie? That's exactly what this feels like right now. It feels like someone killed the real Leilani and replaced her with a robot." After I say it, I wince inwardly. Though the comparison is on point, it still sounded stupid. For the millionth time since I met Lani, I envy her confidence in her opinions. I need it right now if I have a prayer in convincing her to stop this madness.

"Speaking of horror!" She lifts excited hands. "Did you see *Us*? Jordan Peele's new movie? It's about doppelgängers, not robots, but it's..." She smiles wide. "Excellent. Brenna and I watched it last week, and I thought of you. It's so your horror jam."

I stare at her incredulously, my breath coming in pants. "Did I give you the impression that I want to talk about horror movies right now? That I feel like chatting about fucking Jordan Peele and his new fucking movie?" She averts her eyes from mine. "What the fuck is wrong with you? Are you really breaking up with me or is this a joke?"

"I'm sorry if it seems like I'm making light of it. It's just that I made this decision a while ago and I'm already at peace with it."

Suddenly, the oppressively yellow walls of the kitchen start closing in on me. My vision blurs. "A while ago? How could you have made it a while ago?" I gesture behind her. "We just had sex on the counter. Were you planning on breaking up with me then?"

She at least has the grace to look a little guilty when she says, "Yes."

I expel a shaky breath. Feeling almost detached from my body, my eyes dart around the kitchen. "What the fuck is going on here?" I mumble to myself.

"It was goodbye sex. Closure sex." Again that emotionless, clinical voice.

My eyes dart back to hers. "Was that Closure Cake too?" I spit out, hoping the reminder of the night we met will summon some kind of emotion in her. Something... Anything.

"Yes," she says right away. "I didn't get a chance to write your name on it. You got here too quickly."

I scan her face, searching for some sign that she's joking, but I come up short. Her eye contact is as direct and unflinching as ever. "Are you honestly telling me that *that*," I point to the defiled cake on the counter, "is my Closure Cake? That's the Logan Henderson Closure Cake and you made me eat it?"

Her eyes grow hesitant. "I didn't make you eat it..."

"No, but you didn't stop me either. You didn't stop me from smashing it into your pussy and licking it off."

Her eyes soften minutely, but she holds my stare. "I'll admit that in retrospect it seems...sadistic."

"Lani, Closure Cake..." I break off, shaking my head. "That was our thing! Our little joke. Our story about the night we met. The one Armaan or Brenna would have told in their wedding toast." I look away from her as memories of the night we met come flooding back. I knew in my gut that my life would change after meeting her. Unable to stand the memory, I push it away. I meet her eyes, my own narrowing. "It was one of your many quirks that made me fall in love with you, and you took it and made me lick it off of your pussy."

She flinches. Thank god she's finally showing some kind of

emotion. "I just happened to be baking the cake when you texted me. I wasn't planning on having you lick it off of my pussy."

"What the fuck were you planning? I feel like I walked into a trap."

She holds my stare for a moment before she answers. "It was sort of a trap," she says softly. "Almost as soon as you told me you needed time apart, I set out to lure you back. It was all stupid. I regret it now." After taking a deep breath, she exhales slowly, meeting my eyes with that intense gaze that caught me on the night we met. "I haven't taken responsibility for everything I put you through during those months when I was taking so much Ativan—"

I wave a hand. "Let's not even worry about that right now. I can forget—"

"No, let me finish. I want to make amends for it. Don't feel like you have to stick around because you're worried about me, like you did with Brittani. I'll be fine. Let me set you free."

"I don't want to be set free!" I shout.

"Yes, you do. You've been checked out of our relationship for months, long before our break. This is what you wanted two weeks ago, but you felt too guilty to ask for it, so you gave me a chance to 'get my shit together.' But you didn't really want me to. You wanted this."

"I did not want this!"

Her expression softens in sympathy, and it makes me want to shout even louder. She pities me for my loss of control, because she made this decision long before now. She's already "at peace" with it. How could she be at peace about losing her soulmate?

"Logan," she starts in a lowered voice, "I say this out of love—" When I flinch at her use of the word "love," she pauses for a second. Her voice is more stern when she resumes her condescending lecture. "I think it might be hard for you to remember how you felt two weeks ago—"

"Oh my god, no! No!" I shoot her a stern look. "Don't you fucking tell me about my relationship amnesia again. What's that word you use when someone is making you feel crazy?" She frowns in question. "You told me it comes from that movie from the forties about the lady with diamonds in her attic..."

Her face lights up like it always does when we talk about movies. It kills me. I can't be reminded of all those blissful hours spent talking in her bed. It will only make me that much more frantic, and I need to keep my head if I'm going to get her to stop talking nonsense.

"*Gaslight,*" she says in a raised voice.

My eyes dart to hers, realizing I was zoning out and that she repeated herself. "Yes, you're gaslighting me. You're telling me what I really want and what I remember, and it's making me feel crazy. It's fucked up, Lani. Let me tell you how I feel and what I remember."

She lowers her eyes, nodding.

Sensing an opening, I take a step closer to her. "I know that I love you. I know that I want to be with you a year from now. Ten years from now. I remember that two weeks ago I was pissed off as fuck after everything you did and..." My throat closes over at the memory of that night.

God, you're boring! How am I just now realizing it? How have I survived a year of this? Go find yourself another girl and bore her. Better yet, find a vanilla girl like Keira who's every bit as boring as you...

"...everything you said," I finish with effort. "I came home that night and made a decision that would—" I halt when her head darts up. She glares at me, and something in her eyes makes me go cold. A growing sense of foreboding makes the hairs on my arm stand up.

"Is that really what you did?" she asks in a chilling voice. "You went straight home after you left my house?"

I stare at her, too dumbfounded to answer.

"You see, I *heard* some evidence to the contrary."

CHAPTER 26

Past—The Phone Call

Leilani

It was an act of God. Divine intervention. A sign that the universe is not indifferent to us, and occasionally reaches out in our darkest moments, easing our sorrow with small gestures.

There's no other way to explain why his phone called me five minutes ago.

At this precise moment.

To hear all of *this*.

I was in despair when he left here. I stared into that toilet bowl for what felt like a lifetime before I was finally strong enough to stand up. How could I live with myself knowing I had thrown away something so perfect? Then my phone rang, I saw his name, and I almost wept with relief, considering it a gift of mercy from the heavens.

And it was, but not in the way that I thought.

Logan and I never call each other, besides the occasional FaceTime when one of us is out of town. The few times he's called me has been a pocket-dial, and even that I can only recall happening twice. The first time he was on his way home from class with his phone in his pocket. I remember hearing the sloshing of fabric against the speaker as he made his long strides across campus.

And the second time is right now.

I still can't believe it as I stare at the screen of my phone, watching the timer tick past four minutes.

I knew he was with her the moment I picked up the call. I heard her high fluttery voice as she greeted him, both delighted and suspiciously unsurprised to open the door and find him outside at one thirty in the morning. They barely spoke at all before the smacking started. That god-awful sound, so surprisingly crisp through the muffled speaker. And then there was the gasping and the moaning.

Oh god, the moaning.

They've gone quiet for the last thirty seconds. No sounds at all. All I hear is the faint rush of feedback from the air in the room.

I imagine them holding each other, their foreheads touching, eyes shut tight. Staying still to prolong the pleasure. Logan is probably so starved for her by now that he can't move in her for two minutes without coming.

Or thirty seconds.

Pain grips my chest at the memory of the first time we had sex. The stairwell. Is that what this is like for him? He likes novelty, and this is an even greater novelty with the added danger. He's never cheated before. Does that make the pleasure that much more unbearable?

Where are they? Probably on a living room couch where she straddles him. They moved too quickly to have made it to a bedroom, and Logan was obviously too frantic to notice the state of his phone when he tossed it aside somewhere.

Frantic because he wanted her so badly he didn't care to look.

Why don't I feel like crying again? Why hasn't this sent me into another wave of despair?

My body feels tight and alert, electricity buzzing through my limbs. It feels like a high, and not from the Ativan that has now long worn off.

It's a high of fury. A high of injustice. My boyfriend left my house only to go straight to hers, and I've been forced to listen to him fuck her for the last five minutes.

At the murmured sound of their voices, my back straightens in alertness. I smash the phone to my ear, straining to listen closely. I hear Logan's deep voice murmuring something, but I can't make out the words, though I think I might have caught the word "sorry."

Sorry, you motherfucker? You're saying sorry to the wrong person.

I'm filled with the desire to confront them. To speak up into the microphone and admit that I've been listening the whole time.

But something holds me back.

Maybe it's the epic humiliation that was the last eight hours with Logan. Maybe it's the bedraggled state of my appearance, as if they could see my sweat-dampened hair and smell the vomit on my breath as I speak through the phone. Maybe it's that even though it's my right to listen—my right as the betrayed party—I still feel like a bit of a voyeur lurking in the corners as they finally express their growing love.

My chest grows tight. Oh god, why does this have to hurt so much? I take a deep, unsteady breath in an effort to keep my mind sharp.

No, I can't do it. Not yet.

My body grows alert again at the sound of Keira's high, whispery voice. It's an intimate voice, and it makes me want to claw her pretty blue eyes out of their sockets. "Understandable," she said. I know that's what she said. It was the only clear word in her string of murmurs.

"Understandable," you conniving cunt? Is it understandable that my boyfriend put his dick in you because he's disgusted with me?

Emotion grips me so suddenly, I'm unsure if it's rage or sorrow. All I know is that I can't listen anymore. I can't bear to hear another word or noise. Another heavy breath. Another whimper. I click the hang-up button just before throwing my phone on the floor and rushing to the bathroom.

Within a split second of hunching over the toilet, red vomit scatters my vision for the second time tonight.

CHAPTER 27

Present Day

Logan

A cold shiver runs down my spine. Dread fills my stomach like lead. I think I might be sick. I shut my eyes and breathe in slowly to fight the building nausea.

Who would have told her? My scattered mind frantically searches for answers.

Not Keira. There's no way Keira would betray me, but who else knew about it?

A humorless smile rises to Lani's lips. She lowers her chin to give me a hard stare. "You pocket-dialed me," she says, her smile growing as she takes a step closer. Bile rises at the back of my throat as her meaning registers. Oh god. How could that have happened? How could I have been that unlucky?

"That night," she clarifies, as if I needed it. "It must have happened as soon as you walked into her apartment. It was perfect timing, because you started fucking her shortly after." Her eyes grow wide and angry, her smile now a sneer. "I heard *everything*."

The panic seizing my chest starts to ease a little when I realize her misinterpretation. I nearly sway in relief. "No!" I shake my head frantically. "That's not what happened. We didn't have sex. We…" I swallow, hating that this is my defense. "We kissed."

She starts to laugh, and my growing hope is squashed in an instant, leaving me empty. She's never felt this far away before, this unreachable, like if I tried to touch her my hand would sink through. When her laughter subsides, she fixes me with an accusing look. "Do you know what a moan sounds like through a phone speaker?"

Unable to speak, I shake my head.

"It's loud. Very loud."

I shut my eyes in agony, wondering how in the world I'm going to convince her of the truth. "We made out," I say, hating how paltry my defense sounds. "We kissed for…for a while. But I promise you that was all." I grabbed her tits too, I add inwardly, but I shouldn't have to admit that. Not when the universe is obviously so highly stacked against me. I've paid for my sins.

"It must have been a pretty good kiss for there to have been that much moaning."

I shut my eyes in shame. "It was wrong. I felt terrible for it, but Keira and I had an intense conversation about it and we—"

A chill runs down my spine when she laughs again. "You had an *intense* conversation about it," she says through choked laughter. "I'll bet you did."

"I mean we talked about it afterward!" I shout. "We talked

about how it could never happen again. I was in a super dark headspace when I went over to her apartment that night. Do you remember… I mean, this isn't an excuse or anything… But you do remember everything that happened that night, right?"

"Yes, I recall."

Her tone is flat, emotionless—free of any remorse, or even shame. It rubs me the wrong way. Enough to propel me to make a stupid mistake. "Do you?" I ask. "Because I was pretty sure you didn't recall. *I* recall having to tell you about everything you did and everything you *said*."

When she flinches, I hate myself for my impulsivity. I wronged her that night. I seriously wronged her. Now is not the time to itemize her wrongs against me. Like a little kid—tit for tat.

Jesus, is that what I did? Did I think that calling me boring and saying those things about Dean justified what I did with Keira? I can't be that childish, but then why didn't I feel all that guilty? Why is the weight of my sin just now fully hitting me?

"We both wronged each other," she says, as if reading my mind. "The most rational step is to end everything."

"No!" I shout, seized again by panic. "I don't care what's rational. I don't want to end everything. I love you, Lani! I want to be with you forever. I don't care what happened. We'll work through this."

"No, and I actually need to you to leave. I have to shower before class."

I stare at her dumbly.

"If you need to talk more we can FaceTime later, but we'll need to keep it brief. I think we should both focus on moving on."

"Moving on," I say, just catching up to the fact that I'm being dismissed.

"And let's make it our last conversation."

The words don't compute. What conversation? What does she mean by "last?"

When her meaning finally registers, it takes effort to remain standing. This can't be happening.

"Um, ok." I lower my voice in an effort to keep it from breaking. "I guess… I'll just…" I glance at the door then back at her, feeling detached from the world. "I'll call you later."

CHAPTER 28

Leilani

~~Item 1 Makeover~~
~~Item 2 Lure him back~~
~~Item 3 Seduce him~~
~~Item 4 Break up with him~~

Logan: This won't be a brief conversation. I have a lot to say. Sorry.

Me: Whatever. I'll call you at 7.

I expel a listless breath as I set my phone down, dreading having to FaceTime with him. Ready to be done with it all. I should have known it would feel like this. I should have known that as soon as the seduction was over, my high of rage would fade away with my orgasm. It wasn't even fun breaking up with him afterward.

It was just sad.

"Dr. Scott was right," I say to Brenna. "As usual."

We've been laying in my bed for the last hour, alternating between talking and heavy pauses while I stare out into space. She knows I need her presence. I haven't cried, but that's not surprising. I'm too drained for tears.

"About the list?"

"Yes. He didn't overtly say 'This won't make you feel better' because he's always been too afraid of me to speak the truth, but he heavily implied it. And he won't tell me 'I told you so' when I see him tomorrow either." I grab a lock of her dark hair and weave it through my fingers.

"You knew it wouldn't make you feel better. It was about justice."

I snort, shaking my head with a humorless smile. "Justice. I was such a child. He licked cake off of my vagina, Brenna. That was my justice."

"It's incredible!" Brenna grins. "Lani, you made him lick his own Closure Cake off of your vagina. Can you think of anything more feminist? You're a gangster. Just imagine what we would have thought when we were fifteen and made our first cake for Dylan Edwards. We would have bowed to future Lani."

I wish I could find it comforting, but nothing seems to ease this ache at the pit of my chest. "I miss Ativan," I whisper.

Brenna takes my hand in hers. We drift into silence again, her presence soothing me into self-reflection. There's no denying my true intentions any longer. That revenge list was just an elaborate attempt to shield my guarded heart from hurt. Just like

I always have.

I'm a coward.

Brenna interrupts the silence. "Lauren is coming into town. For Logan's sake. Because he's so wrecked over you."

I frown at her, wondering how she found out. As if reading my mind, she says, "I know because Armaan has been giddy since this morning. He's so excited about seeing her, he can't even hide it from *me*."

I squeeze her hand.

"Why am I hanging on to him?" she says, almost to herself. "He's been checked out for months."

I look at her pointedly, silently probing her to actually answer her rhetorical question.

She throws her hands in the air. "I like being around him! It's as simple as that. He makes me feel calm, with his deadbeat stoner ways. I'm attracted to losers."

I only smile sadly at her. I won't scold her for calling him a loser, because I know this is her way. She's deeply hurt by his indifference, and she reacts by lashing out. I'd be a hypocrite to judge her for it. Let she who did not make her boyfriend lick cake from her vagina cast the first stone.

Both of our heads turn at a light tap on my bedroom door. Mia walks in, her face wary. "Logan is on the front porch. He says he's not leaving until you come out."

My mouth drops open. When I look at Brenna, she doesn't look at all surprised.

"Oh, for fuck's sake! I just texted him five minutes ago."

Mia only looks at me, and I can't blame her for not wanting to be in the middle of this shitshow.

I groan as I get up from the bed.

"Don't let him get away with it," Brenna says as I walk out of my room.

"Oh, I won't."

When I open the front door, he's standing near the edge of the porch with his back to me, his hands in the pockets of his hoody. "I told you I would FaceTime you at seven."

"Yeah, I can read." His voice is soft.

"You just don't care about my wishes."

"Not any more than you care about mine."

He turns around, and the sight makes my guarded heart fall into my stomach. His eyes are red. In the blue light of our porch lantern, his usually pink lips are barely visible on his white face. I've never seen him like this, and it makes me want to wrap my arms around him and tell him I take everything back.

Still, my will is iron. "Why are you here?"

"I've just been thinking a lot about everything, and you're not being fair to me."

Of course. Logan is as obsessed with fairness as an eight year old boy. Lauren told me it's a twin thing, an unreasonable expectation after being given everything you've ever owned in a matched pair. "It's not about fairness."

"You're a just person." He looks down. "Or you used to be. At the very least, hear me out."

I glance at my watch. "You have two minutes."

His lips part. "Who are you?"

"Do you want me to answer that or do you want me to hear you out?"

He shakes his head, mouthing what looks like, "Oh my god." Raising his eyes to mine, he takes a deep breath. "I fucked up. I kissed another girl… Made out with her, I mean," he says in a lowered voice, his eyes dropping to the wood beneath his feat. Guilt makes him look away, I think cynically, but then when he raises his head, I see something that looks nothing like guilt. His eyes flare. "I made out with her for five whole minutes. I grabbed her tits too! Under her shirt."

I raise incredulous brows. "What the fuck are you trying to do here?"

"I have nothing to hide anymore, but you're not being fair. You may not have actually cheated, but…" He takes an unsteady breath. "All that shit you said devastated me. Like…" He looks at me intensely, his eyes pleading for me to understand. "Like literally killed me." He flinches. "No. Not literally. Shit. What you said was fucking awful, and you said it first! I was crushed and I went over to Keira's feeling enraged and wanting to hurt you back. The kiss never would have even happened if it wasn't for what you said. And I know it's childish to be like, 'You did first,' but I really think it needs to be said."

He exhales a shaky breath as he concludes. When he lifts his eyes to meet mine, they're wide, hesitant, puzzled even, as if he's just now realizing how much better his little speech sounded in his head.

His vulnerability tugs at a place deep within me, but I can't give in to it. I can't let him off the hook. Not when he's so colossally wrong. "You talk about our betrayals as if they're of equal weight, when it couldn't be further from the truth."

His brow furrows. I feel his growing indignation. He opens his mouth but I halt him with my hand. "What I did was a onetime thing. I said some cruel…terrible things to you. I don't remember saying them, but I know I had the intention of hurting you. I was jealous of Keira that night, so I lashed out at you in the only way I was capable in my drugged...pathetic state. I used Dean because I knew it would make you jealous. It was an awful thing to do, but it was *one* time. What you did was weeks, maybe even months in the making."

When his brow furrows, I take a step closer. I widen my stance, opening my chest to broaden my shoulders, wishing I were taller to intimidate him with my size. "You replaced me. You built a relationship with her while ours was crumbling. You told her everything about my panic attacks and my drug problem. You talked about movies with her, just like we used to." An angry smile rises to my lips when a memory surfaces. "You talked about Marvel movies. You had a multi-paragraph conversation about a fucking fish-man—" I break off, giggling at how crushed I felt over such inanity. "Oh god! She's perfect for you, Logan."

When I glance back to his lidless eyes I realize what a shock that must have been. It probably never occurred to him that I would read his texts during my listless, Ativan days. Of course he didn't. He didn't even bother to delete them. "*Aquaman* is DC," he says, looking dazed. "You read my texts," he finally says.

I nod once. "Every single one."

His lips part before closing again. "When?"

"When you showered." My mind drifts back to those hazy moments when I laid on his bed with his phone in front of my face, half-listening for the sound of the water shutting off in the background that would signal the end of my ritual. I was too afraid of losing him to confront him, so I passively watched their relationship develop behind my back, using texts to piece together their illicit love story like an archaeologist with pottery fragments. Feeling only a dull, distant ache at the pit of my chest as I read the worst of them, thanking the heavens for Ativan for making the whole process bearable, but also fearing how that ache would grow if I ever allowed the haze to clear.

"Your password is 1-1-1-1-1-1," I say, choking on the last "1" with a laugh. "It was my very first guess when my snooping began."

Indignation flares in his eyes. "I had nothing to hide! So we talked about movies. She's a fucking friend! I never even thought about kissing her until—"

"Until you did!"

At the raising of my voice, he cowers a little, his shoulders hunching.

"It doesn't matter. I don't even care about the kiss anymore. Not now that I'm over the initial trauma of hearing your heavy breathing and your moaning and your fucking saliva smacking!" Thankfully he flinches at that. "I care much more about everything that came before. How once you started to doubt your love for me, you immediately sought someone else. I care much more about your emotional infidelity!"

He frowns, ire growing behind his eyes. "What the fuck does that even mean? That sounds like a made-up term! Like you know you can't be mad about my friendship with her so you had to find a way around it. Did I also commit emotional infidelity with Armaan? We talk about movies too. What about Lauren?"

My nostrils flare. "You're a fucking idiot."

"Nope." The ghost of a smile touches his lips. "You just don't have any ground to stand on, and you know it. Look, I admit the kiss was a terrible thing—"

"'It's crazy,'" I quote, "'how much we have in common. I feel like I could talk to you forever without getting bored.' That was one of my favorites of your texts to her. It sounds a lot like something you said to me many months ago. Do you remember, Logan? Or does your relationship amnesia make you say the same things over and over to every new girl?"

He looks guilty for the first time. Still, he holds his ground. "So I like talking to her. It doesn't mean anything."

"It doesn't matter anyway. It's time to put it all behind me. You should too. I meant it when I said I want to make amends to you after all that I put you through with my addiction. Be with her, Logan. Don't feel guilty about it. I'll be fine."

When I start to turn towards the door, he grabs my arm, his eyes almost wild. "No!" he shouts. "What about me? I won't be fine! I don't want to be with her. I want to be with you!"

"That's not an option anymore."

"No, don't say that. Please don't say that. I still love you more than anything. I want to work through this."

"No."

"Stop doing that! I deserve more than this! Don't you even love me anymore?"

When I hesitate, an emotion rises behind his eyes. Something that looks like fear. "I don't know."

"What?" It's a breathless, desolate question and it makes me want to reach out and touch his face.

I soften my voice. "I can't love someone I don't trust. I don't have it in me."

"Let me earn back your trust!"

I sigh. "No."

He scowls. "You're heartless. I don't know who you are anymore. I don't think I trust you either."

His return to petulance hardens all of my earlier sympathy.

I school my face into a blank mask. "Let that be your comfort when you never see me again."

I turn around. This time he doesn't stop me.

Just before I shut the door I hear it. It's faint and unsteady. I don't recognize it immediately because I've never heard him sob before, and it makes me want to cry out at the universe for being so unfair.

Fairness. It's a fixation of mine too, but most of the time I'm able to keep my self-pity in check.

But why couldn't he be as perfect as he seemed? Hasn't my life been hard enough? Did he have to stop loving me after he learned who I really am? Did I really need that confirmation of my deepest fear?

When I get back to my bedroom, something compels me— call it a sickness—to pull out the frayed pink paper in my desk drawer.

Without giving myself a chance to reflect, I grab the list and draw a stark ink line at the bottom.

I don't know if I'm driven by vengeance or my perfectionist need to cross off every item on a list, but the sight of it fills me with a sense of completion.

Item 5 Make him cry

CHAPTER 29

Logan

Street lights. Palm trees. The faint scent of the ocean from the cracked window. The slick leather steering wheel beneath my palms.

Now that I'm standing outside her apartment, I can't remember the drive. She opens the door, looking almost alarmed when her eyes meet mine. "Hey," she says as she lets me inside, and it sounds like a question.

I'm not ready for explanations yet, so I walk toward the hall. She must understand because she doesn't ask any more questions as she follows close behind. I walk into her room, distantly recognizing that it smells like her. After she walks in, I shut the door.

"Are you ok?" Keira asks.

I swallow. "I'm fine."

"You don't look fine."

"I'm just a little disoriented."

She frowns in concern. "What did she do?"

I try to laugh humorlessly, but the sound comes out breathless and strained. I don't even have the energy to laugh anymore. "She dumped me."

Her lips part. "*She* dumped *you*?"

"Yep."

Something flares in her eyes that looks like triumph, but it quickly dies. Of course she's happy about my breakup. She wants me, but she's too good of a person to take pleasure in my pain. "Do you need to talk about it?"

I swallow. "No."

"You look like you need to talk about it."

"I can't spend another second talking about her. Even thinking about her. I'll go crazy. She was awful tonight. She was so…" My voice chokes. With effort, I smooth out my speech. "Heartless. She won't even consider forgiving me."

Keira places indignant hands on her hips. "Forgive you? For what?"

I swallow, feeling the first pang of guilt since I left Lani's house. "She knows about the night we kissed."

Her eyes fill with horror. "You told her?"

"No." A laugh escapes my throat when I think about my colossally bad luck. Of all the times to have butt-dialed her. Before I know it my shoulders are shaking. Keira looks puzzled, but she doesn't say anything. "No, I didn't tell her," is all I say. "But like I said, I don't want to talk about her."

I lock my eyes on hers. It takes a moment before she seems

to understand what I came here for. When I reach my arms out to her, she halts me with her own. "Logan…" Her voice is gentle. "You're a wreck right now. This isn't what you need."

I take a step back, making sure she understands I have no intention of pressing her. "It might not be what I need, but it's what I want. But if it's not what you want, I'll go home."

She hesitates. "You know that's not what I meant."

There's a wealth of meaning in her words. *You know* this isn't the first time I've thought about this. *You know* I've wanted this for months.

"Then why should we wait? I'm not in a relationship anymore." A twisted smile rises to my lips. "Lani even told me I should be with you. She said it would be her amends to me."

Keira scowls. "That's passive aggression if I've ever heard it. She is something else."

"I don't want to talk about her anymore. I don't even want to think about her." My eyes roam her face. "I only want to think about you."

That finally gets her, thank god. I watch the tiny little notch at her throat rise and fall. Her eyes are glazed. I take another step toward her. She stares at me, searching my face. The slight sway of her body towards mine is all the answer I need. I grab her by the shoulders.

Before plunging in, I stare down into her eyes. They're heavy-lidded now. For all her hesitation, she wants this just as much as I do. This is just like that night.

A chill runs down my spine.

This is *just* like that night.

I even feel the same. This ache in my chest. My mouth nearly watering at just the thought of easing it for one brief moment.

"What's wrong?" she asks, but I can hear in her voice that she already knows.

"What am I doing?" It's not a rhetorical question. What the fuck am I doing right now? How am I doing this again? Am I really this stupid?

She exhales heavily before placing her hands on my shoulders and pushing me away. She turns her back to me, as if to gather herself.

I run both hands through my hair. "Seriously, Keira, what the fuck am I doing? I love her! I want to get her back. Why am I here?"

I see her chest expand and contract as she takes a deep breath. "You want to feel better."

"Am I that fucked in the head?"

"No, you're just selfish."

God, she's right. Why the fuck didn't I think about her feelings? Why did I think it was okay to come here for a please-make-me-feel-better fuck when I had no intention of being with her afterwards?

I stare absently into the gray carpet under my feet. "I think I do this a lot."

"Yep, I'm sure you do. I think it probably explains our entire friendship."

My head darts up, and I see her hard blue eyes staring back at me, her jaw clenched.

"Oh god, Keira, no!" I can't let her think that. "That's not what I meant. Seriously, your friendship means the world to me."

Her small smile doesn't reach her eyes. "Just what every girl wants to hear after she's been rejected."

"Shit. I'm being a fucking dick right now, huh? I'm so sorry.

I'm just not thinking right. The last thing in the world I want you to think is that I've been using you."

She chuckles humorlessly. "Logan, this is the definition of using someone. Your whole friendship with me is the definition of using someone. You wallowed over your 'heartless' girlfriend—your words, not mine—and I've been your cheerleader making you feel better. You're *using* me to make yourself feel better. Do you see how that works?"

"Shit." It's all I can say and I feel like an even bigger dick.

We don't speak for a while. She does a small circle around the room while I stare at the wall, wondering how I've been such an asshole moron for the last two months without even realizing it.

"Keira, I'm so sorry. I know it's inadequate, but I really don't know what else to say."

Her expression softens. "It's okay. It's not all your fault. We both have co-dependency issues."

I don't know exactly what she means, but I don't linger long enough to find out. It's clear she wants me out of here. This will probably be the last time we see each other.

On my drive home, a triumphant thrill courses through me for doing the right thing, but it's short-lived.

What am I going to do? Call Lani up and say, "Hey, I almost fucked Keira, but I decided not to at the last minute. Can we get back together?"

And that's when it really hits me.

I lost her.

She's gone.

The despair that descends over me is a physical pain. I tighten my grip on the steering wheel to keep myself from hunching.

How am I going to get through this?

CHAPTER 30

Logan

I remember thinking the world had changed the day my Grandma Louise died.

She was Lauren's and my favorite grandma, and our designated babysitter every time my parents went on long trips. She used to let us stay up all night watching Cartoon Network and Disney Channel. She bought us all the junk food my mom never let us eat, like those pizza Bagel Bites and Flaming Hot Cheetos. I used to sit at the kitchen bar stool while she cooked or cleaned. She'd make me a sugary kid drink along with her routine five o'clock cocktail, and I'd talk endlessly about who knows what, and she would listen. And not in the way adults pretend to listen when they talk to kids, offering a perfunctory, high-pitched "really?" or "no way!" at timed intervals. She would really listen.

She asked me questions. She gave me advice.

I remember running outside right after my mom told us she died. I didn't cry at first. I just wandered around the backyard in a daze, arrested by the belief that the whole world was sad.

It had to be sad. I could see it with my eyes. Our backyard trees looked sad with their long palm leaves swaying mournfully in the wind. Lauren's dirt-crusted lightsaber looked sad and alone and forgotten under the garden bench. I was sad, and the world was sad with me, and I knew with what felt like certainty that we would all be sad forever.

Just like now.

I was wrong of course, because it was just a feeling, and like all feelings, it faded with time. I hardly even think about Grandma Louise these days. And yet...

A part of me wonders if this feeling is more than a normal part of grief, but something reserved only for the loss of what can never be retrieved again. Something that changes you forever, so that even when you don't feel the grief anymore it's still there, because it's a part of you.

I hear a knock at my bedroom door, but I don't feel like moving. Armaan has been nagging me for hours to get my ass out of bed. I've only gotten up twice since last night when I made my zombie-like tread from the front door straight to my bedroom. Once this morning to pee, and then again around noon to pour myself a glass of whiskey.

I couldn't even drink it.

I don't have the energy.

"What?" I ask as I stare at the ceiling, barely able to raise my voice through the door.

The door opens and Armaan peaks his head through. "Let's

go get drunk."

"I don't feel like it."

"You need to stop whatever it is you're doing." He gestures over my lifeless form. "It's pathetic."

When I don't respond, he walks into my room and claps his hands twice. "Come on! I'll go get us a good bottle of whiskey. We'll pre-party here first and then go out to the bars later and I'll be your wing man."

I only sigh heavily in response. Going out to the bars is the last thing I want to do. I'll only feel her absence more. It will be like that long ago apocalypse dream. I'll see her face everywhere, but it will never be her.

I turn my head slightly to get a better look at Armaan. He's staring at the floor, his black brows drawn together, a bewildered look in his eyes. It takes me a moment to recognize his uncharacteristic expression.

Poor guy. He's worried about me. A deep, distant warmth touches me somewhere inside.

Deep, deep down.

He lifts his head suddenly. "Miller got me some hash for my birthday. It's seriously almost as strong as LSD. We could smoke it and watch *2001*."

I consider it for a second. It's the only appealing idea he's had all day.

Oblivion.

"Okay," I say. "But only if you pack me the biggest bowl you've ever packed in your life."

"That's the spirit!" He claps his hands. "I'll get you high, son!"

With that, he darts from my room, likely going straight for the glass bong he keeps in the cupboard under the bathroom sink, skipping like a giddy little kid. If I could feel anything, I'd be touched by his jubilant relief that I'm willing to join him in the land of the living.

***

Oblivion doesn't come. Lucidity flows through me in waves. One moment my troubles are a distant blur and the next they hit me with a crushing force.

The worst part is I can hear her fucking voice in my head, as crisp and husky and self-assured as if she's sitting right next to me. "*Eyes Wide Shut* is better than this," she says. "It's secretly Kubrick's masterpiece."

She would say that too, because it's the dumbest thing I've ever heard. Jesus Christ, will I ever meet someone again who talks the way she does? Will I ever meet anyone who says the dumbest shit ever with the all-knowing authority of a goddess? I fucking love that about her.

"I hate hash," I say to Armaan in a clipped rush.

He narrows his already half-shut eyelids. "Are you having a bad trip?"

"No, but I don't want to watch this anymore. I can't stand another minute of this pretentious as fuck, hipster-ass movie. Turn on *The Office*."

He frowns at me for a few seconds before slowly leaning forward and picking up the remote from the coffee table. I can't blame him for being confused. I don't even know what my outburst was about. I fucking love *2001*. I think I was really asking him to turn off Lani's voice.

To turn off the memories.

Lani and I had a conversation about *2001* on our first non-date. I used it to win her pretentious, hipster favor when she was skeptical of me. But then again, it's not really true that I won her favor, because she still held back for months and months. We had only three months of absolute perfection before everything started to shatter. That day on the beach when she…

What did she do? To this day I'm not really sure. I only know that she infuriated me so much I could barely stand to look at her. She reverted to her old ways, pushing me away by…

Oh shit.

When the realization hits, the hairs on my arms stand up and my heavy body starts to hum. "Armaan, I think I just had an epiphany."

He grins lazily. "Hell yeah! I love your epiphanies! Is it about *The Office*?"

"No, it's about Lani."

His smile falters. "I hope it was something along the lines of, 'It's time to forget about her and move on.'"

"No. I realize…" I try to work out my thoughts, but my words tangle in my jumbled head. "I think Leilani was one of those girls who had blue hair in high school. I mean she didn't literally have blue hair—I've seen pictures—but she was like those girls. You know what I mean?"

He blinks once, a notch forming between his brows. "No."

"They were the kind of girls I always had a crush on too, but they wouldn't give me the time of day. It was like they thought they were too good for me and not good enough at the same time. You know?"

"No."

"Leilani was that girl. She's that girl now. She's just pushing

252

me away and I can't let her do it."

He looks like he wants to roll his eyes. "Logan, she dumped you. I know this is a first for you, so you might not understand how it works. When someone dumps you, you don't get a say."

"I know, but it can't just end like this. I need to get her to hear me out."

He shakes his head. "This is a terrible epiphany. I think you're wigging out."

"No way!" I shout, exhilarated by the first flutter of hope I've felt in two days. "I'm going to win her back! She's been telling me from the very beginning that I'm going to ditch her like I have all of my ex-girlfriends. She's afraid, because she's just like those blue haired girls in high school—like Ali Rivers, god damn you! I'm sorry I never heard of your fucking subtitled anime show that 'changed your life…'"

Armaan looks incredulous. "Who the fuck is Ali Rivers?"

I shake my head. "A girl I went to high school with. Sorry, I think I am wigging out."

He exhales. "I'm glad you realize it."

"But not about Lani! I'm going to win her back. I'm going to wear her down until she talks to me!"

He shuts his eyes. "Oh, Logan."

His response doesn't deter me. I jump from the couch and walk to my bedroom to grab my phone from my dresser. I had left it in there because I couldn't stand its silence. Every buzz of a text not from Lani felt like a punch in the gut.

Elation courses through me when I press send.

Me: I won't let you go without a fight.

CHAPTER 31

Leilani

Forty-two text messages.

Eleven ignored calls.

And three pleading voicemails.

All within the span of two days.

Ghosting someone shouldn't be emotionally taxing. By definition, it's the most passive form of rejection. We communicate our lack of interest by vanishing from their sight. Unfortunately, Logan Henderson has next level persistence, and vanishing isn't as simple as ignoring a few texts.

I can almost feel his mounting frustration radiating through the phone. Logan hates being ignored. He can't stand it.

I should have known he would approach our breakup with the same relentless determination he employed when he pestered me into becoming his girlfriend. He knows how his vulnerability gets to me—the way he so willingly bares himself to rejection—and he's using it in full force to wear me down.

Logan: Lani I'm dying.

Logan: Please hear me out.

Logan: I'm a fucking mess. Just give me one more chance to explain myself.

And then there's those awful voicemails. Each one is whispered—an intimate voice just for me—and he talks as if I'm right there with him. In his room. In his bed. "Remember when I told you about my grandma's basement? I want to live in a house with a basement with you someday." "I want to have kids with you—creepy little kids who are obsessed with death and have your giant, Tim Burton eyes." "Just let me come over and talk to you so that you can tell me I'm weak, unfunny, and have a dumb voice."

I can't take it anymore. I need a distraction, and after listening to one of those devious voicemails just before bed last night, I woke up this morning with a newfound determination to leave Logan Henderson in the past where he belongs. It's time to move on with my life.

It's high time.

When I had an emergency session with Dr. Scott this morning to process everything from the past few days, he asked me if I had reached out to counseling services at IU yet, and I could only stare at him blankly, the full force of my obsession hit me for the first time. For the last three weeks, my only thoughts about graduate school were tied to my revenge list. I haven't given a single thought to my future.

My passion. My career. My hopes and dreams.

How did I dare call myself a feminist?

If I think about it too much, my heart starts to race, and I don't need that. Instead, I'm taking action. I'm sitting here with my coffee in one hand and iPad in the other, searching for housing in Bloomington, Indiana. The flutter in my pulse is from the caffeine, I tell myself, and not the self-loathing from realizing I didn't even think about housing before this morning.

I hear Brenna in the kitchen. I know it's her by the sound of her bouncing footsteps, probably making her usual breakfast—Earl Grey tea and instant oatmeal. After a few minutes, she walks from the kitchen—a bowl of oatmeal and spoon in each hand—and sits on the couch next to me. She leans against my shoulder as she looks at my iPad. "How's the house hunt going?"

"Phenomenal," I say, hoping positivity will calm my frantic thoughts.

"I can live in a mansion at the price we pay for a single room in this crumbling, haunted house."

She points to my phone, speaking with her mouth full of oatmeal. "Is that the price of rent? For a two bedroom? Are you fucking kidding me?"

"And look at it!" I click on the picture reel and scroll. "It has marble counter tops in the kitchen and the bathrooms. I shit you not."

Brenna's jaw drops. "Does Jay-Z own this apartment?"

"Right?"

She places her hand on my forearm. "So, I've been thinking of asking you about something, but I don't want you to get your hopes up 'cause it's just a kernel of an idea at this point."

I turn to face her. "Okay…"

She takes a deep breath. "What if I moved with you to Bloomington?"

My eyes open wide. "You know it would be my dream come true, but I could never expect you to do it. What would you do in Bloomington?"

"Get my teaching credential, like I would anywhere else. It's a better situation if housing is that cheap. California isn't really the place for teaching, unless you want to live in poverty all your life. To be honest, I think I was counting on Armaan's family money whenever I thought about the future. I thought we would live in his parent's beach house or something, which is just sad and shows how stupid I've been, especially since Armaan wouldn't even commit to that with me. He'd probably rather be a squatter with Lauren. They'll probably both smoke weed all day and—"

I place a hand on her arm to stop her from spiraling down this path. "Does this mean you're planning to break up with him?"

She nods slowly. "I have to. This has gone on long enough. I still love him…" When she trails off and averts her eyes, I lift my hand from her arm to her shoulder.

"It's okay to cry, honey. Breakups are hard."

She grimaces, a tear running down her cheek. "I fucking hate crying." Her voice is strangled.

"I do too, but it always feels good after you let it out."

"Fucking Armaan!" she shouts, flapping her hands over her face as if to dry her tears.

We're both alerted to the sound of my phone ringing. I pick

it up from the couch, take one glance at the name on the screen, and throw it to the floor.

"Logan?" Brenna asks.

I only nod, not wanting to take the attention away from her own pain. I stroke my fingers at the back of her neck while she quietly cries. Her head jerks up when my phone chimes. "He left a voicemail this time! Can we listen to it? It will make me feel better. I hope it's really sad and dopey, like everything he does."

I can only smile reluctantly. I lean forward to pick up the phone from the ground. I hold it between us and press the speaker button. When the voicemail starts, Logan is already in the middle of speaking.

"—uck you fuck you fuck you fuck you... Oh shit. Sorry, I didn't hear it beep. To be clear, I was saying 'fuck you' to your voicemail greeting, not to you—"

Brenna rolls her eyes, mouthing, "Oh my god."

"—I've heard it so many times that it doesn't even feel like it's you anymore. It's this asshole cunt bitch who won't let me talk to you, and I hate her—"

"Nice opening, Logan," Brenna says.

"—Anyway, I just need you to know that you will hear me out eventually. You will, Lani! And if you ghost me for another twenty-four hours, I'll be forced to do something drastic. I'll show up on your porch again, and it won't be pretty. You know how you always say you hate the guy at the party who gets out his guitar and starts playing and singing, and that you always want to die of secondhand embarrassment? Well, imagine me showing up on your front porch playing some shitty Sam Smith song loud enough for all your neighbors to hear. Yep. And maybe I'll do it tomorrow during Mia's birthday party too. Oh! You don't think I'd do in front of a bunch of our friends? You think I'd be too embarrassed? Well guess what, I am unembarrassable! But you aren't..." I hear the smile in his voice. "And I'm going to use it against you, because I'm about to lose my fucking mind if you don't talk to me, so just wait for it, Lani. Wait for me to show up at your house and serenade you in front of all your friends. And then when I'm done I'm going to start shouting how much I love you and... No! Oh my god. I have an even better idea. I'll start crying..." He trails off and starts laughing, and he doesn't even sound like himself anymore. The sound is loud and shrill, almost maniacal. "I'll start crying," he says in a voice strangled with laughter, "and then I'll get on my knees and start begging. In front of *all your friends*. I'm giving you twenty-four hours to change your mind and talk to me. Mark my words, Lani—" He lowers his voice, enunciating each word slowly. "*I will embarrass the fuck out of you.*"

Long after the voicemail ends, Brenna and I are still staring at the phone.

Eventually, she speaks, her eyes wide and dazed. "He's unhinged," she says, but there's no censure in her voice.

She's just as alarmed as I am.

He's not doing well. I can hear it in his voice.

Logan's a slow talker—his vowels drawn out, his consonants clipped, like he's so perpetually relaxed that he'll only commit to the bare minimum effort of speaking.

That voicemail was anything but relaxed. It was manic, frantic, and something else...

Painful.

He's in pain.

And he's in so much pain, he can't even keep his worst habits in check.

Just like I was a mere three weeks ago when I wrote the stupid, petty revenge list that sent me on this downward spiral.

You wanted this, a voice says. This was all part of your plan.

My chest seizes with guilt. As if my phone itself were Logan, I set it down gently on the coffee table, brushing it lightly with my fingers.

I sink into the couch, the weight of my sins so heavy it takes effort to breathe.

CHAPTER 32

Logan

Guitar in hand, I walk into Armaan's room.

Lauren is sitting on his bed, engrossed in conversation with him. I fight the urge to roll my eyes at her. This is where she's spent most of her time since she arrived two days ago, even though she supposedly came up here to comfort me over my breakup. My parents even agreed to babysit Cadence for the weekend because of it, and how like Lauren to use any excuse she can get to spend a weekend reliving her partying days. She and Armaan have already talked about going to Mia's birthday party tomorrow without me.

"Hey," I say, and both of their heads swivel in my direction, both looking a little guilty. I don't even care at the moment. I'm too engrossed in my own predicament. "Do you think it would embarrass Lani more if I sang really loud and off key or if I tried to sing really well? If I, like, shut my eyes and rock back and forth and get really into my song?"

"Both," Armaan says. "You should sing really loud and off key and make it look like you think you're really good."

"You're a genius, Armaan!" I look to Lauren. "Which song would she hate more, "Stay with Me" by Sam Smith or "Perfect" by Ed Sheeran?"

A frown forms on her brow. "Can you please not do this? Trying to publicly embarrass someone as reserved as Leilani is a dick thing to do. Not to mention that it makes you look like a lunatic."

I try to stifle the pang of guilt. She's right that it's a dick move, but I'm too desperate to care. I can't be ignored any longer. I'll go crazy. She has to talk to me. "She's the one being a dick," I say, even knowing it's not the truth. "And if I'm a lunatic it's because she's turning me into one by ghosting me."

* * *

That night, I spend about fifteen minutes learning the chords of "Stay with Me" from a YouTube video, practicing just long enough to play a recognizable version of it, but not enough to play it well.

Just when I'm about to put my guitar away and get to bed, Lauren steps into my room, shutting the door quietly behind her. "You're really going to do it?"

"Yep," I say instantly, knowing she's going to try to talk me out of it.

"Armaan and I both think you might be having some kind

of manic episode. Even for your standards, this is a little…
excessive."

"'Armaan and I,'" I quote back to her. "Are you guys a couple
now?"

She hesitates. "Are you annoyed that I've been hanging out
with him?"

"No." My answer is too quick to sound sincere.

"I came to hang out with you, but any time I try to talk to
you, you shoot me down."

I shift in my seat so I can meet her gaze head on. "I'm sick of
being told that I need to move on and forget about her."

"I haven't told you that once."

"No, but you're thinking it."

She stares at me for a moment, as if in indecision about what
to say next. "I'm just worried you'll be disappointed when your
guitar thing doesn't work."

I turn away from her. "Keep your worries to yourself."

When I start to shut my laptop, she asks, "What happened
between you guys? Why won't she talk to you?"

My hands freeze in place. I knew we would come to this
eventually. This is Lauren. I tell her everything, but I'm not
ready for this talk. I'm not ready to reflect on the misery just yet.
I need to wait until Lani and I are back together, when it won't
feel quite as miserable in retrospect.

But something in Lauren's tone holds me in indecision. She's
a good listener. My favorite kind—she gives me her full attention
and she doesn't bullshit me. She's a lot like Lani in that way,
which is why I can't bear to hear her honest opinion right now. I
can't bear to be told that I fucked everything up irreparably.

"I won't tell you to forget about her. I promise. I'm actually hoping you guys get back together. I want someone who will keep Mom in check the next time she tries to humblebrag about your nonexistent modeling career."

Even in my shit mood, a smile rises to my lips. I want that too. I want Lani around at shitty family dinners at Christmas time. I want her around a decade from now.

I want her forever.

And it's still not too late to win her back.

Ultimately, it's hope that drives me into telling Lauren the whole ugly story. She doesn't flinch at any of it, because even my colossal fuck up is nothing worse than things she did in her wild teenage days, and by the time I'm done I feel better than I have in months.

"It sounds exactly like what you did to Becca Keller junior year," she says, almost absently.

Her reflection startles me. "What?"

"She went on vacation over the summer you broke up with her, remember?"

"Not really."

"Well, I remember it perfectly because Mom blamed me for it. She loved Becca and you broke up with her for my friend Jessamyn, remember her?"

"I never dated Jessa!"

"No, you did. Becca went on this whole European cruise thing. She was gone for like a month, and you started hanging out with Jessa and me because you were so lonely, and then you were like, 'Lauren, I'm so torn. I love Becca, but Jessa just understands me.' And of course, I was like 'go for it,' because you know me—"

"I don't remember any of this. I feel like you're making it

up."

"I assure you I'm not." She waves a dismissive hand. "Becca and Jessa were at least twenty girlfriends ago, and you only dated Jessa for like a minute. I wouldn't expect you to remember. The only reason I remember it so vividly is because Becca was the girl you broke up with through email—"

"I would never do that!" I shout.

She looks like she's trying not to smile. "I've been telling this story for years. It's one of my favorites. You dumped poor Becca while she was still on the cruise, and after she got back, her mom called our mom because she was so mad at you for ruining their family vacation—"

"No way! I would never break up with someone through email."

Lauren only looks a little exasperated when she says, "You did, Logan. You wanted to talk to her every day and she couldn't because the calls were so expensive on the cruise, so eventually you just said 'fuck it' and broke up with her over email."

The protest I start to form freezes on my tongue. A memory surfaces that makes the hairs on my arms stand up. *You wanted to talk to her every day and she couldn't.* I remember that. It's not a typical memory—not the sight of my hand dialing her number or the sound of the phone ringing over and over again. It's a feeling. The anxiety of reaching out to someone far away, the mounting dread of being ignored, and the sickening plummet when the fear is confirmed. I hardly remember Becca at all, and yet I know I hated it when I didn't hear from her. I can barely call up an image of her face to mind, but the long-ago hatred of being ignored by her is so strong, I feel it even now.

As if sensing my distress, Lauren smiles sympathetically. "You had me read the email before you sent it. It was really heartfelt."

I'm too in my head to call her out on her sarcasm. At my continued silence, she frowns. "Oh my god, are you really getting upset?"

"I don't know," I say, in a daze.

"It was high school. You were a baby. It's more funny than anything."

"I don't think it's funny. Lauren…" I take a deep breath before meeting her eyes. "Do you think I'm needy?"

Her face freezes momentarily, but then she sucks in her lips, fighting a smile. It's the smug look she gives me anytime I say something stupidly obvious, and it used to make me want to hit her when we were kids, but I can't summon even the slightest irritation. Only anxiety.

"Logan," she begins tentatively. "Is this really news to you? Have I not been telling you that for years? Has Armaan—and all your friends—not said it one hundred times?"

"My friends are just jealous of my game."

She sucks in her lips again, and this time I kind of want to hit her even now as an adult.

"They are!" I shout, inwardly wincing at my childishness.

"You have to have a girl, honey. All the time. You find new girls within minutes after your breakups." Her voice grows tight, as if she's holding back laughter. "Literally, in Lani's case."

Oh shit.

I stand up from my desk and start to pace the room, running hands through my hair as memories of both nights I went to Keira's house come flooding back. I knew even then it was a selfish move. How did I not also realize all of this? How could I have been so stupid for over half of my life?

266

"So, you think I always have a girlfriend because I need attention?" I ask, unable to stop the memory of Lani's words from wrapping around me, squeezing my throat. *Once you started to doubt your love for me, you immediately sought someone else.*

"Well, yeah, and it's understandable. Just think about how little attention we ever got from Mom."

"Yeah, you've said that before, and it's crazy! Mom gave us *too much* attention. She would have controlled our entire lives if she could."

"Yes, but controlling someone is not the same as hearing them."

I nod slowly, straining my brain for even a single memory of being ignored by Mom, and still I come up short.

But then my mind shifts to that recently surfaced memory of Grandma Louise and those conversations at the kitchen counter and the drawling sound of her raspy voice when she called me "honey" or "punkin," and I'm gripped with a longing so powerful I want to be sick.

"Grandma Louise paid attention to us," I say quietly.

A smile tugs at Laurens lips. "She did." Her smile holds as she shifts her eyes away from mine. "I miss her."

"Me too." It's all I can say without crying, and fucking hell I don't want to cry right now. I've been sad enough lately. I don't need to cry over a grandma who's been gone for more than a decade.

"I miss Dunkaroos," Lauren says softly. "Remember those?"

Warmth fills my chest at the memory of Grandma Louise's pantry shelves, overcrowded with cardboard boxes and plastic bags with cartoon characters on them, as if she spent months preparing for our summer visits. She probably did. My lips lift into a smile. "She always fed us such shit food."

"I know! Mom always told her not to, but she didn't care, because she was a bad bitch with her curly acrylic nails and her indoor smoking. Remember how the walls of her living room literally had stains from smoke? God, I miss that."

"I love the smell of cigarettes because of her."

"Me too!" Lauren shouts. "Anytime I see someone smoking, I'm like blow that shit in my face, *honey*!"

When she drawls "honey" with a terrible southern accent, I burst into unexpected laughter. Lauren joins me, and we laugh off and on for several minutes, wiping our eyes occasionally and quoting more of Grandma's southernisms in our shitty southern accents, and then bursting into laughter again.

CHAPTER 33

Logan

It's nine thirty in the morning. Ten and a half hours and counting until Mia's birthday party.

When I hear a ring, I look up from my menu to see Armaan's phone light up on the table. Brenna's name flashes on the screen. Without even glancing at the screen, Armaan picks up his phone and hits the silent button before setting it down on the table again. His eyes return to his menu. When I glance at Lauren, she doesn't seem to notice.

We're out to breakfast because Lauren hounded us both out of bed this morning. Though in retrospect, it didn't take a whole lot of hounding to get Armaan to come, even though he rarely gets out of bed earlier than noon on a typical weekend.

They look like a couple as they sit side by side in comfortable silence, with me sitting across from them as the third wheel. They've been acting like a couple too. Luckily, I'm spared the awkwardness of having to confront them both at the same time, when Lauren asks Armaan to scoot over so she can get up and pee.

As soon as she walks out of sight, I don't waste a second. "You know, I expect this kind of stuff from Lauren because she's been doing it since we were teenagers, but I really thought you were above all this immature high school shit."

He doesn't look up from his menu. "I don't know what you're talking about."

"I know she slept in your room last night. I'm not an idiot."

He exhales slowly, hesitating a few seconds before saying, "We didn't have sex."

"Yeah, I've heard that one before."

"You've said it before," he mumbles.

I slam my menu down. "Yeah, I know exactly what it's like to be a shitty boyfriend, and lose my girlfriend because of it. So, have fun with that. Also, I know my sister a lot better than you do. Don't let her anywhere near Brenna when she's drunk tonight or she'll tell her everything, and you'll be in the exact same position I am now."

He shrugs. "I'll be fine. I'm not as delusional about my relationship as you are. It was fun with Brenna, at first, and then she became my mom. I'm over it."

"If that's the case, stop being a pussy and just break up with her."

Finally, he shows some kind of emotion on his face. It's not quite guilt, but it's better than his almost aggressive indifference. "I'm planning on it."

"Why couldn't you have done it before Lauren slept in your room? It will be awkward for me if Lani and I get back together. She expects me to tell her things like that."

He pinches the bridge of his nose, his face looking pained. "Logan, you need to stop thinking about the two of you getting back together like it's a sure thing. I really don't think your little guitar performance is going to be the winner you're hoping for. I think she's more likely to get a restraining order."

I'm spared the necessity of responding when Lauren returns. "What are you guys talking about?"

"Logan's concert performance."

She frowns at me. "I thought you changed your mind about that."

I shake my head. "I have to talk to her. I need to apologize. I'm not going to embarrass her, though. I think I might try to sing a nice song for her. A song she likes."

Armaan grimaces. "That will embarrass her more!"

I sigh heavily. "I know. I'm not sure what I'm going to do."

CHAPTER 34

Leilani

The ocean breeze cools my hot cheeks as I step outside. The living room and kitchen have grown small and muggy with the steady inflow of warm bodies. I needed to get away, and I couldn't escape to my room like a hermit, so instead I came out to our front porch.

The very place he's supposedly "serenading" me tonight.

The thought makes my breathing shallow, but not because I'm embarrassed. Social anxiety would be like a luxurious day at the spa compared to this crushing guilt.

I have to tell him.

I have to explain my list, and how everything that happened—all of his pain—was part of my calculated plan.

And he's going to hate me.

I wish it were over already.

Armaan and Lauren showed up together about a half hour ago—to Brenna's indignation—and Logan wasn't with them. In fact, Lauren drunkenly insisted that she "talked him out of coming" so I "have nothing to worry about."

I was annoyed with her for many reasons. Annoyed that her carelessness is leading her to hurt my best friend without even thinking twice about it. Annoyed that she's at this moment so drunk that she doesn't even realize how much she's hanging all over Armaan and humiliating poor Brenna in front of all of our friends.

But I was also annoyed that she prolonged my agony by—

I jump at the sound of a shrieking yell coming from inside the house. "Get the fuck out of this house!"

Oh god! That was Brenna's voice. I turn around and rush inside.

The sight that meets my eyes stops me in my tracks. Brenna looks up at Armaan with blazing eyes, her stance as wide as a warrior's, and she's holding a curling iron high in the air. The room is silent. Everyone around seems to have halted in place at her outburst. "Did you hear me?" she shouts. "Get your cheating, fuckboy ass out of my house now!"

"We need to talk." Armaan's voice is surprisingly gentle, though I catch a hint of fear too. "You need to hear the full story."

Brenna glances at Lauren, who is wincing apologetically at Armaan.

"I'm sorry?" Brenna's voice is ice. "Did you do something more than feel her up and down in your bed last night? Did she leave out a few details you want to fill in?"

Armaan shoots a horrified look at Lauren. "I didn't really feel you down—"

"Oh Jesus H. Christ, Armaan, this is not the time for technicalities. Just get the fuck out of my house before I beat you to death!" Brenna raises the iron high in the air like a sword.

I'm propelled into action. I rush to Armaan and grab him by the arm. He looks dazed as he glances back at me. "Come on," I say gently. "Let's go."

He looks at me pleadingly. "I need to talk to her first."

I'm about to tell him no, when Brenna interrupts. "The time for talking is over! If you ever set foot in this house again, mark my words, you will leave here cockless."

Brenna's threat sends Lauren into a fit of drunken giggles. I shoot her a scolding look, but she seems oblivious to it.

Armaan's shoulders drop a little. "Alright fine. Come on, Lauren—"

"Oh no, Lauren is staying." Brenna takes several steps toward Armaan, her eyes wide with menace. "Do you want to know what Lauren and I are doing tonight?" She lowers her voice into a threatening drawl. "We're going to call up one of your dumber than fuck frat brothers. We're going to lure him over here, and then we're going to drag him into my room and fuck him on top of the quilt your mom made me. So, as you put your mouth on your bong before bed tonight, know that both Lauren and I will be putting ours on someone else's cock."

"Girl!" Lauren shouts. "You are my hero! Forget his frat brother. Can we just fuck each other?"

I glare at her again for her tone deafness, but neither Armaan nor Brenna seem to have noticed her outburst.

Armaan looks like he's desperately trying to keep his cool,

but his breathing is rapid. "Brenna, come on. Let's just—"

"Get out of my house." This time she whispers it.

When I shoot Brenna a concerned look, she dismisses my sympathy with a quick shake of the head. "I was ready for this," she whispers, and thanks to my own experience, I know exactly what she means. Rage is a welcome reprieve from months of sadness. Too bad I didn't have the foresight to limit my own rage to a saucy speech about sucking another dick instead of a multi-week revenge plan.

I pull Armaan's arm in the direction of the door, and thankfully he follows, but with a heavy, sorrowful tread. I haven't seen him express this much emotion over Brenna in months. No wonder she's so satisfied.

When we reach the edge of the porch, I let him go. He looks like he's about to make his way down the stairs, but then he turns to me abruptly. "Will you please talk to her?"

I cross my arms. "No."

He sighs heavily. "I really do love her."

"The fuck you do."

"Stop acting like I'm the only asshole here."

"What is that supposed to mean?"

His brown eyes flare. "She's fucking mean, dude! You know it too, and you always let her get away with it. Like, I know I talk a lot of shit, but Brenna's like, 'Hmm, what can I say right now that will still haunt him when he has great-grandchildren? How can I tell him he's a colossal fuck up using the fewest words possible?'" His tone is light, but the words are rapid, as if to disguise the hurt behind them.

So, his infidelity was a retaliation too, I guess. Is this how all men do it?

"What happened?"

I jerk at the interruption.

My heart flutters at the sight in front of me.

He came.

He stands at the base of the steps with his hands in his pockets, his hair wet and floppy like he just hopped out of the shower, looking tall and broad and muscular in that tight red…

Oh my god. He's wearing the T-shirt.

My heart clenches at the sight of that straining red fabric over his broad shoulders, the material barely covering his midriff. He looks ridiculous.

And this will be the last time I see it. That vulnerability I love so much, the willingness to bare himself to ridicule for just the opportunity to make me smile.

I deserve this pain in my chest.

I deserve the hatred that's about to come.

"Lauren told Brenna everything," Armaan says.

Logan laughs humorlessly, shaking his head. "I told you she would."

"I know. I never should have let them go to the bathroom together."

"Is Brenna okay?" Logan asks me, and I bristle at the genuine concern in his eyes.

"What do you care when you did the exact same thing to me? Where was my sympathy on that god-awful night three weeks ago?"

Logan only stares back at me with a pained expression.

Shit. He deserves to feel guilty, but tonight is supposed to be about me owning up to my faults too, not making him hurt worse.

"Alright," Armaan says. "I really am leaving now." As he walks past Logan he gives him a hard pat on the shoulder. "I'm sorry, man. Not that the odds weren't already overwhelming stacked against you, but I think I might have squashed your .1% chance of being forgiven."

"Yeah, thanks for that."

"No problem. And good call with the T-shirt. Pity is probably your only viable option at this point, so take full advantage of it." With that, Armaan turns around and walks away.

I join Logan on the sidewalk. "I see you didn't bring your guitar," I say lightly, in an attempt to hide my inner turmoil.

"No," he says softly. "I realized in the nick of time that embarrassing you into talking to me was…" he squints, as if searching for the right word, "borderline psychotic."

Even in my agony, I can't help but smile.

"I mean, to give myself credit, it was pretty innovative. But psychotic nonetheless." He shakes his head. "Anyway, I still wanted to do something for you. You know, to make amends—"

He cuts off when I wince at the word. He really means it, whereas I used it like a curse.

"To make amends for everything I put you through. So I decided I'm going to do two things for you. And they're going to sound really small. So before you hear them, keep in mind that I'm madly in love with you, and it's going to fucking kill me to do either of them, especially the first one."

My throat grows tight. I give him a slight nod so he'll continue.

"Number one, I'm going to stay away from you."

I want to protest, but I keep my mouth closed.

"And that means in every way. I won't show up here again.

I won't try to call you, text you…" He exhales, biting his lip. "I can't promise I won't drunkenly DM you at two in the morning on some really dark night when I'm fucking dying because I miss you so much, especially if I see a picture of you and another guy…" He winces. "Fuck. I don't even want think about that, but that's why I think you need to block me on all social media accounts, and I mean every account you have because I will stalk your ancient ass Tumblr if I'm desperate enough."

Oh god. His words are like a physical blow. Why does he have to be so wonderful, right now of all moments? Why couldn't he be petty and angry and call me an asshole cunt bitch?

"And the other thing I'm going to do is get therapy. I already made the appointment online today. The psychologist looks perfect for me too. He's got long blond hair and a beard. I can tell just by looking at him that he smokes weed…" He trails off, shaking his head. "Anyway, I know that sounds like it's more for me than you, but I thought a lot about what you said when you were breaking up with me, how someday I would have a conversation with a girlfriend and call you 'crazy as fuck Leilani,' and I don't ever want to do that. Even if you won't be around to hear me say it. I love you too much…" His voice is choked, and when I see the moisture gather in his eyes I want to double over with guilt.

"I love you too much to be the same needy, selfish asshole I've been my whole life. I love you too much to just—"

"Stop!" I shout. "Stop, stop, stop, stop!"

He looks as if I slapped him, his eyes are so shocked.

"I don't deserve any of this! I don't deserve an apology!"

His brow furrows and he takes a step closer to me, lifting his hands up as if to show that he's not going to harm me.

As if I would fear his harm. I'm the one who wrote the revenge list.

"I'm the worst, Logan."

He takes another step, and now I feel his breath against my forehead. "What do you mean you're the worst?"

He's genuinely baffled. I can hear it in his voice. "I was the worst girlfriend to you. I took and took and took and gave nothing back. No wonder you were needy."

Now the tears are streaming down my face. Through my blurred vision, I see his dark brows draw together. "Absolutely not. That's bullshit. You were guarded for sure, but…"

Belatedly, I realize that he's now wrapped his arms around me. I lean into his chest, wanting to feel his warmth one last time before it all goes away. Wanting to savor these last few moments before he knows I'm a monster.

"I'm worse than guarded. I'm vengeful. I thought you fell out of love with me because of my mental illness, and I wanted to hurt you for it." I meet his eyes, not wanting to cower away from what I'm about to tell him. "I wrote a revenge list."

His eyes dart to the side and then back at me. He's more surprised than angry, which means I haven't said enough, and he deserves this. For our last moment together, he deserves my whole, unguarded self. "I wanted to make you pay for abandoning me and falling in love with someone else—"

"I didn't fall in love with someone else." He tightens his hold around me. "I was just needy. It was only ever you—"

He stops when I pat his arm. "Can you halt romantic delusions for one second and let me finish my damn story?"

"Okay," he says, smiling faintly.

I wince. "I'm sorry to snap at you. It's just that when you

hear it you're going to feel differently about me."

"I doubt that, but okay. I'll let you finish your damn story."
Still, that smile and it kills me. I hate that I have to be reminded
of how lucky I was to find this perfect boy with his nearly
limitless patience for my ice-cold, guarded heart.

"I planned to make you fall in love with me again so that I
could break your heart in return. Everything I did was calculated.
Showing up on campus that day. Bringing Dean. I even planned
to seduce you and break up with you..." I trail off when my
throat grows tight. I swallow before starting again. "Logan, I
planned to break up with you while you were still inside me."
His body goes rigid, and now I know I've gotten to it.

Now he really understands my sadism.

And I can't leave it at that. I have to tell him the worst part.
Wanting one last moment in his warmth, I burrow my head in
his shoulder, loving his musky scent, somehow both erotic and
comfortingly familiar at once. "I wanted to make you cry. It was
the last item on my list. 'Make him cry.' And after that night
when you were outside my porch, I crossed it off." He jerks back
and now I know I've done it.

"You crossed it off...because you accomplished it?"

"Yes." Hot shame creeps into my cheeks, making my skin
tingle.

"You've always been really diligent about crossing off your
lists."

My eyes pop open. His tone isn't right. It's strained, but it
doesn't sound angry.

It's not until his arms tighten their hold around my shoulders
that I realize his chest is vibrating.

I place my hands on his chest and push against him. He lets

me go right away.

I see his smile, his shaking shoulders.

Is this really happening? Is he really laughing right now?

He stops laughing abruptly, and his brows draw together as his eyes roam my face. "Oh, Lani. I'm sorry. Oh god, look at you…" He lifts his hand and runs a thumb over my cheek. A sad smile tugs at his lips. "I didn't mean to be a dick, it's just—and don't hate me for saying this but—this revenge list, your little villain monologue, it might be the funniest thing I've ever heard in my life."

I look away from him, placing cold hands on my hot cheeks. I'm not sure if I feel relief or embarrassment.

"And I know this sounds condescending, but it's adorable how upset you are about it—" He makes a gulping sound, as if he's trying hard not to laugh again.

When my head whips back to him, his eyes grow hesitant. Almost fearful.

Oh my god, he's afraid I'm going to snap at him for making fun of me.

And that's when I realize I haven't humbled myself nearly enough. "I want you to have sex with me."

The change over his face would be comical under different circumstances, shifting from fear to confusion to reluctant excitement all in a flash.

"It will be closure sex. And I want you to boss me around like I normally boss you around. You can even spank me. Or not. It can be whatever you want. I told you when we had sex in the kitchen that it was closure sex, but that was a lie. It was revenge sex, and it wasn't fair."

Forcing myself to be brave, I look at his face. I try to read his expression, but I can't. I look away.

I'm startled when he invades my space again. When I look up at him, I see blazing eyes staring down at me. He's not laughing now.

He looks angry.

"You need to explain to me what I'm supposed to get from this *closure sex*." His teeth clench over the words.

Unable to understand his mood, my brows draw together. "What do you mean?"

"I mean you should know by now that I don't just want to boss you around during sex, bend you over my lap and spank you. I want a lot more than that."

The relief that descends over me makes me lightheaded. I shut my eyes, take a deep breath, and relish it when he steps so close that his chest grazes my nipples. "I don't want closure sex, Lani. The fact that you would even offer it makes me—" He takes a deep breath. "Makes me really angry. You must still be on your revenge plan."

When he starts to back away, my heart jumps into my throat. "No! That's not true!" When I draw the attention of a few partygoers now standing on the porch, I lower my voice. "I don't know anything, Logan. I never even understood why you would want me. You're so warm and kind and everyone likes you, and I'm an annoying, cold, vindictive bitch with panic disorder, and now I have a drug problem on top of that. I was always afraid you would find out and leave me."

When his expression softens, my courage rises. "And I don't just want to do this for you, I think I need this too. The idea…" My throat tightens. I clear it before I continue. "The idea of leaving it like this is too painful. I love you too much to leave it like this. I want one more time with you."

Still, his green eyes are expressionless.

I look away, unable to stand it.

"Okay."

His answer makes me jerk back. My eyes dart to his. They're heavy-lidded now, nearly shut. I still can't quite understand his mood, but I know he's aroused, and that's enough to assuage the embarrassment a little.

"But if we're going to do this," he says, his tone hard, "I have a few conditions."

My skin prickles with apprehension. "What?"

His chest rises and falls unsteadily. "Number one, we're not going to call it 'closure sex.' It will just be sex."

I frown. "Okay."

"And number two, we're going to have a conversation afterwards."

I swallow. "What kind of conversation?"

His posture straightens. He crosses his arms over his chest. "A reconciliation conversation."

Reconciliation.

The word leaves me stunned. I think my mouth might actually be hanging open. When I glance back at Logan's face I see the ghost of a smile hovering on his lips. "I can see you're scared shitless," he says. "And I feel for you, I really do, but I have to look out for myself. I don't want closure sex. If this isn't an opening for reconciliation, I'm walking. I'll leave you alone just like I said I would."

I place my freezing, clammy hands over my hot cheeks.

Reconciliation.

It's such a big, scary word. It means opening myself up and

giving him the chance to hurt me once again.

When he takes a step back, panic flares. "Wait!" I shout.

He halts in place, but his expression is still hard. Determined.

"Okay we can do that, but do I have to…" I trail off when my throat grows tight. "Do I have to agree to something right away?"

"No, but I'm not going to let you string me along for five months either."

"I would never do that!"

When he laughs, I realize my blunder. I shut my eyes in shame.

Suddenly, I feel the pressure of his arms around my shoulders and the heat of his breath in my ear. "It's okay, honey. I won't make fun of you anymore. Let's go have our *reconciliation* sex."

I shriek when he grips me by the ribcage. He lifts me into the air and tosses me over his shoulder. "What are you doing?" I shout.

"Taking you inside. Oh, and I think I might take you up on that reconciliation spanking too." He pats my ass with his palm.

"Please do." I giggle, a little hysterically. "I like it hard."

"Oh, I was already planning on doing it hard. You've been a bad girl lately, writing a revenge list and making your poor, needy boyfriend cry."

I smile, my chin pressing against his back as he steps over the threshold of the back door. "In my defense, he was a pretty bad boy."

His voice goes quiet. "He was, but if it's any consolation, he paid dearly for it."

* * *

As soon as we make it to my bedroom, he tosses me onto the bed. The breath I'd been holding releases in a gasp.

He immediately reaches for my pants. He grabs the top button and twists his fingers around it once before letting go. His hands are shaking. "Fuck these jeans," he says. "They've got like fifteen buttons, all the way up to your tits."

I can't help but smile. I love it when he's like this—so frantic that he can't even perform a simple task, like unbuttoning my high-waisted jeans. I grab his hands and give them a tight squeeze before placing them at my waistband. "You can just yank them. You don't have to undo them one-by-one."

He grips tight and pulls my pants open. "Thank fuck," he says as he peels them off along with my underwear. He lowers his mouth to my belly. I gasp as he presses soft kisses down to my navel. When he reaches my pussy, I expect to feel the warmth of his tongue, but instead he burrows his face, inhaling deeply.

"Mmm," he hums. "Your pussy smells so good. I've missed it."

"I don't want you to lick it. I want your cock first."

"I'm in charge, Girard."

I lift my hand to tuck a lock of hair behind my ear. "Oh, I'm sorry. I forgot. Do you want to spank me?" The words feel so foreign on my tongue.

I feel the warmth of his chuckle on my skin. He looks up at me. "I was fucking with you. I don't want to spank you." His smile disappears, his eyelids growing heavy as he crawls forward over my body. When he reaches my face, his lips crash onto mine. "I'm way too impatient for that."

I know exactly what he means. I lift my hands to grip the straining fabric at his arms. "Take this off. Now. I need you naked."

"Oh god, Lani," he says as he straightens, gripping the bottom of the shirt with his fingers. "I think I might die if I don't fuck you soon." He pulls the tight shirt up over his torso, but it gets stuck at his shoulders.

I stiffen. "Logan, be careful. The fabric is really worn."

"I will," he says, but I know he barely heard me. He's too far gone. I wince as he yanks the shirt upward.

The ripping sound echoes across the room.

"Oh, shit," he mumbles.

My mouth hangs open as I stare at the torn, crumpled fabric in his hands.

Oblivious to my distress, Logan tosses the destroyed T-shirt on the floor. "I'll make you another one." With that, he plunges forward, all but devouring my mouth after our lips meet.

When I grab him by the shoulders and push him back, he gasps. His eyes are glazed and a little bewildered as he stares back at me.

"I don't want another one. I want that one."

His bedroom eyes grow wider as they roam my face. A small smile tugs at his lips. "Aww, Lani. Did you really like it that much?"

Unable to stand his piteous smile, I look away. "Of course I did."

He gathers me close, and I catch the scent of his spicy body wash when my face presses into his chest. "That's really cute," he says.

"Don't be a dick."

"I'm not being a dick." I hear a smile in his voice. "I think it's really sweet."

"Just fuck me already."

When he chuckles, I feel the vibration against my cheek.

"Okay, honey."

He doesn't waste a moment. Before I can blink I'm fully naked and he's thrust himself inside me. "Fucking Jesus Christ!" he shouts, looking almost pained. He moves in me and I can feel it all the way to the tips of my toes. I release a low, guttural moan. He lowers his mouth to my chest, grazing his tongue over my nipple. I gasp at the wet sensation. When he moves again, I cry out.

His thrusts become faster. I can hear the slickness between us as he pulls in and out. "I'm sorry, baby." His voice is strangled. "I can't go slow anymore."

"No, this is good! I want you to fuck me. Slam into my pussy. Hurt me with your cock!"

He grows very still, and I feel his shoulders tense beneath my hands. "Oh Jesus, no. Don't do this to me, Lani. Not now. I'm barely hanging on."

Even in my erotic haze, I can't help but smile. I love this about him. I love how he can't stand it when I talk dirty, as if the pleasure is so agonizingly sublime that he has to shut himself off from it.

"I'm sorry," I draw out the words.

He presses a hard kiss against my neck. "No, you know what? It's okay. Keep talking dirty. Tell me everything you want."

When his hard eyes meet mine, I know he means it. I stretch my arm forward to cup his balls. He hisses as I rub the soft skin.

"Okay, this is what I want you to do. Grab me by the hips and pound into me, and don't be gentle, Logan. I mean it when I say I want you to hurt me. Pretend like you're trying to split me in half."

He hisses, as if in pain, but he follows my command. He grips my hips with his large hands, thrusting so hard my head presses against the wall. Heat radiates through my body. "Logan!" I cry out.

He gives me another hard thrust. "Yes, baby."

I grab a handful of his hair and yank his head back. Raising my mouth to his neck, I take a hard bite. He whimpers, thrusting his hips so hard my head bangs into the wall this time. Heat shoots into my abdomen as I lift my hips to meet his. "Touch me," I whisper, and without wasting a moment he places his fingers on my clit and rubs it in the circular pattern he's memorized. I bite his shoulder as the wave of euphoria crashes over me. "Logan," I sob through clenched teeth.

As my body slackens he thrusts harder and faster. As if from a faraway distance, I hear him cry out before collapsing on top of me. His chest heaves against mine. I'm still limp when he lifts his head and presses soft kisses over my face. "I love you," he whispers between kisses.

I press my face against his sweat-dampened chest and nuzzle it. "Mmm."

The pressure of his grip on my chin startles me. When I open my eyes, I see determined green eyes staring back at me. "I love you," he says, his tone firmer this time.

It's not even hard to say it back.

"I love you too."

* * *

Logan

When she starts to close her big brown eyes, I grab her shoulder and give it a squeeze. "Oh no. You can take your orgasm nap later. We're talking now."

Her eyes pop open. When they settle on my face, that vulnerable look returns.

It makes me want to hold her tight, but I won't let it sway me from my purpose.

I only agreed to this for *one* reason. "What do you want?" I ask, my tone final. "We'll strike a compromise."

She lifts her thumb to her mouth and nibbles at the tip of her nail. "Why don't we start with what you want."

"Do you want me to be honest or make up something that won't scare the shit out of you?"

After a moment's hesitation, she says, "Be honest."

"I want everything. Everything we had before. I want to move to Bloomington with you. I want to live together. In a one-bedroom apartment. With one bed. I want to marry you someday."

She winces before covering her eyes with her hands.

It irritates me. "And I want you to stop your bullshit."

She removes her hands, narrowing her eyes. "What exactly is my bullshit?"

I sigh. "You know, it took me a while, but I think I finally know what it is. Do you remember that day on the beach when you were telling me all those stories about panic disorder?"

Her eyes grow alert. "Yes," she says, her voice tight. "Vividly."

It sounds like it was significant to her too.

"Remember how you were like, 'I was the weird kid obsessed with death?'"

A confused frown forms on her brow.

"I was super pissed off at you that day, and it took me a while to figure out why. I realized it was because you were trying to scare me off."

"I guess I was," she says, averting her eyes from mine.

"And I think, deep down, I was scared of what it meant. I was scared you thought you were too weird and dark for me... Like, maybe you thought I was too boring and vanilla for you."

Her eyes fill will horror. "Logan, you are *not* boring. None of those horrible things I said were even remotely—"

"I know. I figured that out too. You were guarding yourself. Closing yourself off to me. That's what you do."

The shame in her eyes makes my heart clench, but I can't let her off the hook just yet. "You can't do it anymore, Lani. It has to stop."

She covers both eyes with the back of her arm.

"You cannot do it anymore." My tone is even harder this time. "With me or whoever. Or you'll be alone forever—"

"You think I don't know all of this?" Her shout makes me flinch. It's only when I see her quivering lips that I realize that she covered her eyes to hide her tears.

It makes me hate myself. I gather her close. Thankfully, she lets me. "Oh, Lani. I'm sorry."

"I have anxiety!" she continues as if she didn't hear me. "I live in my god damn head. I know all of this already. Yes, I was too guarded with you. I was trying to protect myself, and I regret it now, because it didn't make a god damn difference! You broke my heart anyway!"

Those last words end with a sob and now I truly hate myself. I squeeze her body tight as I burrow my head into her neck. "Lani, I'm so sorry. You can't know how sorry I am. You're killing me right now."

She doesn't say anything for a while, and each sob is like a knife in my chest. This is what my fucking needy ass did to her. All of this is because of me.

After the sobs finally subside, she lifts her head to look up at me. Her face is red and splotchy, and her eyes look almost swollen shut. "I'm so scared you're going to do it again." Her voice is barely above a whisper.

"I know, honey." I press a soft kiss against her wet cheek. "I can tell you a million times I'd rather die than hurt you like that again, but that's all I can do. The rest has to be from you. If you want this, you need to have faith in me. I want to change. I want to be better for you. You'll have to trust me."

She shuts her eyes tight. "I'm not very good at that."

Under different circumstances, I might smile at the understatement of the century, but my own anxiety is too high right now. Now we're really getting down to it. In a few moments, she's going to make a decision.

And I feel like I might die if it's not in my favor.

The needy bastard in me wants to manipulate her, to use her trust issues against her. *How many other guys would be patient enough to put up with your bullshit for as long as I did?* I have to clench my teeth to keep the words from coming out.

But I would have been this way all along if it didn't take work to be better. "All I want is another chance," I say, with tremendous effort. "You don't have to make a major decision now."

She's quiet for a while, and I try to retreat into my head to spare myself the agony of waiting on her answer.

After what feels like a god damn eternity, she finally speaks. "Okay." It's just above a whisper. I intake a sharp breath. "Okay?" I nearly shout in her face.

She blinks up at me, as if startled. "Yes. Okay."

As simple as that, her look says, but it's not enough for me. I need more. I stop myself from shifting my hips and sinking back into her, demanding more reassurance before I let the joy unleash. "You need to outline what 'okay' means."

She lifts her hands in a gesture of frustration. "I mean I'll give you another chance." When my face doesn't change, she elaborates. "We can get back together."

I stare at her, unable to believe what I'm hearing. These last few months have been absolute hell. Am I really in heaven again?

I lean in and press my lips against hers, dipping my tongue in slowly as I taste her. She matches my pace, gently massaging my tongue with her own.

This certainly feels like heaven.

When I pull away, I can tell by her softened expression that she feels it too. I smile at her.

This is it.

Our new beginning.

Closure Cake: The Revenge Cake Epilogue
FREE with newsletter sign up!

This **exclusive** 32 page epilogue spans over ten months after Revenge Cake, as Logan and Leilani build their new life in Indiana and grow even more deeply in love.

Sign up here to receive it by email:
https://dl.bookfunnel.com/3ct58hauc4

Author's Note

I can't thank you enough for reading Revenge Cake. You must love angst as much as I do because, let me tell you, that fuckboy Logan gave you a pretty good reason to DNF in Chapter 26 ;-) I'm glad you stayed to see his and Leilani's HEA.

Thank you again for your support and reading Logan and Leilani's story. I'm a brand new indie author and reviews are really helpful in getting exposure. If you enjoyed Revenge Cake, I'd greatly appreciate it if you went to Amazon, Goodreads, or wherever you get your books and told the world what you think.

If you want more Revenge Cake content, go to skylermason. com and sign up for my monthly newsletter. Everyone on my email list will receive Closure Cake: The Revenge Cake Epilogue.

Instagram.com/authorskymason
Twitter.com/authorskymason
Facebook.com/authorskymason

Join my reader group here:
Skyler Mason's Angsty Book Club

Sincerely,
Skyler

Note to Reader

Like Leilani, generalized anxiety and panic disorder have been a lifelong battle for me. I wrote her mental health struggles from my heart.

If you related to either her anxiety or addiction struggles, please know that you are not alone. Anxiety disorders are the most common mental illness in the United States, and addiction to benzodiazepines such as Ativan affects millions of Americans every year.

The Substance Abuse and Mental Health Services Administration (SAMHSA) has a free, confidential, 24/7, 365-day-a-year treatment and referral information service. If you are struggling and don't know where to find help, call 1-800-662-HELP (4357). They can provide you with referrals to local treatment facilities, support groups, and community-based organizations.

Sincerely,
Skyler

Acknowledgements

My wonderful husband Tyson and two beautiful boys, thank you for being patient when I sat in front of my laptop for hours while my mind drifted off to another world, and for only getting mildly annoyed when I finally answered your questions after the third "Skyler" or "Mommy" in a row. Tyson, your support and encouragement to go all in with my romance writing career has meant the world to me.

My amazing editor Rachel Daven Skinner from Romance Refined, I'm so grateful that you pushed me to make this story better. Thanks to you, the final product is what I hoped for when I first sat down to write (and my sentences are prettier).

My Angsty Romance Book Club members Ali, Chanpreet, Leticia, and Rebecca, you were my first ever romance novel community. Thank you for giving me a safe space to talk about my angsty romance obsession every week. And thanks for all your encouragement when I talked through the exciting and scary process of publishing my first novel.

Thank you to my Romance Refined beta readers for taking

the time to read Revenge Cake and give me honest feedback. And to Brittany, thank you for helping me come up with the title. (Only you and Rachel know what a dreadful title I had before.) You were also my very first reader and I will never forget some of your encouraging feedback.

Printed in Great Britain
by Amazon

13204451R00173